The Cake List

By
Dianne J. Wilson

The Cake List

A List Book Romance

~ Book 1 ~

2nd edition © 2023 by Dianne J. Wilson

Contact: dianne@diannejwilson.com

Scripture taken from Holy Bible, New International Version®, NIV® Copyright ©1973, 1978, 1984, 2011 by Biblica, Inc.® Used by permission. All rights reserved worldwide.

Cover Art by Dianne J. Wilson

Edited by Paula Bothwell

Cover Image ID - https://stocksnap.io/photo/GAXFQX8BXD Daria Shevtsova

Back Cover Image ID - https://stocksnap.io/photo/06OAHLI7B4 Eduard Militaru

Feather Logo © designed by Hayley Wilson

The Cake List

Do Something Brave.
Do Something Selfless.
Do Something Kind.
Break a Never.
Stop an Always.
Figure out God.
Some people write a bucket list, you know ...
things they want to do and tick off before they die.
Honestly? Dying doesn't seem half as scary as the
big-O birthday that's hunting me down.
So I've made my own list.
Things I want to do and tick off before I eat that birthday cake.
So far, it's not going too well.

To Wendy

Who always gave me courage to do the 'out there' things.

I miss you, we should do tea.

PRAISE FOR The Cake List

The Cake List was a fantastic read. I was hooked from the very first line. Hilariously funny and entertaining, while still covering some serious issues. We all need to have a cake list like Meg! Well done, Dianne on a brilliant read.

~ Marion Ueckermann, *USA Today* Bestselling Author

"He brought me out into a spacious place; he rescued me because he delighted in me."

~ Psalm 18:9 (NIV)

Chapter One

Monday—60 days and counting

MEG AIMED HER FEET into the satin shoes and realized two things: you can get a muffin top on your feet, and breaking off an engagement makes your feet fat. There was simply no other way to explain why her new ballroom shoes had shrunk. In the shop it was all Cinderella and the prince. One break-up later and here she was—the ugly step sister swinging the daft things on her big toes.

Either that, or it was her looming big-O birthday. Her thirtieth was bearing down on her at the speed of an ovum down a fallopian tube. A few hard pushes and the shoes were on. She fished around in her bag for a camera, pulled it out, and snapped a photo of her feet in the ballroom shoes. Evidence for the list, just in case it all worked out.

She sank back into the dance studio's leather couch and patted it for supporting her. A couple came in wet from the rain, arguing in low voices. The rain was gentle in East London, stuck as it was halfway between the stormy cloudbursts of Gauteng and the freezing, wind-driven, winter rain of Cape Town. The woman's nose twitched and she smacked the man's arm as they disappeared into a side room. Meg fiddled with the empty spot where her ring used to be. Her hand felt naked and she was losing feeling in her toes.

More people drifted in, some more wet than others. Even gentle rain made things soggy. They stowed umbrellas, hung up coats, and knew exactly where to go. Like the ark, they all came in twos. Meg began to feel more uncomfortable in this place than her feet did in satin pumps.

Maybe it was time to take her oh-so-single ugly-sister-toes home and soak them in a tub of hot water. If she thought it through, being here tonight didn't really qualify as anything on The List, not by any stretch of the imagination. It wasn't kind or selfless, it wasn't a *never* or an *always*. It clearly was nothing to do with figuring out God. The only one it came close to being was "brave" but even then—was it swimming a crocodile-infested river to rescue a homeless orphan? Not even close. Honestly, it had been a bad idea from the start.

She pushed herself to a stand, wincing at the pins and needles stabbing her ankles.

"You must be Meg?" The man asking was a head taller than she was in her heels, and slipped his arm underneath hers. She didn't mean to lean on him quite so heavily, but her feet had sabotaged her. The pair of them might as well have disappeared into the other room with all the two-by-twos. Traitors.

"How can you tell?" She eased off his arm, wobbled horribly and grabbed him.

"My staggering powers of deduction, of course." He grinned. "That, and the fact that the next hour is booked for Chad and Meg. He told me to be on the lookout for, and I quote, 'a gorgeous redhead with sun-kissed skin.' That's gotta be you."

Meg rolled her eyes. Chad always thought he had such a way with words, when in fact he oozed more cheese than she liked on pizza. She was not going to let thoughts of him ruin the next hour. It was doing a fine job of ruining itself without his help, thank you very much. "I take it you're the dance instructor?"

"Dominic Kingston, at your service. You can call me Dom, or King." He tipped his head, close-cropped black hair with a dusting of silver over the ears. Easy on the eyes. He checked his watch. "Just joking about King, please don't. Is Chad running late? We can give him a few minutes or we can start if you like?"

The door swung open and for a moment Meg expected Chad to walk in, all confident and charming. Her stomach twisted. It wasn't Chad, but another late couple who waved at Dominic and hurried to the same door all the other couples

3

had disappeared into. As the door opened, music pumped from the room, loud and rhythmical. The woman stopped and poked her head back around the door, making her blonde bob swing. "You coming, Dom?"

"Not tonight, Gina. Go on, you're late!"

She grimaced with a nod and shut the door behind her, cutting off the music midway through a count of eight. It hung in Meg's head, unresolved. They could have kept chatting for another four counts, but no ...

Dominic walked her through to a separate studio. The parquet floor gleamed under the lights, mirrors lined two of the walls, windows covered the third, and maroon plastic chairs lined the fourth. Meg sat down heavily, supremely self-conscious of clinging to his arm. "Chad's not coming."

"No problem. We can do tonight without him. Give you a head start." He turned to her and held out a hand. "Come."

She should really tell him. But that would mean questions. Awful, horrible questions. Meg wasn't ready for those. "What are all those couples doing next door?"

"It's a new project of mine. A ballroom and Latin American formation team." He took off his sweater and re-tucked his shirt. "But we're not here to talk about all that. Let's dance."

Meg gritted her teeth and forced herself to get up and walk towards him. He took her right hand in his, placed her left on his bicep, slipped his other arm around her. Her fingers told her that his arms were musclier than they looked from outside his shirt. Musclier. Was that even a real word? There was a space the size of a dinner plate between them. He was probably trying to protect his toes, which was a wise move considering her history with feet. A tickle started in her left nostril.

"We're going to take it nice and easy, just like walking. Step back right, left then side-close. Yes?" His voice had a soothing quality to it, almost hypnotic. She wrinkled her nose, resisting the urge to rub it on his shoulder. The slightest pressure of his hand on her back warned her he was about to move and she moved, too. Her ankle buckled underneath her and she dropped. Dominic caught her before her knees could hit the floor.

"Wait, let me guess. New shoes?" One look at her face and he shook his head. "I have a better plan. Kick them off."

"What?" Both nostrils were itchy now. Meg's eyes were starting, too.

"Dance without them tonight, stretch them out with potatoes for next week."

"Are you crazy?"

"Look, I'll even take mine off." There were zebras on his socks. Tiny little black and white zebras. What kind of man wears zebra socks? She took the moment and gave her nose a good hard rub. His eyes narrowed. "What's the matter, toe-nails not done? Stinky feet?"

"My feet are not stinky!" She sent her shoes flying. It was such a relief to have them off, she nearly cried. Then the feeling started coming back. "Ow, ow, ow ..." She really did cry. It was all thoroughly mortifying. Chad had probably planned it this way.

"Oh, I get it." He wrinkled his nose in sympathy with her stinging legs. "Let's sit for a while. Is Chad working tonight?"

Meg should tell him the truth. About their fight. Their passive-aggressive, no-voices-raised fight. About everything. She should. "Something like that."

"He's a good guy, Chad. Quite a catch. Lucky you." He tipped his chin in approval, nodding in that sage way people do when being nice about a common acquaintance.

One look at his face and Meg knew she wouldn't be coming back. Maybe the store would give her a refund on the shoes.

"Let's give your feet a chance to recover. We'll start with some theory."

This guy just didn't miss a beat. He helped her into a chair and sat opposite. "What timing is this music? Tell me what you think." He pressed play on the remote that dangled off his belt hook and picked up her left foot. She shot up straight and tried to pull away but he held up a finger, shook his head and asked, "Timing?"

His fingers rubbed circles in each toe, through her arch and her heel. She gave a half-hearted tug. This was awkward, but ... the pins and needles melted away wherever his hands went. Meg felt herself turn to jelly. She focused on the music, one two three, one, um ... "Aaah, I dunno." Her eyes slid closed. Tension was slipping from her back, her neck that had been in constant spasm for as long as she could remember.

"And this one?" He moved to her other foot and changed tracks. The tempo was upbeat, vibrant. She was finding it hard to focus on anything other than her feet.

"Nope."

"Come on, Meg. Focus." Dominic pressed the button again, this piece was smooth and easy. He put her feet down carefully, the pins and needles were gone. She shrugged, eyes still closed.

"I don't think you're trying very hard."

Meg opened her mouth, ready to shoot off a snappy retort but nothing came. Something witty? Nope. Vaguely amusing? Grief, at this stage, she'd settle for two syllables. Meg had grown up in the shadow of the other Meg, the blonde one on the big screen who still dominated the romantic comedy shelf at the DVD store. Redhead-Meg had watched all her movies, rolling her eyes, loudly poo-pooing the guaranteed

7

happy ending thing, all the while secretly nursing a tiny hope that there was one of those reserved for her, too.

Facing Dominic now with a stalled brain, her rivalry with movie-Meg flared. She always had a smart quip. Though, to be fair, she did have a team of professional script writers doing all the hard work. All she had to do was show up, look adorable, and sprout her rehearsed lines at the right time. *Easy for you to be so perfect, movie-Meg. Not so easy for us real Megs.* Her teeth snapped shut with a clack. Dominic was frowning at her.

"Maybe we'll get further when Chad is here."

Sure, and maybe I'll come back next week. Right about the same time it snows in the Sahara. She collected her traitorous satin shoes with a sneeze and hobbled out barefoot, rubbing her itchy nose.

· · · ● ●·● ● · · ·

Dominic was still frowning as he watched Meg leave. Today's setback would cost him a week, a week he didn't have. He hadn't been able to get through enough with Meg for him to judge how quickly she'd learn, either. She had the looks all right, there was no doubt about that. But for what he was planning, she'd need to have a whole lot more going for her than eye candy. He turned off the lights and pulled the studio door closed behind him.

Reception was deserted, but not quiet. They'd cranked up the volume in the room where the team rehearsed and now it would take more than walls to contain the music he'd picked out for their competition routine. He should be in there, putting them through their paces, but he'd trusted them to Gina for this session and he didn't want to go back on that.

Someone had left their shoes next to the couch, pale pink trainers. More lost property. Dominic scooped them up and checked the size. Perfect fit for the feet he'd just rubbed. Meg had left her shoes. He gave a quick whiff—they didn't smell bad, just like her feet hadn't. He dumped them on his desk and picked up a file marked Project Phoenix.

He frowned at the shoes and sat with his zebra feet propped up on the desk. Paging through sections, he turned to profiles. Meg's was filed right on top, a photo of her paper-clipped on. The photographer must have snuck in this shot, she seemed completely unaware, unguarded. Breath-taking. It was a good thing she was taken because a girl like this would be a distraction that he couldn't afford right now.

He checked that calendar and eyed Meg's trainers once more. Maybe there was a way to speed this process up.

Chapter Two

BY THE TIME MEG unlocked her front door, her nose and eyes were streaming. Allergies, ugh. She shut and locked the door behind her and made a mental note to buy oil for the squeaky hinges that broadcasted her comings and goings to the entire building.

She fumbled her way to the kitchen and took out the antihistamine. Who knew what had set her off this time. She downed the small white tablet with a glass of water and thought about supper. If things were normal, fish would go under the grill, veggies in the steamer, and in half an hour Chad would arrive and sniff the air, demanding to be fed. But they weren't, and he wouldn't, and Meg didn't actually know what to do with herself. Cooking seemed pointless.

She took the last chocolate chip cookie from a tin, made a mental note to buy some more, and curled up on the single seater in the lounge, turning her back on the double where they always sat to watch movies. *Used to sit.*

Crumbs fell on the armrest and Meg left them there, counting how many seconds she could resist the urge to brush them off. The phone rang and she picked it up without thinking. Drat, she'd lost count now.

"Meg, how are you, darling?" Alice. If Meg had known, she'd have left it ringing. Alice worked with Chad, she'd become friends with Meg by default. Though "friends" may have been too generous a use of the word.

"I'm doing all right, under the circumstances."

"Hmm. Of course you are. I saw Chad at lunch."

Meg fiddled with the phone cord. A quick tug and she could claim to have been cut off. *Gosh, I wonder what happened? Right in the middle of our deep, meaningful conversation, too. Such a shame.* "That's nice."

"Meg, the poor man is beside himself. How long are you going to keep up this farce? What are you actually hoping to achieve?"

"I don't expect you to understa—"

"What's to understand? He is the best thing that has ever happened to you. This silly game you are playing? You could lose him. Don't you see that?"

Heat rose through Meg in a wave; she felt dizzy and bilious. At least her nose wasn't itchy anymore. She was saved from answering by a knock at the door.

"Sorry, Alice, someone's at the door. Nice of you to care." Meg ended the call without waiting for Alice's response. She straightened the block-mounted photos that lined the wall on the way to checking the door. The photos were all hers, snapped spontaneously in a way that was quite contrary to her cautious nature.

She was grateful for an excuse to hang up on Alice, but when she got to the door, her heart sank. As she stood there, hand on the half-turned doorknob, she realized there wasn't a single soul she wanted to see.

It was too late to pretend nobody was home, unless she could convince whoever was on the other side that the place was haunted by a ghost that *almost* let you in when you came knocking. Yeah, probably not ...

Dominic perched on her welcome mat with his hands tucked behind his back, rocking back and forth on his heels.

"You! What are you—"

He held out her shoes. "You left these and I thought I'd return them. Your door hinges need oiling." He stopped and peered over her shoulder. "Those are great photos, where did you buy them?"

"Photos are mine." She took her shoes from him, half-eaten choc-chip still in one hand. "If you'd let me know, I could have just fetched them." She threw the shoes down behind the door and wished Alice would call back.

"Oh, it was no trouble. Can I oil your hinges for you and is Chad here by any chance?"

"What? Chad?"

"You know, your fiancé?"

"Oh, him! Um." *Anytime, Alice.* "No. He's not and my hinges are under control, thank you very much." Meg was frowning now and not just a few shallow lines either, her whole forehead crumpled up.

"Listen, are you hungry? I need to eat and I hate eating by myself."

Meg held up the choc-chip. "I'm fine, thanks. Really." The man wasn't leaving. There was no way she was inviting him in.

"That is your supper? No, Meg. Put your shoes on, you're coming with me."

"I'd really rather not."

He leaned over, plucked the biscuit from her hand and ate it in two bites. Meg watched it all in shock, empty hand still stuck up in the air like a pirate ship mast. Only it was she who'd been plundered.

"There. Now you have to come." There were crumbs on his lips. He brushed them off and grinned at her. He hadn't even tried to resist brushing the crumbs. Not even for a slow count to one. Meg did the only thing that made sense. She shut the door in his face and locked it.

· · · · ●· ●· · · ·

Dominic felt the lock click into place with a sting worse than if Meg had slapped him. That had not gone well. He considered knocking again, turning up the charm, being his normal persuasive self, but he had a feeling that none of that would work on this enigma of a girl.

He dialed Chad's number as he took the stairs two at a time. If he couldn't get through to the girl, maybe it was time to try a different approach. Chad picked up after the third ring. "Dominic! It slipped my mind to phone you to cancel the lessons. I'm sorry, bro."

"No problem. I can fit you in for a catch-up lesson. To-morrow night? I've got a gap."

"I'd love to but it's not going to work, you know?"

"So, I'll see you both next week then?"

"Uh ... we're going to have cancel the lessons. All of them. Meg dumped me. Not really conducive to couple dancing, you know?"

"What do you mean, 'dumped you'? Are you sure?"

"Bro ... of course I'm sure. I have an envelope with the ring in it to prove it. I always wondered whether she had some messed up masochistic thing going on. Now I'm starting to think that she does. She is one confused, lost, little girl who has just shut the door on a bright future. There's only so much one can do for someone like that, you know?"

"It was wrong of me to ask. Not my business." So Dominic wasn't the only one to have a door shut in his face. The fact that Dom's door had been an actual wood and nails door brought a wry grin to his face.

"Nah, look, it's all good. I've got nothing to hide. I can't understand what gave her cold feet. All our friends said that what we had was the ultimate couple goal. She's messed up big time. Now I've just got to decide whether I'll say yes or no when she comes crawling back. Pulling a stunt like this doesn't do much for one's trust, you know?"

The fact that Chad ended so many sentences with *you know* was getting on Dominic's nerves. He mumbled platitudes and ended the call. So Meg had lied to him. Right now he had two problems: a five-couple team competition to prepare for with only four couples in his studio capable of taking part, and a stubborn young lass upstairs who was fed up with him for eating her cookie.

Chad and Meg signing up had seemed like the answer to his prayers. *What now, Lord?* Should he play matchmaker and try get them back together? Or …

Or there was an alternative which just might work.

· · · · •· •· • · ·

The knock on her door was brisk and loud. Meg stared at the crumbs on the couch armrest and decided to ignore whomever was at the door. She'd had enough drama for one day. Another knock, harder this time. She grabbed two pillows and shoved them up hard against the side of her head. The next knock came through muffled like she was underwater. Kick it up a notch, Meg. Not caring if the knocker figured out that she was home, she began singing at the top of her voice, in a tone-deaf monotone. "LA LA LA LA LAA! WA WA WAAH. CAN'T HEAR YOU, SO YOU DON'T EXIST, SO GO AWAY."

Silence.

Meg removed the cushions and breathed. In. Out. In. Ou—

Knock, knock, knock.

"Oh, for crying out loud, I'm coming!" It was Dominic, with his face all scrunched up as if he expected her to slam the door in it again. Meg's eyes pulled to slits and she stepped back to shut him out with meaning.

"Wait!" He held out a peace offering, laced with chocolate crisps, her favorite brand. Not just one, but a whole new packet-full.

She snatched them from his hands. "Don't think this is going to get me back to dancing with you. All this gets you is a door not slammed in your face."

He brushed his hands off on the back of his pants. "I'll take what I can get. Now ... I'm starving. Please come have dinner with me. You don't even have to eat, or you can even bring those along and eat them if you like." He motioned towards the cookies she had clutched to her chest with both arms.

"Is there nothing I can do to make you leave me alone?"

"It's just dinner." His smile washed over her and ended in her knees, leaving them wobbly. Daft knees. There was no other way to get rid of this man. She retrieved her trainers from behind the door and followed him.

· · • • • • • • · ·

Dominic chose a quiet corner of The Blue Zoo steakhouse. The air hung thick with the aroma of grilled steak, and mushrooms and garlic—a perfect combination. It was still early enough to get a table without a reservation, light enough to scope the room for anyone he knew. Seeing nobody, he relaxed a little. Eating out with another man's fiancée could easily be mistaken for something that it wasn't. Regardless of what Chad had said, he figured it would only be a matter of time till they got back together. Meg was off-limits.

They settled into the booth; Meg hid herself behind the menu. Dominic had thought it would be easier to persuade Meg to join his cause first and then work on Chad. Now, after speaking to Chad and getting off to such a rocky start with Meg, he wasn't sure what to do. According to Chad, they weren't engaged anymore. Meg's ring finger was naked, but she hadn't said anything about a split. By the end of dinner he was hoping for two things: a full stomach, and a bit of hope for his dance troupe. A commitment from one or both of them to be at class the next day would be perfect, but life seldom handed any *perfect* out on a plate. This would take some delicate handling.

Dominic stood to take off his hoodie; curiosity made him peep over her menu. Meg had her eyes shut tight, scrunched up like a birthday girl making a wish. "Uh, Meg ... you okay back there? Have you decided yet?"

Her eyes shot open and she dropped her menu, fumbling to catch it before it slipped off her lap. She missed and curled herself under the table to retrieve it. Her voice came from below, muffled, "Just a piece of grilled fish."

"What kind of fish? Kingklip? Salmon? Good old hake?"

Meg sat up before her head was properly out and thwacked it hard. "Whichever comes first in the alphabet." She poked at her head tenderly, wincing.

"I'm not even going to ask why." He took her menu, placed their orders, and settled back with his thumbs hooked in his denim pockets. This girl was more complex than he'd thought. Asking her outright would get him nowhere, he'd have to try some small talk. The fact that he was useless at small talk was another story altogether. Pretending not to know what he knew, he took a sip of water and asked, "So have you and Chad set a date yet?"

Meg shrank back against the red leather, looking every bit like a cornered animal. Her pulse beat at the base of her throat, her breathing sped up. "Not quite." She cleared her throat and angled herself towards the window, apparently completely absorbed by the fascinating street outside on which nothing moved.

"Have you two had a fight?"

She turned to him, shoulders pulled back, nose high. "What am I doing here? What were you thinking?"

"I was thinking there's not much food value in a chocolate chip cookie. I was thinking that I needed food and so did you."

"Why do you keep asking me about Chad?"

"For the studio—"

"We won't be coming to lessons. I'm sorry."

At that moment their waitress, *Juliet*—according to her badge, brought their food. Meg's hake and greek salad, his ribs and onion rings. Dominic waited while Juliet fussed over their table, arranging food and condiments just-so. His mind ran like a hamster-wheel. He needed Chad and Meg to be fine, so fine that they came to dance lessons and caught up real quick. There really wasn't time for any of this other emotional nonsense.

He sawed off a rib with a steak knife, and picked it up to eat it. Juicy, tasty. Just how he liked his meat. Meg was nibbling half-heartedly at her fish. She poked at it, working it from left to right on her plate and then back again, all without taking another bite.

"Something wrong with your food?"

"No, it's fine."

He put the bare rib bone on his plate and cut off another. "Maybe you should eat some of it then."

Meg sighed, regarding him with cool green eyes. "Here's the funny thing. I don't think I like fish. It's just what I always get." She shrugged, put her fork down and looked sheepish.

"You don't *think* you like fish? That makes no sense. Why do you order it then?" Something shifted, he could see it on her face.

"I just do."

"I'm not following." He picked up his knife, cut off a rib and held it out to Meg.

· · · ● · · ● · · · ·

Meg stared at the rib as if it had her at knife point. She took a deep breath, let it out, and held Dominic's gaze for the first time since she'd met him. Chad always ordered her food. He never asked what she wanted. He just ordered what was best for her. White meat was better than red. *Have the fish, Meg. It's good for you.* Swallowing it as his way of showing love, Meg never complained. It was such a small thing, and his intentions were good. But right now, sitting across from this infuriating man holding out a steaming rib, a sneaky rebellion flowered in her belly. She took the rib and bit. It was good, really good.

"So why are you so keen for Chad and me to come to lessons? Is it a money thing?"

"Are you asking if I'm poor?"

"Not exactly. I guess, maybe. Well, are you?" She put the empty bone on her plate. Her eyes slid across to his plate and she shook herself. Get a grip, Meg.

Dominic speared the ribs, cut off another and handed it to her. "That's quite a forward thing to ask, don't you think?"

"You bullied me into coming. I think I've earned the right to ask at least one awkward question."

"Fair enough. To be honest, there's a competition coming up that I have to win, but I need a five-couple team. I was hoping you and Chad would be my fifth couple."

She swallowed and shook her head. "Even if I wanted to—which I don't—we're not what you'd call competition material. I'm not even sure why I went for that one lesson. I have no rhythm and Chad is worse. But you haven't answered my question." Meg didn't really care whether Dominic's bank account was anorexic or obese, she was keen to see him squirm in too-tight shoes for a change. Only he didn't seem to be squirming.

"Have you ever tried?" Dominic pointed at her plate and his, waving his hands to indicate a swap. "Dancing, that is."

"Well, not ballroom"—she slid her fish plate across the table and made space on her side for his ribs—"other than our lesson. That didn't go so well."

"But that's different. You were wearing your arch enemies in satin. You won't know until you try in comfy shoes."

She snorted a laugh. "Was that an intentional pun?" Confusion wrinkled his forehead. Meg had the unfortunate ability of seeing the funny side where others didn't even see a side. It had earned her many strange stares. "Arch enemy ... feet have arches." There was no amusement in his face. "Well, I thought it was funny. And you still haven't answered my question."

He leaned back, deliberately wiping each finger on a napkin before crumpling it up and dropping it on the table. "Here's the deal. You come to one more lesson and I'll answer your question." His hand shot across the table quicker than a snake strike. The light had dimmed enough for her not to be able to read his expression, a shadow fell across his eyes, cast by the overhead lamp. The same lamp highlighted his jaw, set with a determination that should have made her think twice.

Should have.

Maybe it was the ribs. Compared to forking tiny flakes of fish, tearing in with teeth and bare hands had made her feel rather fierce. It could have been the looming big-O and her sorry cake list. Or maybe the glint in his eyes that took a torch to everything dry inside of her. *Meg. Use your brain. Don't do this.* Her greasy hand met his halfway across the table. "Tomorrow?"

"Seven p.m."

"Deal."

Chapter Three

MEG ENTERED THE TEST results into the laboratory system and hit print. Mrs. Schmidt had some life-changing news coming her way, six weeks along. This was the one part of her job that she liked to pretend didn't sting. She didn't wish any of the other positive results on herself: diabetes, heart disease. She was quite happy without any of those. These pregnancy tests though, they got to her every time. Chad was keen for a baby, too. Was she wrong to have broken it off? She shook her head, brushing away doubts like mosquitoes.

She picked up the next vial—another pregnancy test. Normally, Meg found herself constructing imaginary scenarios of the ladies these test results would go to. *Honey, how about we clear out the study for these—slides a set of booties across the dinner table. Hey, Mom, I guess I need to start calling you "Grandma."*

Happy tears, sad tears. Some miracle babies, some college dreams chopped off at the knees.

Today though, Meg put through her fifth positive pregnancy result without lingering over its recipient. Her mind shifted tracks to yesterday's greasy bet. No matter how she thought about it, she couldn't figure out what had made her agree to go for another lesson. She truly didn't care whether Dominic had money or not.

That left her with only one reason for the daft bet and that one didn't make sense at all because honestly, she never wanted to see the man again. Besides, the first lesson had been awkward enough to dry up any desire to set foot in the studio again, let alone be around Dominic. The man had trouble written all over him. Maybe this is why Chad had kept her away from red meat: it neutralized common sense.

"I just won't go. It's that simple. I don't owe him anything." Mrs. Allbright's sample vial declared its solidarity with her decision by maintaining a stoic silence. Her ever-exotic lab partner, Vashti, chose that moment to come back from tea.

"Meg, stop talking to the test samples. You know it freaks me out."

Meg shrugged. "At least they listen."

"Not talking back does not exactly equate to attentiveness." Behind Meg's back, Vashti was rolling her eyes. Meg didn't have to look at her to know. Years of sharing the same space at Vida-Lab Technologies meant they knew each other better than most close friends.

"Now *that* I can agree with." Meg's thoughts drifted to Chad and how he'd perfected the art of the *uh-huh*. A terrible thing happened today, honey! *Uh-huh.* Pirate aliens from Pluto came down demanding to have their planetary status reinstated. *Mmmmm.* They took me to their ship and impregnated my feet with moon dust. *That's nice, sweetie.*

"You're dissing Chad in your head again, aren't you?" Vashti drummed her neatly trimmed nails on the worktop and even stopped chewing her gum for a moment.

"No!" Meg's eyes slid sideways then blinked rapidly. "Maybe. Oh, all right, so I was. So what? He deserves it. I think."

"He doesn't and you know it."

"So if he's such a catch, why don't you go for him?"

Vashti was outraged, Meg could tell by the way her nostrils twitched. "Megan Davis, I can't believe you just said that! Because he is the perfect match for you. Because you're just being too dim right now to see it. Hear what I'm saying: we each get one chance at getting it right, one chance to be happy. You are busy trashing yours."

"I was joking, Vashti, honestly. Lighten up. Can we change the subject now? I'd really rather talk about something more fun, like Mr. Williams' stool sample that you have there."

Vashti eyed her sideways, probably trying to decide if she really had been joking or not. The deep lines between her eyebrows leveled out and she snorted. "Far be it from me to have all the fun." She slid Mr. Williams' sample across to Meg. "Friends share, right?"

· · · ● · ● · ● · · ·

At exactly 7 o'clock, Meg reached the top of the studio stairs. She would rather be back at the lab doing Vashti's dirty work, but since she'd first sat next to Chad in class at the age of six, he'd drummed two things into her: be on time, and be reliable. Twenty-three years down the line, she couldn't resist the coercion of his voice in her head, even if it meant coming back here. And, of course, her list demanded she do something selfless; maybe after tonight she could tick that one. Tonight was certainly not for her benefit.

Dominic lit up when he saw her. She slipped her feet into her shop-kindly-upsized-ballroom shoes. No muffin top and she could wiggle her toes. Things were looking up. She swished, no! *glided* over to where he waited. Maybe if she lay on the cool, floated around the floor as elegant as a beauty queen, maybe then she could erase the tragedy of their first lesson from his memory.

"Aaah, you can walk. That's an improvement."

"Thanks." Was he not even watching? There was way more than walking going on.

"Let's see how far we get." He pulled her close and took up the classic hold. As his fingers closed around hers, Meg felt the familiar tingle in her left nostril. Oh, no. She chewed her bottom lip. Maybe pain would chase the urge. Her right nostril twitched. She bit harder.

"Remember two steps back, side close, yes? Meg, there's nothing to be nervous of. You don't need to chew your lips."

"I'm not"—sneeze—"nervous." Sneeze. "I—," two more explosive sneezes rocked through her.

"Let me guess. You found some sick friends to hang out with to get off the hook tonight?"

She pulled away from him and dug in her bag for a tissue. At least she'd thought far enough ahead to pack in tissues. "I'll have you know, in my line of work I hang around germs every day of my life. Not just any old germs, fierce ones. The ones that can land you in the hospital. And I never get sick. Ever."

Dominic had his head to the side as if he were studying an oddity of nature. The only problem was, he was looking at her.

"What?"

"That was three sentences without a sneeze."

"So?"

In two steps, he was so close she breathed him in. And sneezed.

"Meg Davis, I believe you're allergic to me."

She scrubbed at her nose and sniffed, trying hard not to grin. "Well, that solves my problem then, doesn't it? I should leave for my own health's sake." She stepped out of her shoes and reached for her bag. As she tugged at her car keys, a crumpled paper napkin fell out. Her list. She scooped it up and shoved it back deeply into the back corner of her bag.

"Wait! I have a plan. You don't have to leave just yet."

"You just don't know how to give up, do you? I can't dance with you. Look at me, I'm a mess." She waved in the vague direction of her smeary face and sneezed. When she opened her eyes, Dominic had his shirt up over his head. He pulled it all the way off and threw it on the table next to the music system.

He turned to her with hand extended. "Come."

"You're half-naked!"

"Call it an experiment. Now get over here, please. Our time is running short."

Meg felt heat rush to her face as she stepped into Dominic's arms. His skin was hot beneath her fingertips as if he'd just walked in off the beach. She was acutely aware of every movement he made; she could see the muscles working beneath his skin. Chad had never affected her like this. Where do you look when all you want to do is look, but you really shouldn't want to be looking? She lifted her chin high left and focused on the ceiling. There were down-lights in every second square and the one in the square closest to the window was flickering and would need to be replaced soon.

"That is the perfect angle for your head. I should have taken my shirt off ages ago." He held her hand too tightly for her to smack him. Meg settled for grinding her teeth. Music flooded the room, Meg stepped off at the first count after the intro. Dominic didn't budge. He didn't look at her, or speak, just pulled her back towards himself this time so close, she could feel the heat from his skin all down her front. Two side sways, a gentle lift and he stepped forward.

Meg followed, allowing herself to be moved across the floor. They made it down two complete sides before she sneezed. Dominic pulled away from her as if she were contagious. He crossed his arms and harrumphed.

"Now maybe"—sneeze—"you can tell"—sneeze—"me why you"—sneeze—"took your shirt off?" She rushed the last bit out, determined to beat the sneeze.

"I thought you might be allergic to my laundry detergent but it seems it may go deeper than that. Never fear. I have plan C."

Meg squeezed her eyes shut, willing the sneeze urge to be gone. "Me too, though my Plan C involves home, an antihistamine, and my book." Even as she was saying the words, Meg felt a tug at leaving her cake list un-ticked. One whole lesson for Dom's sake. Selfless. That's all she needed. Dominic had his hands on his hips and that set in his jaw that was becoming so familiar. "Okay fine. Plan C it is. Lay it on me." She sniffed for emphasis.

"Start in the corner. Walk eight steps forward and stop in a pose like this." Dominic mimicked a flamenco dancer, down to the sultry pout.

Meg snorted a chuckle and sniffed extra loud to mask it. Chad would have been eaten alive by tortoises rather than take up that pose in public. "I don't pout."

"Oh, you will, honey. You will." Dominic's eyebrows shot up and down and the sultry come-hither look slid into his shoulders, still gleaming and shirtless. It was all too much for Meg. She covered her mouth with her hand so he wouldn't see her grin. The last thing he needed was encouragement. Suppressing giggles made her shoulders shake. Seemingly fueled by the crack in her composure, he preened and primped. The absurdity of the man was too much. She shoved the urge to laugh down so hard, her eyes watered.

Holding it in was too much, her eyes streamed and her muscles ached.

"Please stop, I can't ..." She let it out and laughed. Not just a belly laugh, more like a full-body laugh. A minute later, reality hit home with a bat shaped of thick embarrassment and she pulled herself together with heat in her cheeks.

Dominic seemed to sense the shift in her mood as he stopped fooling around. He came over to help her to her feet and quickly backed off so as to avoid her allergies kicking in. By the time Meg left an hour and a half later, he'd taught her twelve counts of eight, all without coming close enough to put a tickle up her nostrils.

· · · · ●· ● · · ·

Gina poked her head around the studio office door. Her blonde bob was tucked behind her ears and there was a faint sheen of moisture across her forehead. "How is our new couple coming along?"

Dominic winced. "How did the team rehearsal go?"

She started to answer, but waggled her finger at him instead. "You know I hate it when you do that."

"You always used to fall for it. Where is the naïve girl that I loved so much?"

Gina ruffled his hair with perfectly manicured hands. Her nails were long and painted in "nude." Why anyone would paint something that was the color of what lay beneath it anyway was beyond the grasp of his logic.

"So ... the new couple?"

"It's complicated. But it will work out fine. Trust me."

"Will they be joining us anytime soon? There is only so much formation work we can do with four couples. You know that."

Dominic shuffled papers on his desk, avoiding her eyes. "I'm sure by next week we can combine." Meg was a fast learner, but the fact that she no longer came with a built-in partner would be a problem for Gina, and rightfully so after the whole Rising Stars debacle. Not to mention the whole too-allergic-to-actually-dance-with-your-partner thing. That would push Gina over the edge, for sure. She had the emotional explosiveness of a redhead at full moon. Handling her took more energy than what he had right now. He shoved the pile of folders in a drawer and fiddled with his laptop cable under the desk.

Gina flopped down in the chair opposite, planted her elbows on the desk, and leaned right into his space. "What are you not telling me?"

"Trust me, okay?"

"I hate it when you say that." Her lips were a tight line of white.

"Monday. We'll do our first combined rehearsal on Monday. Will that make you happy?"

The line stayed tight. "Ecstatic."

He smiled as if she were honestly overjoyed. "Good. That's settled, then. There is somewhere I need to be. Should I lock up, or are you still busy?"

Chapter Four

"I DON'T KNOW, SANDY. Something about bonsai trees just creeps me out." Meg clutched her bag tight to her chest as if one of the tiny trees on display was about to reach out and snatch it.

Sandy yanked Meg's arm, pulled her close, and whispered through clenched teeth, "Shh! Don't say that out loud. These people live for their bonsais." Sandy let go of Meg's arm, brushing at the white marks her fingers had left as is if she could dust them off. "Besides, I haven't seen you for weeks. I wanted to know how you are. This"—she waved at the expanse of the badminton hall that was taken over by tiny tree enthusiasts once a year—"is all just a good excuse to catch up."

Sandy kept her tone light, but Meg knew her well enough to see concern in her eyes. They were only half way down the third aisle of the bonsai display and Meg could feel a vague panic setting in. "Why here, though? We could go walk on the beach." They stopped at a tiny bald cypress and she could have sworn she heard it crying. *All I ever wanted was to be big. I'm a big tree trapped in this tiny tree body. Save me!*

Sandy rolled her eyes. "My mother-in-law is a bonsai fanatic and she put in a good word or two to land me the job of organizing this fine event. Single moms can't be too picky when it comes to growing their event management businesses, you know. Besides, I don't have to grow them, or even like them. I just have to make sure everything runs smoothly. Though, Mom actually wants to give me a tree as a token of appreciation. Honestly, I couldn't even keep the fern in my kitchen alive after Xan was born and she thinks I've got time to tend to one of these. Nuts, I tell you. Anyway, she offered to keep Xan while we came and had a look. I love my seven-year-old, but I'll never say no to a time-out. Hey, you look like you need coffee."

"Well, let's just say that the moment you hear tiny trees screaming for rescue, that moment, right there, is probably a good moment to get some fresh air."

Sandy's nose wrinkled. "I have no idea what you're talking about. I don't think that I want to know, either. Come, I'm buying."

Sitting in the dappled shade, Meg imagined caffeine flooding through her system as she sipped a frothy cappuccino. The tea garden was set up under the real trees outside, big ones that had been allowed to grow as much as they wanted to. Their sheer bigness calmed her. The light filtered through the leaves, casting a green glow on the smooth bark. It was a picture waiting to be snapped and Meg obliged.

Sandy ordered a slice of vanilla-rose cake for each of them, and sat back with her hands folded deliberately in her lap. Sandy had been to some body language workshop and the guru had taught her that crossing your arms made people feel shut out. Now whenever they chatted, she made a point of *not* crossing her arms. It made Meg feel like a specimen.

"So the last time we had coffee, we were making lists of who to invite to your kitchen tea and how long you should wait before having a Xan of your own. Quite a bit has changed since then."

"Come on, Sandy. You don't have to do that euphemistic stuff with me. If you want to know what happened, just ask."

Sandy regarded her in silence, kicked off her shoes, and tucked her legs up underneath herself so that she was sitting cross-legged on the chair. Her hands slid under her armpits. "What I really want to know is if you're happy?"

"Is anyone our age happy?"

"I don't really care about anyone. I want to know about you. How did you get from *I want to have Chad's children*, to *I may need to have my eggs frozen cryogenically* in such a short time? I've watched you two since primary school. Is it just cold feet?"

Meg took her rose cake from the waitress and stabbed it with the fork. "It's cold something. Maybe a little more than feet."

Sandy uncrossed her arms and folded her hands on her lap once again. Meg could almost feel the willpower rolling off her in waves.

"So let me get this straight, you and Chad have been friends since you were eight."

Meg broke off a piece of cake and speared it with her fork, it stayed on the plate. "Known each other since six, but then there was that thing with the glue and eyebrows at seven ..." She shook her head to focus. "Eight's about right."

"You both love each other, enough for him to propose and for you to say yes. Yes?"

Meg squashed the broken off piece of cake with the fork. The mess of crumbs on the plate was growing.

"You are so ready to have a baby, your ovaries basically sing you anthems to wake up each morning, and amazingly, Chad is ready for all that, too. Don't roll your eyes at me."

"What's your point?"

"I'm your friend, so after this conversation I'm going to move on and support you in whatever you choose. But I need to know why you broke it off? And why are you destroying that cake without even eating any?"

Meg was saved from trying to explain by Xan. Sandy's boy ran up at full speed and stopped himself using the table. Meg and Sandy knew him well enough to brace the table before he hit. He grinned at them both with his blue eyes twinkling. His hair was a few shades lighter than his mom's blonde, but he looked like a younger version of her. The boy had more energy than he knew what to do with. His eyes lit up when he saw the cake.

"You want this?" Meg slid the plate across before her friend could object.

He slid into the empty chair. "Thank you, Aunty Meg. What you talking 'bout?"

Sandy's eyes were wide and wild as she watched her boy tuck into Meg's rejected cake. She pulled a cross-eyed face over the top of Xan's head. "We were talking about nice Uncle Chad."

Xan paused, cake hovering half way to his open mouth. "Eeew. Don't like him."

The shock on Sandy's face made Meg laugh, though she was sure it mirrored her own.

"Why don't you like Chad?" asked Sandy.

The fork had made it all the way to Xan's mouth and crumbs flew as he spoke past it, "He'sh a bully."

"He is not! He's gentle and kind." Sandy's hands had crept back up into her armpits.

Xan was shaking his head even as she spoke. "I know bullies. He's a bully."

Meg tucked her own hands into her armpits to hide the shakes that hadn't been there moments before. Sandy stood up, nearly upending the chair. She pulled the cake out from under Xan's nose and deposited it in front of Meg. "I wanted to treat you. You should get some of it at least."

"I don't think I eat cake."

"Excuse me?!"

"Cake isn't healthy. I don't eat it."

"Who told you that?"

"Chad did."

Chapter Five

MEG HAD THE LIST hung on her fridge under a magnet that told her *tomorrow will be better, so don't give up today.* She hated the magnet, but couldn't bring herself to throw it away, like throwing it away would give life permission to smack her with all the *un*-better things it could come up with. She kept the image of her list fixed in her mind as she climbed the stairs to the dance studio. It was Monday night and she was back for more.

Feeling a little smug, she didn't wait in the waiting area, but sauntered straight towards the scene of her first two failed attempts at List Crossing. She snapped a quick pic of the door before walking through it, saw a room full of people and kept going, a perfect circle all the way out.

"Wait, Meg!" Dominic had to run to catch her. He grabbed her by the shoulders, walked her around, continuing her circle back into the room full of people. His arm remained around her shoulders, muscles taut. Getting out of a grip this tight would involve enough squirming to be embarrassing. "Meet the team."

Meg barely heard the names spilling from his lips over the rushing of blood in her ears. Cliff, a buff Asian with a wide, friendly, grin whose partner was Tammy, a gorgeous African lady whose dark skin glowed under the studio lights.

Pale, delicate, Alison stood with a graceful serenity that made Meg think of the lady-elves in movies. Her shoulder-length brown hair was drawn back into a bouncy ponytail that spiked at the top. Her partner was a big guy called Jeremy with kind eyes and a neatly trimmed beard.

Talia was the shortest of them all, a neat, compact ball of muscle and energy, with curly reddish hair and tanned skin that made it look like she lived on the beach. Her partner was Matt, youngest of all the guys. His hair color matched hers and his face was clean shaven. Maybe that's what made him look young.

Reg and Gina. Reg had the pale look about him that people have who live at work in their high-rise offices and never see the sun. That left Gina. Gina with her sharp face and shiny blonde bob, who only wore one expression when looking at Meg: disapproval.

Seven new faces, smiling and welcoming, only Gina stood with her arms crossed, with the barest curl of her lip. Sandy's guru was right about the arm crossing thing. Who would have thought? Their names and faces blurred, too much to take in all at once. Over it all ran one realization—Dominic smelled funny.

The blonde unhappy one came into sharp focus as she stepped forward, hand shifting to her bony hip. "When will your partner be getting here? We can't afford to start late." She'd have been gorgeous if her face hadn't had the pinched look of someone sucking lemons.

Dominic squeezed Meg's shoulder, answering before she could string any words together, "I'm filling in, Gina."

If Gina's face had drawn in any further, Meg thought it may just invert completely. What would you be left with if your face collapsed into some sort of cosmetic black hole? Another shoulder squeeze brought her back into the room where Gina seemed on the verge of hyperventilating. Her chest was heaving and spots of color rode high on her cheeks. She looked like a good candidate for a brown paper bag. Dominic really did smell odd.

"No, Dom, you're not. Have you forgotten the whole Rising Stars Debacle?" The word debacle came out with enough force to warrant its own capital letter.

"Of course not. But this is different."

Gina's one eyebrow clawed its way out of the black hole to ride high on her forehead. The other was still missing in the pinch. "How so? Pray tell."

Dominic relaxed his grip on Meg's shoulder long enough to take his shirt off. He smelled funky, no doubt. "No time to talk now, Gina; you said yourself we can't afford to waste any. Take up starting positions, everyone." He steered Meg past Gina, who still wasn't looking too great, to the same spot she'd started her forward walks and parked her with a wink. He leaned in close enough that only she could hear. "Just do what I taught you and you'll be fine."

"Did you forget to use deodorant?" Her whisper matched his for clandestine-ness.

"I didn't forget. This is Plan D. In case you haven't noticed, you haven't sneezed once." His grin was pure victory as he left her, lined up with the other ladies.

Music flooded the room and Meg felt herself moving with the others. Walks, pose. Hold and circle. The brunette next to her moved her hips in a particular way. Meg fished for her name. Alison! Meg copied the movement and found it allowed her to move quicker and stay in time.

Moving in the patterns she'd learned, she danced in-between the other dancers without colliding. In a few places, she didn't know actual steps, but she managed to walk the patterning enough to stay in sync with the others. The choreography was intricate, and even though her part had felt small she could see in the mirrors how it all meshed together. Synergy like this was addictive.

· · · · ●· ●· · · ·

Dominic held the deodorant lid under her nose. "What about this one?"

Meg shook her head and pulled away before the scent got too far up her nose and brought on a headache. A lovesick soul was declaring his endless devotion over the supermarket PA system. He wasn't helping her head, either. "Tell me again why I'm here?"

"We're overcoming obstacles, Meg." He bent down and picked out another tin, popped the turquoise lid off and waved it under her nose.

Meg sneezed. "Obstacles?"

"Yes! Anything between us and winning the competition must fall. Right now it's that nose of yours." The turquoise lid was followed in turn by an orange, a gray, a midnight blue and finally a dark brown.

Meg shut her eyes and obliged with a sniff. Sandalwood and something else she didn't recognize. She breathed it in again, puzzling over the scent. When she opened her eyes, Dominic had his face millimeters from hers. She shoved him away. "I like this one."

"You're not sneezing and I can live with the smell. That's a complete win." He smiled as he said it.

"You should try it now. You really should."

"What are you saying? The *au natural* man-odor not doing it for you?" Dominic mock swaggered, holding out an armpit for her approval.

Meg grabbed her nose and pushed him. "Oh, my word, stop it! You twit." There was something vaguely ridiculous about how happy Meg felt in that moment. No logic could explain it. Practice had been hard and she had been pushed to absorb steps and patterns on the fly. By the time they did the last run-through, she'd held her own and managed the entire way through without crashing, tripping anyone, or landing on her rear. She was a long way from knowing all the steps, but the patterning had stuck in her brain.

She wasn't sure who was more surprised, the other couples or her. If Dominic was surprised, it was well disguised under a thick layer of smugness. He was delighted. Seeing him so proud of her caused a tiny *something* to bubble in the pit of her stomach. The laugh bubbling from his belly right now stirred that same bubble. She clawed to get back to safe ground. "Anyway, you told me we were just popping in to get food."

"Oh my, this looks cozy." Chad strode down the aisle with phone-call-Alice, his co-worker. Alice stared down her nose at Meg with the same expression on her face that Meg used for a cockroach in her kitchen. Chad's face turned an interesting shade of red.

"Chad, I assume. Good meeting you in person." Dominic reached for a handshake but Chad left his hand stuck out, swinging like a tree limb.

"What is going on here?" Chad's face gave away no emotion. His eyes though, they cycled thoughts like a slot machine, coming to rest on a single conclusion. The wrong one.

Meg felt herself folding inside, re-tucking layers of herself into tiny fragments. Blood rushed through her head and the lights spun. Fainting seemed like a good option.

· · · · ·•·•· · · ·

Dominic recapped the deodorant and slipped it into the basket Meg was carrying. It crashed to the floor before he realized that it was more than the basket falling. He caught Meg just before her head met tiles. Chad stood frozen, a tightly coiled fury playing through every muscle in his face. Alice hovered, her hands fluttering like moths.

Dominic brushed hair away from Meg's neck and slipped his fingers to find her pulse; it was low and skittish.

"I should have known. I've been such a fool." Chad had one hand on his hip, the other seemed intent on strangling his hair.

"Does she do this often?"

Chad's chin stuck out. "You seem to know all about her. Why don't you tell me?"

"Oh, come on, this is not the time." Dominic dismissed him and his melodrama, his whole focus was on Meg who lay in his arms as pale as a porcelain doll. Just then Meg's eyes opened, swimming and unfocussed. "Hey, welcome back."

He saw consciousness return as panic and she pushed herself upright. "Where is he?"

"He's gone." Dominic hadn't seen him leave but the spot where he'd stood frothing was open.

"This is terrible. He thinks ..." Meg fought herself out of Dominic's arms and onto her hands and knees. Her legs shook as she pushed herself up straight and her eyes were wide and panicked.

"Meg, I don't care what he thinks. If he'd cared enough to listen, we could have explained. I have my doubts that he would believe whatever we'd said anyway."

49

"I have to go. I can't do this. I can't …" She pulled out of his grip and ran.

Dominic fought the urge to run after her, catch her in his arms and hug her until she felt better. *Perfect timing, Chad. Thanks, buddy.* There was something about Meg that brought out a fierce side that he hadn't known was in him. If it didn't seem creepy, he'd have bought a sword and stood guard outside her apartment. Her neighbors might have thought it odd, but he could live with that. But then again, it was her heart he longed to protect and a sword wouldn't do much good there.

He made his way to the check-out, mulling over his next move. He needed Meg for the competition, that much was true. But seeing her after tonight's rehearsal had convinced him that she needed this as much as he needed her. He may have to tell her the real reason the competition was so important. *What do You think, Jesus? Can I trust her with this?*

The singer on the in-store radio crooned on about *love not living here anymore* as Dominic paid for Meg-friendly deodorant, hoping that he'd get a chance to try it out on her.

Chapter Six

MEG LOCKED THE DOOR to her apartment, knowing the click meant the world had to leave her alone for the next twelve hours. It was a deeply satisfying thought. She'd considered changing careers at least five times today. One for each positive pregnancy test she'd processed. That was a mere coincidence, of course. Of course!

She picked an apple from the bowl on the counter and hunted in the drawer for the peeler. If she were to change jobs, the most logical thing would be to open a quaint little bookstore. One of those on a corner that sold obscure second-hand books with people's phone numbers penned onto the flyleaf in the hopes that destiny would do its thing and reunite fated lovers. She'd run it at a loss and drink cheap coffee out of recycled cardboard cups. It would be nice to be part of the meant-to-be's for a change. Besides, if the romantic comedies were to be believed, running a bookshop was a sure way to meet Mr. Right.

She peeled the apple in one long, curly strip and toyed with the idea of leaving the peel on the counter. Her heart pounded at the thought and she scooped it up and threw it in the bin. No point pushing the boundaries, not after today's scene.

There was every possibility that Chad was her Mr. Right and she had bombed her bridges. Not a homemade petrol bomb either, but one of those heat-seeking, guided by a satellite in space, leaves a decade of nuclear fallout-type bombs. Seeing the scene through his eyes—her and Dominic giggling over buying toiletries together—it didn't take a great leap of imagination to read into the situation. Add to that the fact that Chad had never fully grasped her reason for breaking it off. Meg felt her stomach twist.

She set the apple aside, untouched, and felt ... dirty.

· · · · ·•·•· · · · ·

Dominic stood outside Meg's door and found himself praying. He could only do so much, the rest would need Divine Intervention of the most miraculous sort. A full five minutes later he rang the bell. As he did so, his cellphone buzzed in his pocket. He checked it out of reflex more than interest.

Plz com now. Buntu.

The message was short, but not one he could ignore. Buntu never messaged him unless there was trouble. Meg opened the door, peering through a tiny gap, saw him and shut it again. He heard the jingle of the chain before it swung open a tiny bit wider than before.

"What do you want?"

"I wanted to check on you after last night."

"Well, I'm fine. Thank you for asking."

"Good." The *now* in Buntu's message meant urgent. He felt it in his spirit too, the urgency. "It was good seeing you, Meg." He stepped away from the door before he changed his mind, and ran.

It took twenty minutes to get through the traffic in town and onto the road that led to the squatter camp where Buntu lived. The road degraded to a dirt track, pockmarked with deep pot-holes. Taking a pothole too fast would guarantee a damaged wheel; he slowed way down and had to come to a complete stop for a goat that decided the grass did indeed look better on the other side and chose to cross over. Grass was too generous a word. The sidewalks were no longer neatly mowed lawn, but mud interspersed with rough scrub-brush and thorns.

Shacks dotted the roadside, rough structures built from sheet metal and stolen road signs. Most had no fences between them. It was after 9:00 p.m., but there were kids still playing outside. The road was a walkway, jammed with milling groups of teenagers.

Buntu lived off to the left edge of the camp. By the time Dominic pulled up outside her house, the small African woman was out the door, face wet with her tears, wringing her hands. She was a tiny person, compact and powerful. Her chiseled cheekbones were highlighted strong and proud in the muted moonlight. Wood smoke hung thick over the area. Those who couldn't illegally tap into the power lines lived around a fire for warmth and cooking. Buntu carried the smell around herself as if it had been rubbed into her skin.

"What's the matter? Is it one of the kids?"

Buntu nodded. "Isaac didn't come home from school." Her voice was deep and strong, a slight tremor the only hint that she was concerned. "I'm so scared."

"We'll find him, Buntu. The others all fine?"

"Sleeping." She waved in the direction of the shack behind her. "Isaac has new friends. Bad boys, not good. They make trouble."

"The sooner we get you out of here, the better."

Buntu had a hand over her mouth as if she could stop words from coming out, words that would convince her that Isaac was truly in danger. A boy came out of the shack and ran up to hide behind Buntu's legs.

Dominic bent low and waved. "Hey, Ernest."

More bones than muscle, Ernest responded with a flash of white teeth before slipping himself under Buntu's arm and hugging her. He barely reached past her waist, his clothes had more holes than fixed bits. Buntu enfolded him in her arms, tucking him close to her fiercely, as if protecting him could keep Isaac safe by proxy.

Dominic gestured towards the boy. "Is he talking yet?"

Buntu shook her head. The boy tugged at her clothes and went off in a complicated series of arm waving and hand gestures. Not a single word passed his lips through all of it. Buntu shrugged. "It's impossible to understand him."

"I'm not so sure. Ernest, do you know were Isaac is?" The boy's eyes stretched wide and his chin dropped in a single nod. "Can you take me to him?" Ernest looked up at Buntu, waiting for her approving nod before agreeing.

Buntu's eyes shone bright with tears as they met Dominic's. "Keep him safe. Find my boy. That's all."

· · · · ● · ● · · ·

Meg washed the kitchen floor, replaying Dominic's visit over in her head. He must surely be the weirdest person she'd ever met. With all his strange habits and things he'd rather not speak about, Meg couldn't help but wonder what kind of secrets the man was keeping and why.

A clear voice broke the silence outside with an old tune, "Time In A Bottle." One of Meg's neighbors could sing, and did so every day round about this time so regularly that Meg could set her clocks by it. It sounded like a woman singing, but Meg hadn't quite figured out which neighbor it was. Surely it couldn't be grouchy Mrs. O'Riley from next door.

She reached up into the cupboard for goldfish food and crushed a few flakes into the bowl on the kitchen counter where one sorry little fish called Ebb swam laps all by himself. He had fish problems which made him swim sideways and sometimes upside down. Sandy had given him to Meg as she couldn't bear to watch the fish struggle, knowing that he could go belly up at any second. Meg, however, liked his courage and kept him, rooting him on every day that she woke up to find him still breathing.

She leaned on the counter now, wishing he could talk back. "Hey, buddy. So what do you think? Who in their right mind would knock on someone's door at this time of night, ask if they were okay and then leave? That's not normal, don't you think?"

Ebb didn't answer but bobbed to the top and did some awkward gymnastics to get the food floating on the surface.

"You may have issues, Ebb, but you never give up. I'll give you that much. And to think Chad wanted me to flush you. Honestly." If Dominic's visit had done one thing, it had taken Chad out of her head. Except now she'd just thought of him and he was back. Ugh.

A realization settled over Meg as light as snowflakes. She hadn't been able to pin down what made her break it off with Chad, but now she knew. It was a simple thing, not a relationship deal-breaker by any sane person's standards, yet it had flicked a switch in her heart, mind, and soul as effective as a master trip switch on an electricity panel. One suggestion and it all shut down.

Flush the fish, Meg. Put it out of its misery.

She was throwing away her relationship over a broken goldfish that could be one breath away from dying anyway. That didn't make sense at all.

The doorbell rang and Meg wondered where her screwdriver was to disconnect the thing. On her way to the toolbox, she opened the door out of habit to find Dominic with mud on his face cradling an African boy who was bleeding from a cut on his head. A second, smaller boy hid behind his legs and peered up at her with big eyes.

"I need help."

"Why me?"

"C'mon, Meg. Medicine is your field."

"Fine. Come in. Put him on the couch." Meg ran to fetch her first aid kit, caught sight of herself in the mirror and stopped. *What am I doing?* Her cheeks were flushed bright pink, hair scraped back in a ponytail and her pants had a hole in the left knee from scrubbing floors. *The boy is bleeding, holey pants will do.* Right. She found her kit, dusty and unused from the time she'd bought it.

By the time she got back to the living room, the boy was stretched out on the couch she and Chad used to sit on to watch TV. Dominic knelt next to the boy, gripping his hand tightly, the other arm looped around the small boy who hugged Dom's neck and had big teardrops collecting on his lashes.

Meg knelt next to Dom, leaning in close to the injury to get a better look. Blood seeped from a deep gash from eyebrow to hairline, the skin was already bruising. Meg took out a small pile of gauze swabs and pressed them against the wound. "My 'medical' work is not quite what you're thinking."

"Medical is medical, surely. It's all bodies."

She pressed down harder, absorbing the blood. "Let's just say if you stuffed him in a test tube and brought him to me, I'd be fine." Her mouth pulled in a grim line as she watched the blood soak through the gauze in seconds. Keeping pressure on the wound, she frowned at Dominic. "Or you could say that if this guy were pregnant or suffering meningitis, I could confirm it for you. That's about the extent of the help I can give." She pulled the gauze away and motioned for the bottle of disinfectant and a ball of cotton wool.

"You work in a lab."

"Bingo." She wiped the wound down with disinfectant and tossed the cotton wool to one side. She wadded up a thick pad of gauze and pressed it against the wound. "Pass me the bandage, please. No, not the white one. Give me the flesh-color—the wide one. It's stretchy." She finished dressing the wound and watched for seepage before letting out a breath she didn't know she'd been holding. "If he bleeds through the bandage, you might have to take him for stitches. I need tea. You want some?"

Dominic hugged his legs, his forehead on his knees. The blood on his hands had dried and he had red marks all over his pants. When those bloody hands started shaking, Meg knew he wasn't okay.

"Let's get you cleaned up." She helped him up off the floor and he leaned on her as if all the strength had gone from his legs. They shuffled through to her bathroom, a room so small you had to be careful not to bump your head on the wall as you sat down. She guided his rear onto the toilet seat with enough dexterity to keep his head safe and ran a basin full of warm water. Using her lilac face cloth, she washed his hands, one at a time. Normally, he'd be full of chirps and swagger, but his face was pale and tight and he sat quiet. Meg rinsed the cloth, wrung out the excess and wiped mud off his forehead, his cheeks. Using a spare towel, she dried his hands and face.

She was so focused on the task at hand—mud, blood—that it was only as she wiped the last traces of moisture from his forehead that she realized how very much in his space she was. Being so close on a dance floor was one thing, here in her tiny bathroom was quite another. Meg panicked.

"I'm going to put the kettle on." She walked out of the room and realized she couldn't leave him there. She swung back, took his arm between two fingers and guided him through to the kitchen where she propped him up on a barstool and filled the kettle.

"Who is he?" Unresponsive, Dominic sat staring at his hands. Meg bent over and stuck her face in his. "You with me?"

Dominic stirred as if she'd woken him up from hibernation mid-winter. "My friend's son, Isaac. I don't know what happened, I found him behind a dumpster like this."

"And the little guy?" She tipped sugar into a glass of water and stirred. The granules swirled around and surrendered to the liquid, dissolving without much of a fight.

"Isaac's brother, Ernest. He doesn't say much."

"Here"—she slid the sugary water across the table to Dom—"drink this. I think you're in shock."

"Is he going to make it?"

"He'll be fine. You'll need to watch for infection and he'll probably have quite a scar for the rest of his days, but he'll recover."

"There was so much blood."

"One of the main arteries got nicked, so blood was literally being pumped out. That's always impressive."

Dominic blinked and she saw a pull to his lip that she was beginning to recognize.

"What's that face about?"

"Impressive. Impressive is you picking up a routine in a single session. This morning's sunrise was impressive. I don't think of blood as impressive."

"I guess that's why you teach ballroom and I work medical. Why didn't you take him home?"

Dominic took a swig of sugar water and grimaced. "I needed to know that he'd be fine. For his mom's sake." He downed the rest of the water and pushed the empty glass across the table to Meg, shuddering. "That was gross."

He cared about the mom enough to make sure her boy would live before taking him home. Isaac was his best friend's son. That made Isaac's mom Dominic's friend. Meg wasn't too sure how she felt about that. "You've got color back in your cheeks. Seems to be helping."

"How did you know?"

"About sugar water? Everyone knows that for shock—"

"No, I meant washing my hands"—he wiped a hand over his face—"and everything. How did you know it would work?"

Dominic was staring at her with an intensity that made her squirm like there were fleas between her shoulder blades. She busied herself pouring a cup of hot chocolate for Ernest, and answered simply, "Did it?"

· · · · ·· · · · ·

Dominic curled his hand around the warmth of the teacup. How would he answer that? *I was falling down a black tunnel with no hope of stopping and your small act of kindness brought me back.* She'd think he was a flake for sure. "It did."

"Good. We should check on the patient." Meg carried through the cup of chocolate and set it in front of Ernest on the coffee table. The boy hadn't budged from his brother's side, balanced on the soles of his feet, hugging his knees as if trying to take up as little space as possible.

Meg put her hand on his back. "Ernest, this is for you." The boy flinched, eyes on the carpet. Meg knelt down until she was at his eye level. "Your brother is going to be fine." She spoke in the soft tone one would use to soothe a scared animal, her mouth turned up in the slightest smile. Ernest looked up from the carpet long enough to catch her eyes. Dominic saw the boys shoulders relax. He must have seen something that told him he was safe here as he allowed Meg to lead him closer to the table where his drink waited.

"You know this will be his first cup of hot chocolate?"

Meg frowned at that but kept her thoughts to herself. She was glowing, radiant. Dominic had never seen her look so beautiful. It wouldn't have surprised him to hear a choir of angels launch into the "Hallelujah Chorus."

The doorbell rang and Meg ran to answer. She peeped through the hole, and came back into the room looking green, like someone had stolen her lunch. The angels hung back on the song and two words escaped her lips and fell over her like a lead catch net.

"It's Chad."

Chapter Seven

THERE WAS THE USUAL squeak from the front door hinges, Chad was letting himself in. Dominic watched Meg slam the living room door shut just as the front door clicked closed.

"What are you doing here?" Meg's voice came out high and squeaky, muffled but clear enough that Dominic could hear every word through the closed door. He eased himself onto his rear and motioned Ernest to silence with a finger to his lip. Ernest was too absorbed in stirring his hot drink to notice. Dominic realized what a truly wasted gesture it was, given that the boy never spoke anyway.

"C'mon Meg, don't be like that. I practically lived here." Chad voice was low, persuasive. He'd turned on the charm.

"Things have changed."

"I figured that out when I found you cavorting in the toiletry aisle. I feel like a bit of a fool. How long has that been going on?"

There was a pause, Dominic could imagine Meg sighing, hunting for the right words.

"I'm running out of ways to say this, Chad. There is nothing going on. Don't give me that look. Why won't you believe me?"

"The thing is, I couldn't understand why you ... did what you did. We are good together. We have been for so long. At first I thought it was cold feet, which is understandable. But you wouldn't listen to me, you wouldn't see. No, no! Let me finish. But when I saw you that day, it all fell into place. It all became clear. Wow, Meg. I never thought you had it in you to be so heartless."

Heat flooded Dominic's cheeks, fueled by a rage in his chest that spread to his hands. Rearranging Chad's face seemed like a perfect way to stop the itch in his fists. He forced himself to stay sitting next to Isaac, held back purely by knowing it would not help Meg if he barged out there now.

A flicker of consciousness pricked Isaac's eyes, he was coming around. Pain crumpled his face and a low moan escaped his lips.

The voices outside the living room hushed.

"Are you finished?" Meg's voice had climbed even higher. "Because I think it's time you leave."

"What's in the living room? Why is the door closed? You never close the door."

Isaac thrashed on the chair, the low moan growing to a wail. Dominic grabbed his shoulders, whispering, "Shhh! It's okay, Isaac. You're safe."

"I'm watching TV and I'm missing the end of my movie, so if you wouldn't mind, I'd like to get back to it."

"But we're not done talki—"

"We really are."

Isaac moaned and Dominic thought for sure it would filter through the door like someone being tortured.

"What are you watching? You know how horror movies affect you. Maybe I should watch with you."

"No!" It came out forceful, too strong. Enough to make Chad suspicious for sure. "I'm really fine, just need my space." Dominic heard the door slam shut, cutting off Chad mid-whine.

More than a minute later, Meg came back to the living room with her hands shaking, a butter knife clutched in her fist. "I think it would be best if you left."

"Do you have anything for pain?" Dominic had Isaac by the shoulders, keeping him steady as he thrashed on the couch, still not conscious but surfacing enough to feel the sting of his cut. Ernest stared at his brother with wide eyes.

Meg shuffled the knife from one hand to the other, frowned and put it down on the bookshelf. She dug in her handbag and inched closer to Dominic to hand over a blister pack of anti-inflammatory, anti-pyretic, anti-allsorts painkiller capsules and grabbed him a bottle of water from the kitchen.

Dom turned the pills over in his hand. "I don't know how to give this to him while he's out of it; he'll choke."

Meg shook her head and muttered under her breath. She took the blister pack out of his hand, popped out a capsule and opened it. She tipped the powder into her palm, rubbed her finger in it. "Hold his head still." Isaac had his mouth opened, mid-wail. She pressed her powdery finger onto his tongue, repeating the gesture until most of the painkiller in her hand was gone. Using the water bottle cap, she tipped tiny sips of water down his tongue to wash the powder into his system. Within minutes, the pain killer started taking effect and Isaac relaxed.

Dominic wanted nothing more than to hug her, but when he looked up the butter knife was back in her hand and he got the message. It was time to go.

The door clicked shut. Meg felt the cold metal of the knife handle in her palm and instantly felt stupid. How was she planning to defend herself with a butter knife? Smear them to death? Chad had a way of loosening all the muck that she tried to keep buried. Even a few minutes with him was apparently enough to dig up her old friend Suspicion and send it floating to the surface of her consciousness like poisonous seaweed.

Isaac couldn't even walk by himself, let alone attack her or rob her house. Ernest was young and innocent. Besides, the cup of hot chocolate had won her his undying devotion. He wouldn't harm her. That left Dominic. She wasn't always sure what was going on in his head or why, but if he'd wanted to do bad things to her, he'd already had plenty opportunity.

So why the butter knife?

She could ask that same question for a hundred things she did around Chad.

Meg took her Cake List off the fridge and flopped down on the couch, feeling worn thin. She toyed with the idea of crossing off *Figure out God* but she just couldn't do it. As much as she felt she knew enough about Him and how He worked to make the call, she shied away from actually putting pen to paper. The List went back up on the fridge under the irritating magnet and Meg took herself off to bed, feeling strangely hollow.

· · · ● ● ● · ● · · · ·

The sun had barely peeped over the horizon as Meg walked into the lab, put her bag in the cupboard, turned to her workbench, and screamed. Right there, in between her work notes and test tubes, sat a potted plant. She had no trouble with those generally, but this one was a bonsai.

Vashti came running in. "Who's dying?" Her cheeks were flushed.

Meg had no words, so she pointed with a finger that shook.

"Where did that come from? Oh, my gosh, it's so cute." Vashti cooed over the little thing, feeling the leaves between her fingers. It was just bigger than Meg's coffee mug, but it had more wrinkles than a collection of grandmas.

"I don't know. I walked in and it was just ... sitting there. And no, it's not cute. Kittens are cute. Baby hamsters are cute. This thing is an abomination."

"Aboma-what? You're staring as if it might climb out the pot and dismember you. I don't get it." Vashti's face wrinkled into a question mark. "There's a note. You should read it."

Meg shook her head, waving her finger at Vashti's chest. Vashti rolled her eyes and plucked the note from between the miniature leaves. "Look! It even has tiny fruit." She rolled her eyes again at Meg's squeak and opened the note.

Vashti read it out loud. "I'm sorry about the other night. Please meet me for coffee at lunchtime. I would like to make it up to you. Roxy's, one p.m."

"Who's it from?" Meg chewed her lip.

"It doesn't say. It's all very vague. What happened to you that would need an apology like this?"

My life was interrupted by a bleeding boy, his mute brother, and their misguided angel. "Not much, really. I think I know who sent that."

"You've got a lunch date! That's a first."

Meg ignored the sting. Vashti always had a man in the wings, lurking, waiting for the perfect time to pounce. With her high cheek-bones and tanned skin, it was no surprise to Meg that she didn't understand.

"It's not a date and anyway, who says I'm going?"

"Don't you want to?'

"That's not the point. Why are you so keen?"

"Meg, darling. I think if you had a man in your life, someone with real flesh and blood, you would no longer need your test tubes for company. I'm right and you know it. Are you even listening to me?"

All Meg could see was the plant, in its stunted smallness.

Vashti scooped it up and waved it under Meg's nose. "How about this: I'll take this little creature off your hands and you go for coffee. Deal?"

Chapter Eight

ROXY'S BUZZED WITH THE lunchtime crowd to the sound of Norah Jones crooning over rain on a tin roof. Meg stood at the door, clipped her hair up, and chewed her lip. She had a debate going with herself that had started the moment the lab door swung shut behind her with enough force to smack her rear. No matter how far her thoughts drifted, meandered or stomped, it all came back to one question: Why was she going to have coffee with this man?

It wasn't to do with the fluttering in her belly when she stood too close to him, or that she'd *almost* had fun shopping for deodorant. At least until Chad showed up. None of that was enough to make her leave the safety of her lab.

She noticed a young man staring at her, bobbing up and down on his toes. He wore a beige cotton apron with a pen and notebook poking out of the deep pocket along the front.

"Are you a waiter?" The man bobbed and nodded at twice the speed, clearly relieved that she'd noticed him. "And you're waiting for me. Ugh. Sorry, lots going on. Can I have a table where it's easy to get out and leave quickly?"

"Ma'am?" His eyebrows bunched together in the middle of his forehead.

"Not without paying of course! Oh, never mind. Anywhere will do."

He led her to a table buried deep in a suffocating corner of the coffee shop, exactly the opposite of what she'd been hoping for. It also seemed to be the only open table left. The note had said 1 p.m., so Meg had made sure she was there by 12:40 p.m. That gave her enough time to change her mind without the embarrassment of bumping into him on her way out as he was heading in.

She settled in the stiff-backed mahogany chair, popped her bag on her lap, and opened the menu to give her hands something to do. Her eyes hadn't adjusted to the dark and it was too gloomy in her corner to read anything in it anyway. The waiter fussed over the condiments, nearly tipping the salt. He caught it just before it spilled its guts on the table. "Would you like me to open the window shutters for you?"

Meg shrugged; it probably wouldn't make much difference anyway. The waiter must have taken her vague gesture as a yes as he squeezed in behind her, his round belly brushing the back of her head. Meg cringed and hunched over her bag. After a few bolts, some nudging and another belly brush later, she sat in a pool of glorious light with enough fresh air flowing in through the open window to grow crops on Mars.

"I give you a few minutes, yes?"

The poor boy left without any response from Meg who sat lost in her thoughts. She dug out her camera and twisted around to snap a photo of the open window. The camera was old, a hand-me-down from an aunt who saw she had an eye for light and composition. Meg still used it, partly to remember her aunt who she'd been fond of, but she also liked the challenge of producing a good shot within the limitations of older technology.

The faint breeze carried in the scent of jasmine and cooled the back of her neck, blowing through the fluffy bits of hair that always rebelled against being tied up.

It made her feel light, free. Happy.

The heady combination of wind and light seemed to have air-lifted her thoughts up and out of the maze of her mind and in a moment she knew there were two reasons to have coffee with Dominic. Two reasons that were a direct contradiction. On the one hand, he made her happy. There, she'd admitted it. Whether he was rubbing her feet, covered in the blood of his friend's son, or bullying her on the dance floor, something about him warmed her. On the other hand, he was obviously hiding something. Unless he truly was just a money-grabbing egomaniac, there was more to winning this competition than he was letting on.

Charming and deceptive. She should get out now while she could. Yet the combination tickled the sleuth in her, the same sleuth that had her combing through corpuscles for diagnoses every day.

Meg checked the time on her mobile, 12:58. She looked up as a man came through the door and stopped to speak to her pot-bellied waiter. It was Chad. Her mind ran over the words on the note ... *I'm sorry about the other night. Please meet me for coffee at lunchtime. I would like to make it up to you. Roxy's, 1pm.*

Not from Dominic, but from Chad. Stupid. Stupid. Stupid.

Meg stowed the camera and hooked her bag on her shoulder. She checked the window behind her for a quick getaway. It led to an alleyway and out onto the street. A good escape route but for the thick jasmine creeper that grew from wall to wall below the window sill. It would be impossible to get over it in her skirt without getting hooked up or showing off more of her underwear in public than she'd like to.

Pot-belly was pointing towards Meg's table and she panicked. Another waiter came past, carrying a milkshake on his tray. Meg ducked in front of him, took the full glass off the tray, stuffed it into the man's free hand and took his tray.

"I need this for a moment." She left him clutching the shake in both hands as if she might just turn around and steal that, too. Meg hid behind the tray and threaded between the tables, slowly working her round-about-way towards the door. As she shuffled sideways, trying to be small enough to fit in behind the tray, she berated herself for being so dim. Not for a moment had she considered that the note and the abomination had come from Chad.

Her view was limited to people's legs from the knees down. She shuffled past a pair of hairy feet shoved into dirty flip flops. The toenails were yellow and curled from being ignored. Sitting opposite were a dainty pair of pale feet, nails polished and buffed in delicate sandals the palest shade of yellow. *Run while you can, girl.* Two pairs of trainers at the next table seemed like a better match. Closer to the door sat low-heeled suede pumps and matte moccasins. *Hmm. No calling that one.* A strip of sunlight from the entrance stretched across the tiles like a runway to freedom. She might just make it.

"Meg! You came. I wasn't sure you would. Here now, give this man his tray back. Look at that, we're in luck! There is one empty table open." Meg let herself be dragged back to the table she'd just left.

"This is too bright and windy, let me fix that quick." Chad squeezed past her, drew the shutters and bolted them, then slid the window closed. "There, that's better. Now we can talk."

· · · • · • · · ·

Vashti put a pile of reports on Meg's desk. "I take it lunch didn't go too well." She parked herself on the edge of Meg's desk. "Judging by the state of your face, I should probably give you your plant back. You can throw it out the window or hack it up with a pair of scissors or something. I thought this Dominic might be a keeper. Either I was wrong, or you need to lower your standards."

Meg rubbed her eyes, peering into microscopes made them tired. "It was Chad. Not Dominic."

"What the heck?"

"I know. I've seen them both this week, I just never thought." Meg grimaced and took the pile of reports Vashti had dumped. "You'd think by now I'd have learned not to assume."

"What did he say to you?" Vashti's eyes had narrowed the same way they did when she was on the trail of a particularly malicious strain of bacteria. There was no throwing her off the scent now. Trying to fob her off in this state would have been a complete waste of time.

"He closed the windows. It was awful. Don't pull that face. I tried to explain how Dominic and I ended up toiletry shopping together but—"

"You went toiletry shopping? With your dance teacher?"

"It's a long story; it doesn't matter."

"Okay, so let me guess. I'm thinking Chad wasn't thrilled about you going for dancing lessons without him. Was he angry?"

Meg saw the moment in her mind for the hundredth time that afternoon. No, it wasn't anger. She could deal with anger. "He laughed. For about a minute non-stop. Then he choked on his drink and kept saying it as if it were the funniest joke he'd ever heard." *You? Dancing? Meg, Meg, Meg. Dancing with me for our wedding is one thing. But in a demonstration team? With your coordination? What were you thinking?* "Anyway. It doesn't matter. I'm probably going to go to crochet lessons or something. I can learn how to make bed socks. Everybody loves bed socks."

"Meg, I don't how to say this. I hate bed socks."

Chapter Nine

TEAM PRACTICE WAS MORE than two hours away but Dom was taking no chances. He knocked on Meg's door and waited. He heard footsteps coming closer, the locks clicked open, and there she stood with a crochet hook, a ball of canary yellow wool, and what looked suspiciously like half a bed sock.

Dread and excitement took turns on her face and it came to rest on something he could only describe as confusion.

"Hey, Meg. What is that?"

"It's obvious. What does it look like to you?" She swung it around with her nose wrinkled disdainfully.

"I couldn't possibly guess, but it's looking good for whatever it is. Listen, I thought I'd fetch you early so we can break down some of the routines before the others get there. You ready?"

"I can't do it, I'm sorry. I have this to do." She held up the wool and hook. "It's ... urgent."

"Life or death crochet. I get it. What I don't get is what changed between our last practice and now. You can't tell me that you weren't enjoying yourself." He moved her out of the doorway and let himself in, pulling the door shut behind himself. "Let me make you some tea then we can chat." Meg stood like an island, hook caught in mid-stitch, her cheeks flushed red. But her eyes were sparkling. That was something. "Do you take sugar in your tea?"

"Wait, I'll make."

He followed her to the kitchen where she dumped the wool on the countertop and filled up the kettle. He slid onto the barstool and leaned on his elbows. "So, how have you been, Meg?"

She wiped the top, lined up two mugs so that their handles faced the same way, swung around and frowned at him. "Okay, I guess. How is Isaac?" *And his mom. How is his mom? Not that I care one way or another.*

"Okay, I guess."

"No infection?"

"Nope. Healing well."

"Is this small talk?"

"I can leap right in and ask what's going on. Why swap *batucadas* for bed socks? Would you prefer that?"

"Not really. Wait! You could tell it's a bed sock? That's brilliant!" She wouldn't look at him, but kept fidgeting. Moving but not going anywhere. A balloon with a cut string. Something had her spooked. He slipped off the seat and moved right up close to her. Maybe if he could get her to stand still she would answer his questions. A pulse beat in the base of her neck, faster than a normal pulse should.

"Fine. Chad says I can't dance. He's known me most of my life, so I think he has a point."

Dominic stuck his hands in his pockets and kept them there, out of temptation to hold her shoulders. "Has Chad seen you dance recently?"

"Well, no, but—"

"Then you shouldn't listen to him. Simple."

"But wh—"

He held a finger to her lips and shook his head. "I like your goldfish by the way. He is one brave little soul."

Meg stirred and moved the cups across to the counter next to the fish bowl. "I didn't know you'd even noticed him. His name is Ebb. He has some challenges."

"So I see. He's doing good, challenges and all."

"You really think so? Or are you mocking me?"

"I wouldn't say it if I didn't mean it, and why would I mock you about your fish?"

"So you wouldn't flush Ebb?"

"Flush him? Why? He's still alive, seems healthy apart from not being able to keep his upside up. Are you considering it?"

Meg didn't answer, but sipped her tea. "Give me a few minutes to get changed."

· · · · ● · ● ● · · · ·

Sunset lit the polished wood of the studio floor with a bright glow that made Meg squint. Even through slitty eyes, she could see the frown on Dom's face.

"Batucadas, samba walks, *then* rolling-off-the-arm. You need to remember that." Dominic had his teacher's voice on, part-patience, part-encouraging, part-bully. Though right now bullying seemed to be winning.

"I can't decide what's worse. The pain in my feet from seven blisters, the pain in my thigh muscles from dancing in these heels, or the pain in my butt from you!" Meg's fluffy bits of hair were plastered to the nape of her neck with perspiration. She was also tired and frustrated at not getting the steps in her head.

Dominic grinned. "Well, someone has lost her filter."

"Stop laughing and fight with me. Then I can throw a tantrum and leave."

"Let's take it from the top. I'll put music on and we can mark it out, yes?" He didn't wait for her to agree, but walked to his starting position and clapped twice.

Meg fought the urge to stamp her foot. The music started and she scurried to her starting place, picking up the steps half way through the first bar. Samba rolls ...

"No! Batucadas first! C'mon, Meg, you've got to get this right. We have to win."

"I'm not going to get it. We should just give up now." The man was obsessed with winning. Whether it was ego or money, either way didn't make sense to Meg. Their priorities in life were clearly light years apart. She glanced across to where her bag waited patiently next to her shoes.

"No, you're going to get this. You can't give up now." He paced a few steps, one hand on his hip, the other scratching his head. "Okay, okay. This might just work. Before you quit, buy some rolls."

"And now you're hungry? How would rolls help?" This man made her brain ache. She frowned at him and aimed herself at her shoes. "I'm sorry, I just don't get it."

As she brushed past him, he caught her wrist and spun her into his arms, his face so close to hers, she had to squint to focus. He leaned in closer still, tipping her backwards so that the only thing keeping her from the floor was his arm around her waist. His voice dropped low and husky. "The only thing you need to get are these steps. Listen closely. *Buy* for batucada. *Some* for samba walks. *Rolls* for rolling-off-the-arm. Yes?"

"Oh." Meg shut her eyes tight and tried to slow her pounding heart. This new deodorant they'd picked out smelled good. Really good.

"Oh my, this is cosy. Should we all come back when you're done?"

It was Gina. Somewhere in the middle of Dom's bizarre shopping list, the whole team had arrived and let themselves in. Gina stood with her bony hip jutting out and a sneer on her face. Meg had never felt judged by a hip before. It was all quite fascinating.

Dom pulled away, settling her back on her feet before removing his arm. "Hey, Gina. No, come right in. We've just managed to nail an entire section. Right, Meg?"

Buy some rolls. Got it. Meg didn't trust her voice, so she nodded. *Buy some rolls.*

"Good. Let's see it." The word "good" rolled out of Gina's mouth as if it were a lemon she'd been sucking.

· · · ◆ ◆ · ◆ · · ·

"Twenty minute break, then we'll take it from the top. I need more energy, people." Dom had lost his normal happy face and it was probably her fault. Meg snuck off to the ladies' room before he could corner her with the list of corrections that seemed to pile up in his head like dirty laundry on a teenager's floor.

"Wait! I'll come with you." Talia ran to catch up with Meg before she disappeared around the corner. "My feet are killing me." Talia barely reached past Meg's shoulder, a compact ball of energy wrapped in toned muscles and skin that drank in the sun. She brushed back the stray bits of hair that had escaped the single plait that had most of her curls under control. The plait hung halfway down her back and swished as she walked.

Meg took Talia's foot gripe as permission to hobble. "Tell me about it. I've stopped counting how many blisters I have on each foot. For each practice I seem to grow at least one more."

"I remember those days! I don't get blisters anymore, but these babies"—she leaned on the wall and tilted her heel upwards—"are slaughtering me. My muscles aren't used to the extra heel height. I had to buy them to make me taller so that I'm a better match for Matt." She pushed open the door to the ladies' and waved Meg in first. Talia shut herself in a cubicle and kept on chatting through the thin walls. "So where did Dom find you, anyway? You are heaven-sent! Was it from the ad in the paper?"

Meg stood, stuck halfway into a booth. It didn't feel right to keep chatting while answering nature's call, but apparently Talia had no such hang-ups. Should she chat first? Talk while busy? Come back by herself later? "Something like that," she mumbled as Talia flushed. She ducked in and shut the door as Talia's swung open.

Water ran, soap squirted from the dispenser. "And you've never danced before?"

"Um, not this style." *Come on, bladder. It's just another girl. A small one at that.*

"You're picking up really fast! Impressive!" Loud blowing from the hand dryer. "I'm going back, are you fine here by yourself?"

"I'll be fine. No probs." *Please go!* The door swung shut and Meg's bladder got over its stage fright. At last.

She came out to find Gina resting her rear on one of the basins, blocking off the soap dispenser. *Hey, Gina. What's up?* "I didn't hear you come in. Excuse me, can I get to the soap?"

Gina slid sideways, bony hip still doing its thing. "I thought we could chat before we go back in. Have you thought about what you are doing, Meg? What makes you think you can pull this off? I mean, don't get me wrong. It is super-sweet of you to try, but I think it's time you face reality. You aren't a dancer, never will be. This competition is stiff. Why set yourself up to be humiliated? Trust me, I am probably the only one honest enough to say this to your face. The rest are all too ... polite."

Meg frowned at the soap bubbles forming patterns on her fingers. Talia did seem sweet enough to say nice things when pushed into a corner. Only Meg hadn't even started the conversation. Talia had. It didn't add up. It didn't help that deep in her heart, actually with her whole heart, Meg agreed with Gina.

"So what do you think?" All Gina's angles seemed to have softened, even her hip was now *the friend who cared enough to confront.*

Meg opened her mouth to answer but no sound came out. Her brain blanked.

"Do you like him?"

"Sorry, what?"

Gina pushed herself off the basins and sauntered across the floor to tower over Meg. "Dominic. Is he why you are here?"

"No." *I don't think so, anyway.*

"Good. For your sake. You don't want to get entangled there. Trust me."

"Sure. Whatever."

Gina turned to the mirror and re-clipped her fringe. "Also, if you chose to pull out, you'd be saving us all time and trouble. Nobody will tell you to leave because they are too nice, but let's just say you won't be letting us down if you quit."

"But I thought you needed a minimum number of couples—"

"Not your problem. I have that covered."

"Bu—"

"No, really. That is no longer a problem."

Chapter Ten

IT WAS 10:00 P.M. when Meg finally unlocked her front door and ran a bath for her aching body and fried brain. She breathed in sandalwood-scented steam, rolling her shoulders to ease out the stiffness.

She'd left dance practice with one new blister on her left foot, miraculously none on the right, at least ten counts of eight sandwiched into her brain, and a business card of a seamstress that she had to go see for her team costume. She'd shoved the business card under her Cake List on the fridge with a shudder. Something about the words "dance costume" filled her with the same amount of dread that "baboon spider" or "poopy diaper" did for other people. Sequins and bare skin. Ugh.

Meg lowered herself into the bath water, wincing as the water stung the popped blister on her big toe. She sat down quickly to get her feet out of the water and prop them up on the side of the bath. Lying back, she scooped up bubbles and fashioned a quasi-snowman on her left knee. The steam swirled in lazy curls and her mind began to pick at the ball of tangled thoughts of the day. *Yeah, maybe not.*

Careful not to drown her soap bubble man, she sank down low enough to get a good mouthful of water and squirted a stream of steaming liquid towards her creation. Her aim was good and soon he was reduced to nothing more than a shapeless blob of the stuff that he'd come from, leaving her with the bitter taste of soap bubbles on her tongue.

Bitterness slipped down her tongue, landed in her heart and she wondered if that was how God spent His days. Creating people, setting them up and then taking them out for fun.

Look what a happy life you're having! You're getting married! You're going to have babies! Oh, wait. That's too perfect. Let me wreck it all for you and see how long you last. I'll start by drowning your fiancé's sister. That will mess him up real good. Oh, wait! It can be worse! I'll do it while he's a small boy and make sure he's right there watching and not able to save her. That will wreck him so badly he'll never recover. Fast forward a few years, hook you up with him, and let one damaged one destroy the other. One spurt of soapy water and I can take down both of you at once.

She could tick it off her list—she had God all figured out. Meg sank below the surface feeling hollow. List ticking should feel better than this.

· · · · ● · ● · · ·

Dominic rubbed his eyes and knuckled the small of his back. The lamp on his desk did its best to push back the shadows in his office, but struggled, only managing a dim pool that reached as far as the papers on his desk. For once he was keen to go to bed. Rehearsal had used up most of his energy and maybe tonight he'd sleep. A full night's sleep was almost too much to hope for, given that most nights saw him lying awake, watching whatever mind-movies his busy brain coughed up for him. Often he would use the time to pray, but tonight he wanted to switch off.

The door swung inwards and Gina let herself in, shutting it behind her.

"I thought you'd left with Reg." Dom moved so that his desk sat squarely between them.

Gina shook her head. "You know Reg. When work calls, he runs. Always some IT emergency or the other. I was wondering if you could give me a ride home?" Her tone was light, but she slipped across the room with a roll of her hips that made him twitchy. She draped herself on his desk and leaned across towards him. "What are you working on now anyway? It's late."

"Oh, I just needed to pick up the Phoenix files. I'm on my way home." Dom dug in the drawer and found the files that he didn't actually need and bundled them up together. He felt cornered, a bug trapped on a spider web. "You know what? Let me call you a cab. It will get us both to bed sooner. Was there anything else?"

Gina studied her nails. "Actually, there is something. I have a *proposal* for you." Her eyes flicked up lazily on the word proposal. She settled into the chair opposite him, in no hurry to leave.

"Can it wait? It's late. You look tired." Now that he'd mentioned it, Gina had dark circles under her eyes that he hadn't noticed before. "You really do look beat. Are you sick?"

"Well, that's a bit rude, don't you think?"

Dom shrugged and stayed standing, hoping she'd get the hint. Some nights he could take her drama. Not tonight, though.

"Well, I'm fine. Never been better. Okay, if you're in such a hurry, I'll get right to it. I don't think your little redhead is working out. She will never be ready in time."

"Are you kidding me? I know it's a lot to expect from a newbie, but she's a fast learner. You can't deny that."

"Oh, for sure, but I don't think it's enough."

"It has to be. We don't have a choice."

Gina leaned back, resting her head on the chair. She was a beautiful woman when stress didn't get involved with her face. "Before you argue, hear me out. What if we ditch the idea of the formation team and enter as a couple? Just you and me." She sat forward, eyes sparkling. "I think we'd be fabulous together. Face it, Dom, you are the best guy in the studio and none of the girls come even close to me." There was no boasting in her tone, she was good and accepted it. No false humility there, either.

"The prize-money isn't enough in that section. You know that."

"If it's money you need, you can keep my share of the winnings, too. I know what you want the money for, I just don't understand why."

Dominic shrugged into his jacket and picked up his car keys. This was not a conversation he wanted to be having. Especially not with Gina. "It's late. We've got to be back here in a few hours." He reached out to help her up, but she ignored his hand. As she stood, her eyes rolled back and she fainted, landing in the chair hard, nearly knocking it over.

"Gina!"

Seconds later, her eyes rolled open. "What happened? Oh, I feel sick."

"Just take a moment. Breathe. You probably just stood up too quickly."

"I need a bucket." She clamped her hand over her mouth and Dom ran for the dustbin. He got it to her just in time.

"Bring the dustbin, I'm taking you home."

Gina let herself be led out of the studio and into Dom's car, as meek as a newborn kitten. It would seem that something had triggered her eating disorder again.

· · · · ·· · · · ·

Meg checked the clock. Two minutes until lunch break, which was usually more a time of day than an actual event. Today would be no different, not with the heaps of blood work she had to get through. The phone on her desk buzzed; it was Lou the security man from downstairs.

"Miss Meg, there's a man here to fetch you."

Lou was getting old, his hearing was becoming more cotton-wooly by the month. Meg would hate for him to feel bad about it. "Lou, I think there's been a mistake. I don't know anything about that. Are you sure he wasn't asking for Peg in accounts? You know, Peg ... Meg ... easy mistake."

"Nope." His voice dropped low and she could imagine him hunching over the phone in his glass cubicle, loving the intrigue. "He's quite a looker. You should get down here before he changes his mind."

"Lou!"

Muffled talking. Meg could only think the phone was being pressed up against Lou's ample belly while he conferred. The voice that picked up from the belly was not Lou's voice.

"Hey, Meg, it's Dom. We have a fitting appointment with the seamstress. I thought you might want some company. You know, a hand to hold ... someone to barricade the door shut so you can't run away ..."

She snorted a laugh despite herself. "Sounds fun." *Not.* "I'm sorry, I can't leave, I have so much work. I didn't even know I had an appointment."

"It was written on the back of the business card I gave you. Didn't you see it? Wait, give me a mo—" The line went dead and Meg stared at the phone in her hands as if it were a snake. She hung up and reached for the nearest sample.

"So this is your kingdom! Nice!" She hadn't even heard his footsteps up the stairs. The man must be part hobbit.

"Dom, what are you doing here? Lou never lets anybody come up."

"Oh, I knocked him out and handcuffed him to the desk. He'll come around in an hour or so."

"What?!" Pins and needles prickled across her scalp.

"It's a joke. Calm down. He let me up because he can see what an enormously trustworthy person I am." He grinned so wide, more than half his teeth showed all at once. "Actually, I took a guess that he's a Dean Martin fan. As it turns out, I was right. We traded favorite song lyrics and here I am. Come on, you can't miss this. This woman is impossible to get an appointment with."

Vashti, who hadn't breathed a word all day, stuck her head around the corner. Her eyes rolled up and down Dom. "Meg, go with the man."

"But—"

"Just go. I'll do the urgent ones. Besides, it's lunch time. This place owes you about three trillion lunch times."

· · · · ● · ● · · · ·

StarDust Dancewear was nothing more than a staircase behind a glass door, wedged between a bookstore and a coffee shop with enough cheesecake on display in the window to dimple your thighs before a single bite crossed your lips.

"Look, Dom! Cheesecake! And there's a bookstore. It's a sign. We should get some. They have the blueberry one. Oh, my word. I love blueberries." Meg stood rooted, close enough to the window that her breath misted it up.

"Focus. We're not here for that." He took her by the elbow to guide her towards the door, but Meg dug in her heels.

"No, but I really *really* want this. Look at it. It's beautiful."

"Dress first, cheesecake after. Now come!"

Meg allowed Dom to pull her away from the cake and followed him up stairs of sparkly white stone. Demure wall lamps led the way upwards, a firefly trail luring the unsuspecting into the lair of a beast, a beast armed with a measuring tape and pins, living in a cave of wicked down-lights that existed only to highlight every bump and wobble.

"I really, *really* don't want to do this." They'd reached the top of the stairs and Meg felt sick to her stomach.

"Uh-huh." Dom ignored her whispered hiss. He squeezed her hand absently and tapped on the glass door, squinting to see inside. The door clicked open and Meg felt her legs quiver. The shop was done out in bluish-white with accents in jewel colors. Tall dress shelves lined three of the walls, surrounding couches and a coffee table in the center of the room. Each of the cupboards was filled to bursting with sparkling garments arranged in the color order of a somewhat drunk rainbow.

Only then did she notice the short girl waiting patiently for her to stop gawking. She was an odd duckling with fuzzy red hair that reminded Meg of a feather duster. Her clothes were a shade of purple so dark that if you squinted and tilted your head, you'd swear she wore black. She only reached as far as Meg's shoulder, but her eyes were steely gray beneath perfect eyebrows. And she looked young. Very young.

"Shouldn't you be in school right now?" Meg peered around, waiting for the real designer to appear and take over.

The girl ignored Meg and her question, turning to Dominic. "Is she the one?" Her eyes scraped up and down Meg, who promptly felt naked and resisted the urge to cross her arms over her chest.

Dom stepped forward and slipped an arm around Meg, at once drawing her closer and preventing any escape attempt. "So good of you to squeeze us in, Caz. This is the one, yes."

Caz squinted and twirled her bony finger in a circle. This seemed to be code for *I want to see her butt* because Dom swung Meg around fast and kept a firm hold on her shoulders. Meg leaned in close, her voice dropping low, "She's a baby. Is this a joke?"

Dom avoided her eyes, but leaned in closer still. His breath brushed her cheek. "She's the best. Trust me." He was wearing the new deodorant again. She sniffed deeply, half-expecting the tingling to start up her nostril.

"Hmmm. This is not going to be easy. Are you sure you can't get the other one back?"

Dom cleared his throat and Meg could swear she saw a blush creep along his hairline. "No, Caz. That's not going to happen."

"Well, that's a real shame. The dress really worked on her. Aah, well. We take whatever challenges come our way, even if they are pear-shaped. Come this way. Not you, Dominic."

Dom swung Meg around and she followed the girl, frowning furiously and mouthing *I am not pear-shaped* at Dom who sat himself down on the snowy couch, looking suspiciously like he was trying not to choke on his tongue.

The room Caz led Meg to was small, naked-white, with only a three panel full-length mirror in one corner. Above the mirror ran a circular curtain rail complete with drapes. The drapes themselves—thin muslin—hooked on either side of the mirror, forming soft cloud-like bellies of fabric. The lighting was as dimple-highlighting as Meg feared.

"Right, no time to lose. Keep your underwear on, take all the rest off. I'll give you a moment then I'll come measure you." Before Meg could object, Caz withdrew on ninja-silent feet.

· · · · ●· ● · · ·

Dom squirmed on the sofa, trying to get comfortable. How could something look so good, but feel so wrong? Maybe it was the fabric. All he achieved for his wriggling were some impressive squeaks. He, too, had been worried that Caz was too young the first time he'd met her, but she soon proved that ability wasn't linked to looks or age and the studio had used her services ever since. He leaned back, wincing at the couches griping. The door swung open and Meg stormed out, her face red and fuming. She stalked straight past him and down the stairs.

Caz followed, as peaceful as when she'd gone in earlier. "Quite a temper on that one."

Dom shrugged. "Can't say I've ever seen it before. What did you do?" Dom stood and pointed both thumbs towards where Meg had made her spectacular exit.

"Just what I always do. I've got what I need. I'll be in touch. When do you need the outfit by?" She rolled her eyes. "I'm pretty sure you're going to tell me by the next competition and then I'm going to tell you it's impossible, then you'll offer to double my fee ..."

"Caz, have a heart! You know I can't do that."

"A girl has to try. Anyway, you'd better go get your girl. She was moving pretty fast." Dom hugged her around the head. Caz mock-punched his belly and pushed him off her. "Go!"

· · • • · • • · · ·

Meg peered up and down the road, willing a taxi to appear. Her ears burned, she was so angry. She turned to yell at the cheesecake that taunted from the shop window behind her, but as she opened her mouth, Dom ran down the stairs and burst through the door.

"Meg, wait!"

Meg shut her mouth and stuck her thumb out to hail an approaching cab, but Dom reached over and grabbed her hand in his, hiding her thumb. The cab slid past and she stamped her foot.

"Let's get you that cheesecake you earned." Without waiting for her to agree, he turned her around and aimed her at the coffee shop, ordering two blueberry cheesecakes and cappuccinos on their way past the front desk. He led her deep into a sheltered recess towards the back of a room that seemed deeply committed to the color purple.

He seated her at a table and plonked himself opposite her with his chin on his hands. "So, are you going to tell me what happened up there?"

"If you think I'm going in public wearing that, you've got another thing coming," she spluttered, tripping over her words as red crept up her neck.

"You're going to have to help me here. Wearing what, exactly?"

The blush bloomed all the way up her cheeks this time. "That see-through body-stocking thing. It hides nothing! *Nothing!* I thought this was a dance school, not a nudist colony."

Dom frowned, then his eyes popped wide. "Oh, I get it. She tried the under layer on you."

The waitress brought their cake and coffee. One slice of cheesecake was big enough for three people. Tears clouded Meg's eyes.

"Are you crying?"

"No. Yes. Maybe just a little."

Dom put his cake fork down and reached for her arm. His thumb rubbed circles on the inside of her wrist, making it hard for her to think. "Talk to me, Meg."

She pushed her cake a few millimeters away. Only a few. "What is an under layer?"

"First tell me, did the see-through thing you tried on fit you?"

"Well, yes. But I can't go in public like that. Is that what all the ladies wear?"

"Pretty much. But—"

"Then I'm not doing it. I'm sorry."

"Just listen—"

"Are you completely insane? How can you even—" Dom reached over calmly, scooped up a forkful of cake and shoved it in her open mouth. Blueberries flooded her senses. Her train of thought crashed and all she could do was savor the tastes that danced on her tongue. She leaned back and shut her eyes, losing herself in the moment. The air moved and when she opened her eyes, Dom was right up close in her face.

"The naked thing? It doesn't stay like that. That is just the bottom layer that Caz uses to make sure she's nailed your size and shape. There are still layers to be added. Many, many layers."

Meg swallowed and felt her righteous indignation shrivel into something small enough to fit into her pocket, and not just any pocket. The tiny one in jeans that's good for nothing but small change. "Oh."

"You panicked for nothing."

"Oh."

"Eat your cheesecake, Meg."

"Okay."

Chapter Eleven

MEG'S CHAIR SEEMED DETERMINED to inflict pain on her. It would probably have killed her if it got the chance. One of the wheels had broken off, so she sat lopsided. No matter which way she twisted or moved, her back ached. Normally she didn't even notice it anymore, but there was nothing normal about the hours she'd spent prancing around in high heels. She adjusted the microscope and slid forward to see better. That simple movement got her thigh muscles burning.

"I'm such a wreck."

Vashti snorted. "That's what you get for pretending you're sixteen. I'm going to come watch that competition, you know. When is it again? I must buy tickets."

"You really don't have to. Like *really*." The thought of being watched by people she knew made her feel sick. "Actually, please don't."

Vashti shrugged. "We'll see. Here, please do these for me." She slid a tray of test vials halfway across the counter top they shared. "I have an eye appointment, but there's a special rush request on some of these pregnancy tests. Vial one is due for surgery, vial two is meant to be going on skin treatment, and vial three is a non-specific urgent."

"No watching and I will."

"It's the first three on the left. Later!" She turned back. "Oh, I nearly forgot. Our email is down again. You'll have to get the driver to deliver the results to the doctors' rooms."

"Again? You dodged my conditions!" Meg's words slammed into the back of the lab door as it swung closed. She reached for the first one on the left, a pregnancy test. Ms. G. MacMillan. "Righto, Ms. G. MacMillan. Let's see if you have a little bun in your oven." She left the vial to one side and processed the others before hitting print and waiting for the results. She ripped the page off the printer. *And today's lucky winners are ... dun-dun-dah! MacMillan and Louw. Myburgh gets to go on her skin treatment without fear of all-those-things-that-could-go-wrong to a baby from acne pills.*

Meg braced herself and phoned Reception. "Can you send a driver up to collect? I've got some urgent results that need to be delivered." The receptionist was new and Meg couldn't remember her name, but she was a classic new-broom-sweep-clean who did everything by the book without any allowances for anyone being remotely human.

In her head Meg thought of her as Broom and was secretly terrified she'd call her that to her face.

"I'm sorry"—Broom sounded anything *but* sorry—"there is only one driver available and he is in the yard packing to leave on his next round. If you run you might catch him."

"Could you stop him for me? I'm on my way down."

"I'm sorry, I really can't. I can't leave my station."

Meg hung up, grabbed her urgents and bolted down the stairs two at a time. She rushed past Broom with an extra bit of leg-swinging and puffing for dramatic effect and nearly slipped on the tiles. The door handle saved her, and she swung herself upright with a quick glance over to where Broom sat texting on her phone, completely unaware of all the action put on for her benefit. Honestly.

Meg let herself out and realized that dancing must be doing some good for her body—she wasn't dying or panting for breath as she ran down the steps, caught the driver just as he was about to pull away, and shoved the results into his hands.

She was so impressed with herself, this deserved a reward. One of those ginger and beetroot smoothies from the shop on the corner that she always watched others drinking but could never bring herself to buy—that would do. As she crossed the street, a small boy begging further down caught her eye. He rested against the STOP sign on the corner wearing holey pants. His bare feet were cracked and dry. There was something familiar in the way his bony shoulders held up the scraps of his t-shirt like a wire hanger. He was far too small to be out on the streets alone.

A car stopped and the driver handed him some coins through the open window. Sheer happiness flashed across his face and in an instant Meg recognized the hot chocolate smile. It was Ernest. She checked both ways for traffic and crossed over to him.

"Ernest, why are you here? Shouldn't you be in school?"

The boy's eyes dropped to the pavement as she came close. His hands slunk behind his back, hiding the money he'd been given. Meg knelt down in front of him. "Do you remember me?"

A flick of his eyes, the briefest nod. There was no way she could leave him here. "Are you hungry?"

Ernest frowned, still not meeting her eyes. Meg checked her watch. She still had a bit of time until she was due to be back in the lab. She held out her hand. If he took it, she'd buy him food and make sure he was delivered somewhere safely. If he didn't ... If he didn't, then what? Back to the lab pretending she hadn't seen him? Spend the day obsessing over how many bad things can happen to a small boy on the street? She was saved from facing that dilemma by a small brown hand that slid into hers.

A few minutes later they queued to pay for a steak pie, bananas, a shiny green apple and a bottle of water. While they waited, Meg sent a quick one-handed text to Dom. *Are you at the studio?*

Meg paid and hauled herself back across the road towards her car, dragging Ernest along behind her as fast as his little legs could go while shoving banana into his mouth. She hadn't heard from Dom, but she was out of options.

· · · ● · ● ● · · ·

The studio was quiet compared to its normal buzz. Meg could hear the faintest strain of "The Blue Danube Waltz" coming from the main studio.

"Come, Ernest; Dominic will know what to do with you." Her smile at the boy was wasted as he'd just peeled back the wrapper on his pie and was staring at the warm pastry balanced on his palms reverently. He was so in awe, he hadn't even heard her speak.

Meg steered him onto a couch in the waiting area, unfolded a tissue on his lap to catch crumbs, and went on a Dom-hunt. She checked the two smaller studios first; both were empty. She peeped into the main studio where the waltzing was underway. Gina was putting an elderly couple through their paces. Still no sign of Dom.

The last place he could be was the office. She rubbed her hand over Ernest's springy curls as she walked past him through the waiting area to the office. The boy had eaten half his pie but was just as hypnotized as before. The door to the office stood ajar and she knocked before going in. The desk was messier than she thought it would be. She tapped her cheek, wondering what to do now. She couldn't leave Ernest here without Dom knowing. Gina was about as motherly as a paper bag. Unless Dom showed up in the next minute, Meg would have no choice but to take Ernest back to the lab with her.

She searched the desk for some paper to leave a note. Nothing. *Come on, Dom.* Every desk should have a notepad or something. She put her hand on the knob of the top desk drawer, glancing around to make sure no-one was looking. It was ridiculous to feel guilty for snooping, even though her reason for snooping was completely valid. After all, if he'd just been here as he should have been, none of this would have been necessary. With a shake of her head at her silliness, she slid the drawer open and found her own face staring back at her.

Meg blinked hard and shut the drawer. She breathed deeply and rubbed her eyes in case they'd gone squiffy. Squaring her shoulders, she pulled the drawer open again. It was still there. A dog-eared photo of her glued onto a folder. Pins and needles prickled up and down her arms. Why was this here?

Blood pounded her eardrums. She lifted it a fraction, torn between looking and running. Gina's photo stared up at her from the folder beneath, her name written in strong, black print. Gina MacMillan. Meg reached out to open the folder but heard footsteps. Too shocked to think straight, she shoved the folder back in the drawer and slid it shut as Gina walked in.

"What are you doing here?" The smile on her face was a pseudo-friendly, glued-on sort.

"Is Dom around?" Meg's hands fluttered like moths and she tucked them under her elbows.

Gina stood in the doorway blocking her escape. Fine tendrils of blonde stuck to her damp temples, the only indication that she'd been dancing. One dab with a towel and they'd be gone, unlike Meg who needed a shower and fresh clothes after a session. She couldn't tell if Gina had seen her closing the drawer or not. Heat flushed through her face.

She needed time to think. Safe ground. *Ernest.*

"Ernest!"

"What?"

"I found him begging on the corner of the street. I couldn't leave him there. I figured Dom would know what to do with him. I was just looking for something to leave him a note. Anyway, he's clearly not here and I have to get back to the lab." She took a few steps towards Gina, hoping she'd get the hint and move.

Gina didn't budge. She tilted her head sideways and eyed Meg with her lips pursed. It was all Meg could do to not stare at her belly. *Are you the same G. MacMillan?*

Gina's face softened. "I understand, you know. Dom is a good-looking guy."

"Excuse me?" *Not the belly.*

Gina shifted and crossed her arms, leaning lightly on the door frame. "I just don't want you to get your hopes up. I'm not sure what he said to persuade you to stick to the competition team, but have you asked yourself why he wants to win so badly?"

"Prize money. He's already told me that."

"So, he hasn't told you. I see. I won't give away his secrets, but weddings are awfully expensive these days." She paused, cleared her throat. "I'm not the type who will settle for anything less than the best." She picked at a carefully manicured cuticle.

"I really have to go. Excuse me, please." Holding onto the scraps of her composure, Meg pushed past Gina. Ernest would just have to come with her, she wasn't staying here another moment. Only the waiting room was empty, the crumbs on the chair being the only evidence that Ernest had ever been there.

Chapter Twelve

CONFLICTED.

Meg watched Ebb doing his contortions to get to his food and couldn't help feel a bit jealous. The fish had one simple challenge, get to the food. It was always a struggle, but at least there was only one choice involved. Get to the food and eat it, or die.

Nothing like what today had thrown at her, all wrapped in enough secrets to split her head in two. To find her face staring back at her from the inside of Dom's desk drawer had been odd, no—worse. Creepy. Granted, she wasn't exactly an expert on how to run a dance school. Maybe it was standard practice and she was being freaked out for nothing.

But maybe it wasn't.

She would have loved nothing more than to cut ties, ditch this whole crazy ride, and hopefully find herself again. The Meg she knew colored in the lines and was always five minutes early. None of this joining a dance team nonsense.

And yet to quit now would leave her with questions. Unresolved things that would hang over her, sniggering when she tried to sleep at night. Carrying on meant more opportunities to peep inside that folder. It also made life impossibly complicated and put her in the face of a frustrating man who she wasn't sure she could trust.

At least he liked her fish, or pretended convincingly enough to fool her. She was going to have to color outside the lines for a little longer to get to the bottom of this mystery.

Her phone buzzed at her and she jumped. She really needed to change that tone to something more relaxing. She'd been added to a group and the message was short.

Dancers - qualifying round this Saturday. Extra practice tonight from 6pm.

Seemed like a potential snooping opportunity had just landed in her lap.

• • • • • • • • • •

The knots at the base of Dom's neck curled tighter. He tilted his head for relief but that sent a shooting pain up his neck. Gina was digging through a box of leotards, muttering to herself. Spots of color stained her cheeks as if someone had slapped her or gone overboard with blusher.

Dom sighed, trying to exhale quietly. "Gina, please stop. It's too late to do this now. Let's get on with practice, the others will be here soon. Maybe there'll be time afterwards."

"They should be in here. I put them in myself." Gina straightened up and her eyebrows shifted. The glint in her eye should have been enough warning, but he'd been known to be more stubborn than wise. "Did you loan them out to someone?"

"Er, no. Not that I can remember."

"That's so typical of you. Honestly. Next time you pull a stunt like this, I'll let you figure it out." The red blotches on her face had deepened. Dom noticed but chose to clamp his mouth shut. Pins and needles prickled through his cheeks.

"Let's get some help and tackle it together after practice. Okay?"

Gina sniffed and allowed him to drag her away from the exploded entrance hall to the cool studio.

· · · · •• • •• · · ·

The studio reception resembled a refugee camp with clothes strewn everywhere. Meg picked her way through the clutter, resisting the urge to fold everything she stepped on. Messiness made her heart beat faster, and not in a good way. She tiptoed through the last stretch at a speed that would have flipped her sideways if her ankle rolled.

As she pushed through the doorway into the studio, she slipped into sleuth mode. All she needed was time and a good excuse to go snooping in Dom's office.

All the dancers were spread out on the dance floor and Dom waited at the music system. Strangely, his ears were red. The only time she'd ever seen them glowing that way was while they'd faced Chad while picking deodorant. The connection shot unreasonable panic through her and she scanned the room in case.

"Meg, good of you to join us. The warm up has started." Dom's tone was cool and Meg's mind ran wild with things that she might have done to annoy him.

She slipped into socks and joined the line of dancers to warm up. The moisture trailing down her spine said it was quite warm enough already, thank you, but Meg knew better than to open her mouth.

Gina faced them all, looking like a skinny rhino ready to charge. Or bolt. Was that fear lurking behind all the bluster? Meg's head tipped sideways as she examined Gina, it always did that when she puzzled over a conundrum.

"Rises. NOW, please." Gina glared holes through Meg who nearly swallowed her tongue in fright and shot up onto her tippiest of toes to make up for her lapse in concentration, wobbled, and sank back to flat.

"Sorry." Even as the mumbled word lemminged off her lips, she knew. She had the unfortunate ability to turn a rhino into a fire-breathing dragon. Maybe she could hire herself out for parties. Talia shot her a sympathetic shrug.

Meg could almost see the torrent of words build up in Gina and burn bright red on her face. She opened her mouth as Dom walked over and patted her shoulder. Meg homed in on the pat. Was it to calm her, or was it a secret lover's signal? Was he lingering a little? Did he know about the baby? Cue soap opera music.

She tried to focus through the rest of the warm up, but her mind kept looking for clues. Lunges, squats and cat-stretches later, Dom shooed Gina to join the rest of them and clapped. "Places, please."

Music filtered through the system, trickling into Meg's veins. Slow intro, saxophone with a rumba rhythm. Meg knew it well now, four sets of eight.

Chapter Thirteen

Saturday—40 days and counting

THE LEOTARD STUCK TO Meg like a shy toddler. Black, long-sleeved lycra with a flared skirt tacked on just above her hips. Meg pinched it away from her skin and it snapped back with a sting that quickly turned to an itch. Their actual costumes were still under construction, so they'd dressed as penguins for the qualifier. Penguins in heels. Lovely. Where was Dom?

Other groups milled about in tight clusters, their outfits glittering in the semi-gloom. Compared to them, Dom's team were definitely underdressed. Their dancing would have to make up for the lack of sparkle in their costumes. Meg wanted to go home.

Talia grabbed her shoulder for support as she adjusted her shoe. "You'll get used to it. This is your first time doing something like this?"

Meg braced herself to hold up the tiny dancer, unsure of how to respond. *Oh no, daaah-ling, I do this all the time. My lab specimens love to see me perform.* She settled for a shrug that nearly tipped Talia off her feet. "Oops, sorry!"

Talia waved off her apology and cringed. "Here she comes. Stand up straight."

Meg followed her eye-line and her insides folded in on themselves. Gina. With bright spots of fury tangoing on her cheek bones. The grumpiness of the woman seemed to be increasing exponentially, though her stomach remained a flat, hard thing. If there really was a baby in there, the poor little sausage was going to have to fight for living room.

Gina marched right over, a general inspecting an army. But in heels with a swishy skirt. Meg bit back giggles. Gina's finger in her face made Meg squint.

"No messing up." Gina moved on to Talia who didn't get the finger of doom, but a single nod of approval.

Meg leaned close to Talia. "Remind me again, why are we doing this in a shopping center?"

"Built-in audience, publicity for the actual event, I guess? It's also good prep for us. Nothing like having to put it all out there for a bunch of harassed shoppers who would rather be home watching cricket on the telly."

Meg would rather be home watching cricket on the telly, too, and she hated cricket. "Wait. Are you saying we're not dancing in here?" She tapped her foot on the cement which suddenly seemed perfect. "We have to go out there to dance? Out there where people can see us?" She peeped out the door. A lady stalked past carrying multiple shopping bags, tipping over slightly to one side as she walked as if all the heavy ones were on one side only. Her face was sweating and scrunched up. Meg doubted she'd stop to watch a bunch of penguins do the samba.

"That one might not stop," said Talia, "but usually we draw quite a crowd."

A dull pain started at the base of Meg's skull. She knew these headaches, in a few hours it would have her head throbbing in a skullcap of pain. Their waiting room was an unoccupied shop with a hastily rigged overhead lamp for light, dusty tiles under their feet, and non-existent AC. Not even a window for some airflow. This might have been the daftest thing she'd ever done.

A cool hand slid onto the small of her back. It was Dom, looking a bit annoyed as he tugged at the collar of his stiff, white shirt.

"Are we all ready?" He glanced over his team and his face gave nothing away.

Meg had to admit that they all looked pretty-darn smart together. The girls had their hair slicked back into buns. Talia had done Meg's in a minute flat. She'd been a ballerina all her life and apparently they came out of the womb with bun-making skills. The make-up was heavier, bronzer than she was used to—Talia had fixed Meg's attempt with a good-natured *tsk-tsk* through her teeth—but it all came together and Meg quite liked the end result.

"We're up in twenty minutes. Warm-up time." Dom flashed a smile at her and for a moment a sneaky sort of happiness popped in her belly that dulled the pain in her head by a fraction.

· · · · ●· ● · · · ·

Dom led his troupe through the Saturday morning shoppers with his mouth so dry that swallowing seemed impossible. A section of floor close to the food court had been marked off as the dance floor with chairs set up on three sides. The DJ—surrounded by sound equipment—and the judges all took up the third side. Dom had brought their music earlier and they'd done a quick sound check. Technical gremlins aside, that part was under control. Now it was up to the dancers to bring it.

He'd gone through the routine in his head, orienting them towards the judges.

The others were used to this, he wasn't concerned for them. Meg. There was his unknown. He stole a quick glance at her face. She was breathing fast, her eyes were wide and her nostrils flared slightly as she walked. The pulse in her neck fluttered under her skin. He reached for her hand and squeezed.

"You've got this."

She focused on her shoes and pulled her hand away to adjust her skirt. It made no difference whatsoever to the skirt that was securely tacked on, clearly she was dodging his hand. A small nod without any eye contact was all he got. This girl was a bundle of nerves held together by resolve as flimsy as a breeze.

He kept a close eye on her as their music filled the open space. Shoppers were collecting in tiny groups, dumping their bags at their feet and leaning on shop windows. The rhythm kicked in and he saw it. The weeks had been fraught with what-ifs and doubts. But there was this one moment that had sparked hope in his belly and he saw it again now. Meg's face lit up, her eyes sparkled as their music pumped through the speakers. She was feeling the music. Maybe—just maybe—she'd get through this.

· · · · • · • · · · ·

Music coursed through her veins. The steps she'd been eating, sleeping, and drinking had been well and truly massaged into her brain and muscles. The skirt swished around her ankles like a living, breathing, thing and it all felt like flying.

Three minutes flew past in a breathless rush of adrenaline.

By the time the notes trailed off, Meg buzzed full of endorphins. They held their end pose as they'd practiced, a slow count to five. She'd made it through the entire routine without face-planting, ripping her leotard, or losing a false eyelash. Maybe the routine wasn't quite perfect, but she'd got through it without anything embarrassing happening. That made it a complete win in her book.

The crowd was on their feet, whistling and cheering. Meg turned a slow 360 degrees taking it all in. Faces blurred into a happy smear. Except one. One face came into sharp focus. One not smiling or cheering, lip curled as if curdled around an unpleasant odor. She'd lost count over the years of how many times she'd been on the receiving end of that face.

Chad.

· · · · ● · ● · · · ·

Dom reached for Meg to hug her, but she stood frozen like an introvert in a spotlight. He followed her gaze and saw a man in the crowd glaring at her. Chad. Seeing that tomato face, all puckered and angry, flipped logic upside down in Dom's head. He might get her into trouble for this hug, but if what she was saying was right, Chad no longer had a claim to her anyway. The man should know what he'd given up on.

Dom stepped in between them and drew Meg into his arms. Meg shook her head as if a spell had been broken and stiffened. He held on and whispered, "You did great. Well done, you. I think that's enough to get us to the next round." It was like hugging an ironing board.

Meg side-stepped his arms, blinked three times and patted his shoulder awkwardly. "I have to, um. I ... have to go."

The rest of the team had already moved off the performance square, but Gina came back and clicked her fingers in his face. "Earth to Dominic. Hey, sunshine, are you in there? Let's go, buddy, the next group would like to start."

She got behind and pushed him until his feet hooked and he nearly tripped. That brought him back.

"I have to go get Meg."

125

Gina hissed in his face, "No. You need to stay here and wait for adjudication. You're the team leader after all."

Talia grimaced in sympathy. "Don't worry, I'll go see if I can catch her. You guys stay here."

Dom leaned on a pillar watching Talia shuffle off after Meg in her latin dance shoes. His legs felt shaky, like they might not keep him upright.

Chapter Fourteen

MEG SAT IN HER car wondering if it was safe to drive yet. Nameless emotions boiled in her chest like heartburn. Well, not nameless in all honesty, she just didn't care to admit to being embarrassed and ashamed enough that her ears might burn off her head.

Her phone buzzed and she jumped before opening the message. She read it without thinking.

Meg, I get it now. I understand everything. You are going through some big-0 crisis. Don't worry, I'm here for you. I'll see you soon and we can figure out how to fix this. Together, like old times. Yours in spite of everything, Chad.

Pure anger flared in her belly, burning her embarrassment to a crispy little thing that lurked on the edges. She drove home fuming and nearly took out the post box on the sidewalk as she pulled up outside her apartment. How dare he?

Meg avoided the elevator and ran up the stairs two-at-a-time. She let herself into the apartment and froze. There was a smell in the room that hung like a cloud of unresolved notes. Was something moving in the kitchen? Fiddling with the kettle ... Maybe a large rat?

Her mind darted like a goldfish. Ernest? No, surely not. Had Dom found her spare key? A sneaky double thump in her pulse rate gave her the courage to tiptoe down the hall. There was definitely something moving in the kitchen, the kettle clicked on. This was like every horror movie Chad had forced her to watch with him. The people were always dumb enough to keep walking straight at the scary thing.

And they always died.

Wait, what? Meg stopped outside the kitchen, imagining watching herself on the screen. Don't do it! Don't walk into the room. With a loud snort, she rolled her eyes and strode purposefully into the kitchen to see what was going on.

"Chad! What are you doing here?"

"It's called making tea, I believe." Chad had two cups ready and stood with a foot tapping waiting for the kettle to boil the way he always used to. The handles of the cups faced different directions and it made Meg's scalp itch. The familiarity of him in her space settled over her like an old blanket. "It took you a while to get here. Where were you?"

Meg bit her lip to stop the words queuing on her tongue. "Why are you here?"

Chad stirred in a sweetener pill before handing over the steaming tea. "I assume you still drink tea?"

Tea, yes. Artificial sweetener, no. But you should know that after spending most of our lives together. "I do."

"Ironic, those words." Chad crossed the kitchen in two steps and stood too close for where they were. A month ago, this would have been normal. Now, it made her palms sweat.

"Why did you come here?"

"Honestly? I think I know what's wrong with you. Would you like to hear what I'm thinking?"

Meg resisted the overwhelming urge to step away from him. She would show him that she wasn't intimidated. Or affected. His voice was gravelly and low and it reminded her of when they were both teens and it broke. She would start up random conversations about trivial nonsense just to hear him speak. Before long, he'd get annoyed and stop speaking altogether.

Something about those memories made her feel like she was paddling on the edge of a whirlpool.

"You're going to tell me anyway."

He trailed a finger down her jaw-line. "Simple, really. You're facing a big-O birthday. That usually sends a woman into a spin. Kinda like an early mid-life crisis, you know? I just don't think it's altogether fair for you to punish me for the fact that you're a bit freaked out."

Her brain froze and hung like her old cell phone used to. Three things she wanted to say, but they all muddled into a spaghetti mess that didn't make it out. *Why is it always about you? I'm not freaked out. Walking away from you is the best thing ...*

Chad must have misread her silence. He stepped in closer to whisper in her ear, "Let's be honest. You don't really think you fitted in with the real dancers, do you Gem-gem?"

He hadn't called her that in years. Backwards Meg makes Gem. Backwards. She turned the word over in her mind. It felt like an insult, actually. His aftershave had a woody undertone to it that used to make her think of being deep in a forest. It filled her senses. Over his shoulder she caught sight of Ebb, more down than up. An upside down fish and a backwards girl. Quite a good mix. A backwards girl pretending to be a dancer. It was nothing that she hadn't known already, but seeing herself through his eyes twisted her gut. She couldn't argue, but facing it still stung like hot water on sunburn. It was time for a serious conversation with Dom.

She stepped away from Chad and it hit her. Mushrooms. His aftershave was no longer just a forest. It was a forest full of mushrooms, not the nice ones that you threw in salad or ate on pizza, but the toxic ones that could take you out with one bite.

"I think you should leave now."

· · · · ● · ● · · · ·

Dom sat in his car debating the wisdom of the move he was contemplating. The back seat of his car was hidden under packets of groceries that he needed to drop off for Buntu, but he had two hours before he could do that safely. He opened up the email and read it one more time. This was not something to deal with alone, yet showing up on Meg's doorstep unplanned didn't seem to go down well with her.

Genius plan! He'd call ahead. That way she'd expect him, and he wouldn't have the door shut in his face again. He dialed Meg's number, not completely expecting her to answer.

"Meg's phone."

Not Meg, but a guy. "I want to speak to Meg. Is she there?"

Scuffling, some muffled conversation. "Meg speaking." The strain in her voice was unmistakable.

"Hey, Dom here. Sorry for interrupting. I have some news that I thought you'd like to hear."

"The weather is lovely, thanks for asking."

"Meg?"

"No, I can't take you up on your offer right now. Thank you." *Click.*

She'd put the phone down. Something wasn't right.

·········

Meg ended the call and blanked the screen.

"Who was that?"

"Someone trying to sell me something I don't really want."

"You shouldn't be so rude to someone just trying to do their job."

"I suppose you think I should call back and apologize?"

Chad's head tilted and bobbed at the same time as if he were trying to get water out of his ear after swimming. "That's actually not a bad idea."

"What? No! I wasn't serious." She scrambled for words, familiar frustration crawling through her chest and threatening to choke her. She had to get this man out of her home. "I'm tired, my head is sore. Please just go."

The doorbell rang.

"Leave it, Gem-Gem. We're not done."

With a squeak, she ducked beneath his arm and dodged him to get to the door. Without stopping to check who it was through the peephole, she threw it open.

Dom stood with a fist in mid-air, ready to knock. "Hey. I've come to tell you some news."

Meg panicked. She pushed him off the doorstep, slipped out behind him, and pulled the door shut. "You can't be here."

"What's going on, Meg? That phone call?"

"You-know-who is inside and any second now is going to come outside and then I'm never going to hear the end of it." The words were barely out when Meg heard footsteps coming down the hall. Dom grabbed the door handle. Meg caught on and shoved her thumb against the peephole.

Dom leaned in close, his breath tickling her ear. "Is he bothering you? Are you safe?" He pulled back quickly to look in her eyes.

The handle jiggled, but Dom held it still.

"What is going on? Meg! Let me out." Chad sounded less than happy. Distinctly unhappy, in fact.

Meg mouthed silently. *You need to go.*

Dom shook his head and hissed, "No."

He's going to kill me. Meg pointed at the door and slit her throat with her finger.

"That's exactly why I'm not leaving." Dom managed to look smug while door-handle-wrestling Chad.

"Open this door! Now!" Chad was fuming. She hadn't heard him this angry in years.

Only because you're here. If her eyes stretched any wider, they'd pop right out.

Dom glanced down the corridor, nodded, and beckoned her closer. "Pick up a rock from the potted plant. On three, throw it down the stairs, run, and hide behind the dustbins behind you."

Meg stretched to pick up a rock while keeping her thumb on the spy hole. As she straightened up, Dom nodded.

"One, two, three!"

She threw the rock and heard it bounce down the stairs as she ran towards the bins. Dom ran behind her and they both slammed into hiding as the door flew open and Chad spilled out. He stood listening for a moment before taking the stairs two at a time.

Dom put a hand on her arm. "Let's stay put for a few minutes."

Meg leaned back against the cool bricks. Her belly had turned to jelly and the headache was back in full force. This was someone else's crazy life. Not hers. "What did you come here to tell me?"

Dom's worried face split into a grin. "We made it through! To the next round of the competition." He was beaming, glowing. "You did good, Meg. Aren't you going to say anything?"

Meg heard the words. They were in her head, sizing up against Chad's disdain. *Ding, ding, ding. Round 1.*

"Meg?"

"Sorry." She mentally swatted the bikini-clad, number-carrying lady out of the boxing ring in her head. "I don't even know what to say."

"Why is Chad here?"

Meg lost focus, seeing his face in the crowd again. The scorn in the pull of his lip. "He was at the mall." Her lip quivered and she bit it and she felt the pull of tears in the bridge of her nose. She pinched it to stop them but they collected on her eyelashes anyway. Traitors.

"And he's jealous?"

"No, not jealous." She bit back a laugh, a gallows laugh. Embarrassed, ashamed.

"If he makes you so uncomfortable, why did you let him in?"

"I didn't. He was inside when I came home." The adrenalin from that was still lurking in her veins. The last few minutes had pumped a fresh dose.

"Does he have his own key, or do you keep a spare outside somewhere? Neither of those options is a good plan, Meg."

"I don't keep a key under a flowerpot outside and I never gave Chad a key to my place. I can only think he had one made on the sly. Why are you attacking me like this? Anyway, I don't want to talk about him. What are we going to do?"

Dom cleared his throat. "I wasn't attacking you, I just want to know you're safe." He coughed again. "We are going to get ready for the next round, of course. Tighten up the routines, do a couple of costume rehearsals. Be as ready as we can be, then go clobber it."

"Not that, silly. Now. We are hiding from my ex behind a bunch of garbage bins. I can't say this was how I intended to spend my evening."

Dom settled back against the wall as if it were the comfiest chair. "Oh, I don't know, this is nice. We should do it more often."

Meg groaned. "My rear is freezing, my head is aching. I just want to go home and be there safely."

"Would you feel safe if Chad came back?"

Meg imagined being alone with Chad in her kitchen and her belly twisted. Words escaped her, so she shook her head.

"Right. We need a plan."

Chapter Fifteen

VASHTI WAS WATERING THE bonsai when Meg hurried into the lab, stowed her bag, and put on her lab coat.

"You're late."

Meg buttoned up her coat and sighed. "A whole minute, I know."

Vashti moved the tiny plant to the window sill and frowned at Meg. "You're never late and you look rubbish. Busy weekend?"

"Chad was in my flat, then Dom came over and we ran away from Chad. Dom took me to get new locks. Did you know there was a twenty-four-hour department store that sells new door locks? I didn't, but there is. Then we stopped off somewhere in the bushes where Dom delivered groceries." She paused at the absurdity of that. "Then he took me home, changed my locks and I got to bed at about two a.m. Oh, and we qualified for the next round of the competition." She plonked down on her chair. Delivering the sound bite of the weekend's drama had wiped out her last bit of energy.

Vashti took it all in with a slow blink. "I understand why you look like rubbish." Her mouth worked silently and she shrugged. "Groceries to the bushes?"

"It was weird. I didn't ask."

"You got through! That's great. I've got my tickets. I'm bringing the new receptionist along. I feel like I should get to know her. She's not the happiest person. Do you get that vibe, too?"

"You invited Broom? I can't believe you did that." Meg's nose crinkled. "You should see about a getting a refund. I'd hate you to waste your money."

"Broom? Her name is Liesl, with no second e. Not Broom. I won't even ask." She waved a hand between them as if warding off all the crazy coming from Meg. "I'm not getting a refund, I'm going to come watch whether you like it or not."

"You don't understand. I'm not doing it. I can't."

The phone rang, it was Liesl-with-no-second-e. "There's a man here to see ... oh wait." Her voice muffled and Meg heard her shouting in the background. "Sir! You can't go up there."

Her heart sped up so fast she saw stars. "If it's Chad, I'm not here."

Vashti waved at her. "Quick! Hide."

Meg dodged the corner of her desk and threw herself down next to it, blocked off from view of anyone coming in the door. The familiar swish of the door opening sent a cold shock through her.

Vashti's chair scraped as she stood up and gasped. "Oh, my word! That is gorgeous! Meg! Get out here, now."

Meg stayed in her corner, squeezing her knees together to stop them shaking. Vashti appeared in front of her and grabbed her by the arm.

"Come on. You've got to see this."

Meg wriggled up the wall, not trusting Vashti's slim frame to counterbalance her weight, muttering under her breath the whole way up. "If you're hauling me out because he brought flowers, I'm going to shove them up your left nostril one petal at a time."

Dom stood at the doorway, holding up a sparkling charcoal-colored dress that twinkled as the light caught it.

Meg's breath caught. It reminded her of the dress the big-screen Meg wore on the night she announced her engagement to John Mellen-what's-his-face. Delicate trails of sparkles on a chiffon-like mesh, a demure cut that covered all the bits she was so desperately angry about sticking out on that one visit to the seamstress. It was so beautiful, it made her heart sore.

Vashti was still holding her hand. She pulled her closer and squinted at her face. "Meg, are you crying?"

"Maybe just a little bit."

Dom was beaming. "Soooo?"

"It's exquisite. I'm speechless."

He shut his eyes and breathed deeply, mumbling something she didn't quite catch.

Vashti fluttered around them like a hummingbird around a daylily. "You have to try it on."

"Vashti! No. I can't do that now." She waved a hand in the general direction of test tubes and printouts. "No. All this is waiting." She stared Vashti down with a silent plea for her to shut her mouth and keep it that way.

Dom seemed to take his cue from Meg and folded the dress carefully over one arm. "There'll be time later. I just wanted to see if it would work for you. I'll see you at practice tonight, Meg. We'll have a full dress rehearsal. Have a good day, ladies." He stepped back and left so fast it made Meg's head spin.

Vashti rounded on her the moment Dom was out the room. "You can't possibly pull out now. That dress! Oh, Meg."

Meg couldn't help wondering how the dress would make her feel. A dress is just a dress, right? Not like it had special powers or anything. She'd turned to her table, trying to focus on what she had to get through today. Maybe she'd try it on. Just once.

• • • • ◦ • ◦ • • • •

Dom took the stairs to the studio one at time, balancing his sparkly cargo carefully across two arms to keep the hems of the dresses from trailing on the ground. He hung them in his office for later and went hunting for Gina. He found her curled up on a couch in the waiting area lounge, fast asleep. Her head was at a funny angle and a tiny snore buzzed from her nose each time she breathed in.

Was the woman sick?

Dom leaned over the back of the couch and poked her shoulder. "Gina, wake up." Nothing, apart from a grunt. He knew how to get through to her. He leaned in close and whispered, "I've got a dress for you to try on."

With a grumble and a moan, she rolled sideways and swung her feet off the edge of the couch. "My dress? What's it like?" She rubbed her temples and brushed sticky tendrils of hair away from her neck.

"You can try it on if you want."

She sat up straight with her eyes scrunched up against the bright sun streaming in the windows and held out a hand. "Give."

Dom fetched her dress from his office and handed it over. Gina shuffled down the hall to the change room, yawning all the way. This wasn't like Gina, at all.

"Hey."

Meg had actually made it. "Hey, yourself. So you came." He fought hard to keep his mouth in a subdued little smile when all he wanted to do was yell *Hallelujah!* and hug her.

Meg coughed behind her hand, a subtle *obviously* in the shrug of her shoulders.

"Well, you might as well go get dressed. We're going to do a run-through in costume just to make sure nobody's outfit has an issue."

Meg followed him to the office and hesitated before taking the dress from him. "But what if it doesn't fit?"

"It's a forgiving design. I doubt you'll have any problems. Off you go."

A faint flush washed through Meg's pale skin as she shuffled out the office and unknowingly followed Gina.

· · • • • · • • · ·

Meg cringed as the bathroom door slid shut behind her. Some-one else was in here already, grunting behind a closed cubicle door. She'd so hoped to do this alone. The dress went on over her head without giving her trouble and as she zipped up the side, Gina burst from the cubicle, red in the face and sweating.

She huffed when she saw Meg, but waved her closer.

"Zip me up. The stupid dressmaker got it wrong."

Was that a hint of a tear on her lashes? "Are you sure it's your dress? Maybe you got Talia's by accident." Meg reached for Gina's zip and for the first time, she saw it—a soft roundness to the girl's belly that wasn't there before.

Trying hard not to stare, she tackled the stubborn zip. She pulled and tugged, secretly terrified of ripping the delicate fabric. No matter what she tried, it was not going to close.

"Just pull the thing. It's not that hard." There were definite-ly tears now. She wriggled and squirmed, sucking in her belly as much as she could.

"I'm going to pinch your skin if you keep moving like that. Hold still." Meg squeezed the two edges of fabric together with one hand and pulled the zipper with the other. Suddenly, in one smooth swoosh, it was up.

Gina slid a quick glance at herself in the mirror. She had the stuffed look about her that women in corsets used to have as they floated around in dresses that made breathing optional. The quick brush of her hand across her stomach was not lost on Meg.

"You know that you probably won't fit in this in a week or two's time. What are you going to do?"

Gina froze. "What are you going on about?"

"Babies generally don't shrink. They grow. You've got to give that poor little thing some space." Meg sucked in air. She hadn't meant to say it out loud. Had she said it out loud? Gina's face flitted between spine-melting rage and disbelief. Apparently Meg's brain had blurted.

"What are you saying?"

Meg considered her options. Deny saying it. Run. Laugh hysterically, slap Gina's shoulder and pretend it was the funniest joke she'd ever made. "I work in the lab." She shrugged.

Gina's anger froze over and the icy cold that followed was twice as terrifying. She leaned in so close that Meg saw a filling in her molar. "I don't know what you think you're going to achieve by playing this game. Whatever it is, you will not win. I see right through you, Meg. All sweet and kind on the surface but I know what is brewing underneath. If you start spreading this lie, you will regret it."

She stepped away from Meg and drew herself up tall, breathing too fast.

The wrong McMillan. Why, oh why, could she not keep her mouth shut? Now the woman truly hated her.

"I'm sorry, I assumed—"

"Wrong. You assumed wrong. You are so dumb."

Meg frowned at Gina's sparkly back as she shut herself into a cubicle.

Meg considered staying to reattempt the failed apology but if she were on the toilet, she'd want some privacy, too. She walked back to the main studio consumed with one thought. Had she really been mistaken? If so, why didn't Gina's dress fit? And what about Dom? If he had a baby on the way, surely he had a right to know about it? Her imagination had always run on the wild side. She shook her head and groaned.

Dom let out a grunt as she stepped into the studio. "Let's have a look. Why is Gina taking so long?"

Meg stepped out and twirled dutifully, her mind consumed with whether or not to tell him of her suspicions. The skirt was made from the softest shimmering charcoal fabric and spun off her hips in a wide circle, catching the air and floating around her legs like delicate petals.

Dom squinted and tilted his head to the side. He said nothing, but his lips pursed as if he were contemplating a particularly stubborn math problem. Or a dirty stain.

"Is it that bad?"

Dom still said nothing, but waved her towards the wall of mirrors.

Meg braced herself, breathing deeply three times before opening her eyes. "It's exquisite." She eyed herself in the mirror critically. The cut of the dress suited her figure. The color, while subdued, offered a perfect contrast for her red hair.

"So, what do you think? Was I wrong telling you to trust the small lady?"

"Small *young* lady, and I suppose you weren't."

Dom grinned. "Suppose?! My goodness, girl, be honest. She's done a seriously good job. You need glasses if you can't see it." He stared at her for a split second before his face crumpled back into itself. "Where is Gina? I swear that girl can dress in minutes flat when she wants, but she can also use up hours. I don't have time for nonsense. Surely she knows better?"

Meg opened her mouth and stopped. Dom might have a baby on the way and he was clueless. Or Meg had cooked up this little drama all by herself. Either way, it wasn't her place to say anything.

She settled for a shrug.

· · · • • • • · · ·

Meg threw some veggies into the electric wok and stirred them into the chicken and sauce that was already mostly cooked. She'd struggled at dancing tonight. She'd never been good at keeping secrets. She also hated secrets being kept from her. It didn't make keeping her mouth shut any easier.

Her doorbell rang and her heart-rate picked up. She'd come to expect either Chad or Dom, neither of which she was particularly excited to hang out with. It was Sandy with Xan in tow, bouncing on his toes with a big piece of bright-yellow cardboard tucked under his arm.

"Meg, please say you've got power. We're out at home, some sort of fault at the power station, and this one has a poster to do for school. I just don't have the energy for the lifecycle of a butterfly by candlelight with no coffee." Xan clutched the cardboard a little tighter and stared up at Meg with a tragic look on his face as if his poster had been the sole cause of the power station failure.

Meg hugged her friend, relieved. "I'll put the kettle on. Can I make you hot choc, Xan?" She grinned as the little boy's face lit up.

Xan settled in the living room and spread out his crayons, while the two ladies headed to the kitchen. Meg flicked the switch on the kettle, stirred her stir-fry, and cringed as Sandy homed in on the list stuck under the offending magnet on the fridge.

"What's this?"

"Just a list."

"This looks like goals. You're going to have to get more specific if you want to meet your goals. You know that, right?"

"I know that, obviously. I just feel like I'll know when I've met each one of these."

Sandy wasn't listening, she had her phone out and was typing into the search bar. "Look." She shoved the phone under Meg's nose. "Wait, I'll read them for you. How to set goals. Goals must be specific, measurable, attainable, relevant and time-based. SMART. See? I'm not wrong. There is nothing specific, measurable or attainable about any of these." She frowned at the crumpled list as if it smelled bad.

"You're also not listening to me. And anyway, why would I take advice from the internet? Who does that?"

"Mommy, this doesn't look a caterpillar." Xan stood at the door with his nose crinkled up, his thumb waving in the direction of the living room.

Meg saw her escape and grabbed it. "I'm good at that sort of thing. Come, Xan, I'll help you figure it out."

She fled the room and the sound of Sandy's nail tick-tick-ticking on the list as it hung limply on the fridge door.

Chapter Sixteen

MEG YAWNED AND THE butternut pasta on the shelves in front of her blurred. Sandy's visit the night before had left her unsettled and sleep had eluded her. She picked up a different packet of pasta (it was purple), and popped it in the shopping cart. No, it wasn't just Sandy. It was Gina and her secret, too. Meg picked up a can of baked beans and held it against her forehead, hoping the cool metal would remove some heat from her skin.

A small African boy pushed past her and hurried down the aisle. Meg recognized him—Ernest. His shoulders were hunched and he kept his head down, moving fast and looking guilty as if he were up to no good. Curiosity got the better of Meg. She parked her cart and followed him with the can of beans still in her hand.

He picked out a box of oats, wrapped his arms around it tightly and headed down the aisle. Meg followed, trying to blend in. Just an ordinary shopper, nothing strange happening. Her pulse was racing and she wanted to giggle. Mystery at the grocery store.

Ernest ran up to a slim African lady who was waiting in the queue to pay for a few things. Her cotton dress was worn and faded but clean. Her limbs were lean and smooth; she had little more body fat than Ernest. She clearly missed more meals than she should. Ernest held out the oats to her and Meg watched as her face fell. She looked over her few things, counted the coins in her palm and shook her head at Ernest. He sighed and studied the box he held, the bottom of it pressed up against his bony ribs. The woman said something too soft for Meg to catch and Ernest nodded and walked her way, still tracing a finger over the picture of the steaming bowl of oats on the box but without a fuss.

Could this be a list thing? Meg's heart was pounding enough for it to be. She just had to figure out how. Ernest was heading straight for her, walking slowly, too engrossed in the box to notice her. Meg took out the little notebook and pen that she kept in her bag and quickly scrawled a few lines. She took some money out of her wallet, way more than the oats' cost, and folded it up in the note. As Ernest reached her she crouched down in front of him, blocking his path.

"Hey, Ernest. Do you remember me?"

He nodded and nearly smiled but his eyes were too sad to join in.

"Is that your mom?" Ernest nodded again. Meg took a deep breath and put the folded up note into his hand. "Take this note and the oats and give them to the teller. Don't tell your mom who gave it to you. Have you got it?"

Ernest tucked the box under one arm and frowned at her before taking the folded up note. For a moment she thought he wouldn't, but then he turned and ran to the teller. She was taking money from his mom as he got to her. He shoved the note and the box of oats into her hands and ran to his mom's side, biting his lips the whole time.

The teller read the note, looked around, and held it out for Ernest's mom to read. A queue had built up behind them and Meg had to stretch her neck to see what happened next.

Ernest's mom was putting up a fight, but the teller sighed, pointed out the growing line of people waiting to be served and rang up the oats. She forcibly folded the wad of change into Ernest's mom's hand, added the oats to the women's one tiny packet and waved them off. Meg wondered what she'd said because Ernest's mom didn't argue. She slipped the packet on her arm, took Ernest's hand, and left the shop.

Meg hung around the cereal aisle with a grin so big it hurt her cheeks. Do something kind. She felt like she was floating as she walked towards the dairy fridge. That had been a kind thing to do, right? She'd actually nailed one thing on her list.

· · · · ●· ●· · ·

Dom slipped through the rusted gate, ignoring the "no entry" sign. He knew it was there, but the sun had set hours ago and it was too dark to see it now anyway. He latched the gate behind him and breathed the fresh air deeply. It was such a weird contrast to the tangled mess of overgrown weeds in the grounds surrounding the derelict building he'd come to visit.

He picked his way through the damp soil towards the empty shell of a house that waited for him in the distance. The insides were in darkness, but one window showed a room lit up, glowing with moonlight. The roof over that particular room was clearly no longer intact.

Dom felt the familiar tingling in his belly. This place had that effect on him. Butterflies, some might call it, but Dom had his own opinion. God's way of saying pay attention. "I'm listening. Show me."

The house had been looted of every part that could be removed. The window frames stood empty like eye sockets in a skull and the doors were missing, too. Dom crossed the threshold and a cold shiver passed through him.

As he walked through the house in moonlit gloom, his imagination ran riot. The moment splintered as his phone rang, loud and jarring. Mom.

"Hey, Ma."

"Dom, you have that tone to your voice. Are you back at that house?"

"I don't know what you're talking about."

"You are there. Oh, Dom. You need to let it go now."

"Why are you calling, Ma?"

"Your father would like to talk to you. There's an opening at the office for an architect and he wants to put your name down as a candidate. I know teaching dancing is fun, but you've got to be practical. That's not really a good way to make a living, not long term."

"I know what I'm doing, Ma. I know what God has been saying to me and I'm happy to do it. You've been in the mission field, you should understand."

His mom sniffed, an injured little sound that at once broke his heart and boiled his blood.

"My boy. My dear, stubborn boy. I get it. You want to serve and lay down your life, but all that doesn't really fit in with today's economic climate. It was different for me, I was young and your nana was happy to find the money to let me chase those wild dreams. Your dad and I? We simply can't fund wild dreams."

"I know. That's why I'm not asking you to. I don't expect you to understand either."

"Oh, but I do!" She clucked her tongue in frustration. "I just want more for you. Anyway, how's that lovely friend of yours? What's her name again …"

"Gina. Gina is fine, Mom. Not that it's any of my business."

"You could make it your business you know; she is a fine young woman."

"Ma, you sound like every cartoon queen ever, trying to marry off your son so you can have some grandkids. Seriously?"

"Well, all those queens had a point. Come on, Dominic, make a good choice. That's all I ask."

Dom closed his eyes and felt her words rain down on him like arrows tipped in cold poison. He fished a receipt out of his pocket and crinkled it between his fingers close to the phone. "Aah, sorry, Ma. You're breaking up." More crinkling. "Chat soon." Crinkle crinkle. Finger aimed at end call. Beep. Silence.

· · • • • • • • · ·

Meg sipped her tea and smoothed out the list on the counter in front of her. This was a moment. An occasion. A tiny, mini, victory-dance-worthy celebration. She was about to legitimately cross something off The Cake List. She ignored the last entry on her list, figure out God. She pretty much had that one wrapped up, but still couldn't bring herself to cross it off.

She sipped her tea again and slipped the cap off her pen. Pausing for a moment, Meg imagined a room full of cheering people who she modestly tipped her chin to. *Yes, it's true, people. I am about to cross something off my list*. Even Ebb cheered her on from his front seat view in the glass bowl. OK, Ebb was actually chasing a fish flake, but if he'd had a clue what was going on, he would have been cheering her on, no doubt.

She held her breath as she touched the tip of the pen to the paper napkin, pressed down, and ripped the list.

No!

Her list was in three pieces. How was that even possible from one small line? Was it the pen that had caused so much trouble? The doorbell buzzed and she shuffled over to open up, still frowning at the pen.

It was Dom. His cheeks were flushed as if he'd run a mile in the cold. "Hey, Meg. Can I come in for a moment?"

Meg waved him in, still glaring at the pen.

Dom tapped her forehead and bent down low to look her in the eye. "I'm putting the kettle on."

Meg followed him to the kitchen and slid onto a barstool, feeling gutted. As she rearranged the pieces of her list, a sick sort of dread hovered over her. If this was a sign, it wasn't a good one.

"Is that a shopping list? You should get an app on your phone for that sort of thing. My virtual list has never ripped before."

He leaned on the counter, grinning at his own cleverness. Meg sighed.

"You could just rewrite it on some proper paper. It will last longer than that flimsy thing."

"But I can't do that. Committing to paper is like throwing out a challenge to all the opposing forces in the universe."

Dom reached over and, before she could stop him, slid the pieces out from under her hands. His eyes flicked across her scrawl and without a word, he flipped the pieces over and lined them up. He held out hand, palm up the way a surgeon would demand a scalpel. "Sticky tape."

"Wait. Aren't you going to judge me and tell me I'm being nuts?"

Dom shrugged. "I can if it will make you feel better. Meg, you're nuts. Now find me some sticky tape."

"You know that that could actually just cause more trouble, right? If it sticks wrong, you won't be able to get it off without ripping it more."

Dom waved his flat palm in her face and Meg found sticky tape to put in it. In fewer than thirty seconds, her list was back in one piece. Dom popped it back on the fridge under the magnet she hated so much, and switched the kettle off.

"Come with me, I want to show you something."

· · · · •• • • · · ·

Dom parked outside the rusty gate for the second time in one evening, hoping his mom wouldn't phone again. Meg sat frowning in the passenger seat. He opened the door for her, but she stayed put with her seatbelt firmly clipped. He hadn't planned on bringing her here, but there was a vulnerability to her list that touched him. It was a simple, honest list, more heart-felt than anything he'd read in ages. It made him want to share this with her.

She hissed, "What are we doing here?"

"Trust me. Come see."

"Fine, but if we get arrested, I'm saying that you kidnapped me. Is this even your property? Is it safe?"

He reached over, unclipped her safety belt and took her hand. "You worry too much. I do this often." Too often.

Meg almost squeaked when she saw the "no entry" on the gate, but he rushed her past it and then they were in. There was an urge in his gut to see her response to this place, maybe even the Holy Spirit? It was nothing logical, just an overwhelming urge.

Meg still spoke in a rushed whisper, her shoulders all hunched as if she could make herself smaller, invisible. She tiptoed across the grass. "Dom, I need some context. I'm freaking out."

He stopped and hunted for words. "I want to know how this place makes you feel." He shrugged. That was exactly what he wanted.

"Feel? Is that it?"

"That's it. Come on, we're wasting time."

He offered his hand as they crossed the bumpy lawn and she ignored it, tripped, and grabbed his arm. As they stepped over the threshold into the building, he watched Meg's face. She breathed, her eyes narrowed, and the anxiety in her features melted into wonder. Her finger tapped her cheek and she nodded. She ran her fingertips along the wall as she walked. Her feet took her to the room with the holey ceiling.

Meg dug in her bag and held up a camera. "Do you mind?"

Dom shook his head and watched as she stretched out on the dusty floor and wriggled until she got an angle that she liked.

She pushed off the floor, handed him the camera and walked straight into the puddle of moonlight, lifted her face to the light and twirled. The moonlight caught her hair and her skin as she spun, glowing and twinkling. Dom couldn't help grinning. A twirling girl, a camera in his hand … the moment was too good to pass up. He clicked for rapid fire, catching the movement across a bunch of frames.

Just as quickly, she stopped and ran to the next room. Not a word crossed her lips, but he watched the emotions play across her face. Within minutes he'd followed her through the entire house and they stood back in the hallway leading to the front door.

She grinned at him. "I don't know what this is, or what you want to do with it, but I love it."

Chapter Seventeen

MEG PLUGGED HER USB data stick into the self-service machine at the print shop. She scrolled through the images to make sure she had all those she wanted and clicked on *print*. A buzzer went off and she panicked. Trust her to do it wrong.

The skinny, pale girl behind the counter came running and patted Meg on the back with a fluttery hand.

"Have I broken it? I'm so sorry, I can pay to get it repaired." Meg felt a bit sick.

"No, ma'am. You are our winner for today!"

"Oh? What have I won?"

"Pick out your favorite photo and we'll print it on a canvas for you." The pale girl grinned widely, clearly expecting Meg to be overjoyed.

Meg preferred life to come with a bit of pre-warning. Even good things needed time to sink in. "Uh ..."

The girl wiggled a finger towards Meg's photos. "Which one?" Her foot was tapping on the floor.

Meg scanned through them, feeling the pressure. Her feet at the studio on that first lesson maybe? The photo of Ernest and his box of oats? She scrolled a bit further and goose-bumps raised all down her arms as she got to the moonlit hole in the roof at the rundown house Dom had taken her to. This was it, no need to look any further. The contrast between the dark texture of the ceiling and the glowing light from outside breathed mystery into the image that gave Meg butterflies in her tummy.

She tapped the screen and the pale, impatient girl nodded vigorously.

"Good choice, I like that one, too!" She whipped Meg's memory stick out and disappeared behind the counter. A few minutes later she appeared again and stuck a slip in Meg's hand. "You can fetch it tomorrow after two p.m."

· · · · ● · · ● · · ·

On a whim, Dom typed out a message to the dance team group and clicked send.

Dance Team: no practice tonight. Social @ my place tomorrow night instead. I'll provide snacks and entertainment. Just bring yourselves.

He grinned in satisfaction. It was his birthday and they'd all forget, but he didn't really care as long as he had some great company. Then he remembered that catering wasn't exactly his strong point. Gina would usually have had all that covered, but he didn't feel up to all the drama that went along with anything to do with her. That left Meg. Whether she had any catering skills or not, at least she'd be good company.

He messaged her next.

I need help. I'll fetch you at 6pm.

He sent the message then thought he should probably have asked instead of assuming. Meg might have other things to do on a Friday night. She also wasn't a fan of being bullied. He opened up his messages.

Meg is typing ...

Quickly before she could hit send, he typed out:

Only if you're not busy and your heart is big enough to help a guy out, of course.

His message sent before she could reply to the first one. Phew.

He waited, watching to see what would appear. There was the longest pause before she started typing again.

Not sure how much help I'll be, but okay.

Dom punched the air and let out a whoop. His phone flew out his hand and landed in the bin.

· · · ● ● · ● · · ·

Meg faced Dom in the grocery aisle and shrugged. "You must have had something in mind when you planned this thing?"

Dom rubbed the back of his neck. "Planned isn't quite the word I'd use. It was more of a spur-of-the-moment thing."

It was Friday evening and the shop buzzed with pre-weekend shoppers. A couple brushed past Meg, arguing over lasagna or goulash for supper. Meg stopped herself from offering them helpful advice—goulash is less work to cook—and turned her attention back to Dom.

He stood with his head at an angle, studying her as if she were a specimen.

"We could get away with pizza? We buy the dough and make them ourselves. It's easy and it goes far."

Dom patted her on the arm. "Great idea! Where do we find dough?"

Meg sighed and led him to the fridges where the uncooked dough stood stacked in bulging plastic bags. She kept going down the fridge aisle and added cheddar cheese and some bacon. "Do you like weird cheese and olives?"

Dom shook his head. "Nah. I'm more a bacon and pineapple kinda guy."

They stuck their heads in the soda fridge at the same time, picked out two different flavors and popped the bottles into the trolley. This was fun.

"How about we make finger salads?" Dom held up a cucumber for Meg's approval and she shrug-nodded.

Her phone buzzed as a message came through. It was Talia.

Heads up. The social is actually for Dom's birthday. He doesn't like to be alone so he always makes something up. See you there!

· · · · ● · ● · · · ·

Dom's apartment was on the top floor of a square building in a quiet part of town. Meg intended to be early, but she'd stopped to pet the neighbor's cat and then had to go the long way around the building to avoid having to talk to her actual neighbor. The old lady was apparently a complainer and would latch on to any available ears. Meg had never actually chatted with her, but according to the neighbor on the other side, once she got going, getting away without being 100% rude was impossible.

As Meg rode the elevator, she slipped into super-sleuth mode. Today was the day she figured out exactly what was going on between Dom and Gina. Solving the mystery of whether Gina was pregnant or not would be a sweet bonus.

She shifted Dom's awkward present underneath her arm. She'd had no idea what to get the man, but when she'd fetched her block-mounted canvas photograph, she thought of how much he seemed to love the old place and maybe this canvas would be good for him. They'd even gift wrapped it for her at the shop.

The others were there when she arrived, all spread out on Dom's leather sofas. Jeremy was telling a story, his face lit up and animated. He was a big guy, larger than Meg thought dancers to be, but he moved with grace and ease that impressed her. She missed too much of the story for the punch line to mean much, but the others chuckled.

Dom's place was smaller than she expected, but organized and neat. Floor to ceiling glass took up one whole side of the living room looking out over the ocean. It took Meg's breath away.

Dom came out of the kitchen wiping his hands on a cloth tucked into his jeans. He grinned when he saw her. "You're here. Now we can start."

"This is for you. A little birdie told me it was your birthday." She handed him his present, cringing a little inside.

"Was it a little Talia-birdie perhaps?" Dom took the present with a mixture of you-really-shouldn't-have and pure delight on his face.

"I'm not telling, but it's a weird present. If you don't like it, you can pass it on. I won't be offended. Actually, I might be offended. So you'd better pretend to like it a lot."

Dom laughed and stowed the wrapped present in his bedroom.

Meg was about to apologize for not being there to help set up when she saw the dining room table all laid out with the snacks they'd bought. Gina hovered, fussing over the bowls and plates, looking harassed as usual. Her face was flushed and the viscose dress she wore flowed over her curves softly without giving away any secrets.

Dom waved everyone closer. "Drinks are on this side. Fill your plates and get something to drink, we'll eat while we chat. Make sure you sit near your partner." This might have been a social, but Dom still had his teacher voice on. Clearly this was a social with a purpose other than just hanging out.

He disappeared into the kitchen and Matt followed. Meg grabbed the moment to make up for not helping set up and followed them. Dom had a montage of framed photographs up on the wall just outside the kitchen. The one that caught her eye most was an amber sunrise over the sea. It was an exquisite photo that captured the first rays of sunlight through the smooth crest of a breaking swell. The other photos were taken in exactly the same place but at different times of day with different tides and sun-rays. She lingered to look for landmarks and see if she could recognize which beach it was. It made a beautiful wall decoration.

Dom and Matt were already deep in conversation. It sounded like they were picking up on a conversation they'd started earlier.

"So you reckon I should tear it all down and start again?" Matt asked.

Meg hung back; walking in would have been rude.

Dom's response was instant. "Old things have to be torn down to make way for newer, better things. Sometimes the old things might need to be razed to the ground completely to make space for new. Do whatever it takes, it will be worth it."

Cold passed through Meg. He was going to tear down the moonlight house. Granted, it was old and needed a good bit of fixing, but to tear down a building with that much charm seemed criminal.

Heat flooded Meg's face and she bailed on the idea of helping them make coffee and tea. She hurried back to the dining room table, put a few things on her plate and quickly took the corner two-seater. It gave her the best view of everybody without being obvious. Dom came and squeezed in next to her and helped himself to a mini muffin off her plate. He chewed twice, swallowed and cleared his throat before speaking.

"Time for some partner work. You'll be introducing each other and you'll have to tell us one obscure fact about your partner. But before all that, you have two minutes to come up with your couple name. And ... go!"

Meg frowned at Dom for the muffin as much as the task. "Couple name?'

•••••••••••

Dom was having trouble not staring at Meg. Late afternoon sun streamed through the glass panel of the front door and set her hair ablaze. He focused on keeping his voice low and normal. "Yeah. I thought we could be MeggaDom. It's got a nice ring to it, don't you think?"

"The image in my head is huge and stupid. There's got to be something better."

Dom waved a hand in her face. "Stop being a hater, it's better than DoMeg. Have you got a better idea?"

"Not right now. Give me a minute ..."

Dom tapped his watch and waited. "We could do a spoonerism and go with DegMom?"

Meg snorted and nearly dropped her plate. Her laughter warmed him.

Dom checked his watch, grateful for something to take his focus off Meg and her hair. "Time is up! Let's hear from Talia and Matt. Give us your couple name and tell us what you know about your partner."

Pixie-like Talia patted Matt's leg. "You talk." Matt had floppy bangs and a clean-shaven face that made him look fresh out of school.

Dom held out a finger and waggled it like a school teacher. "You have to introduce each other. Sorry, Tals."

She scrunched her nose at him. "Fine. This is Matt." She backhanded his chest. "He knows more about computers than anyone else I know. He hates sushi, but is a fan of Mexican food. He started dancing to meet girls." Her eyes slid sideways and Matt shrugged.

"She's not wrong."

"Now he still dances because it's an excuse to spend time with me." Talia ended with a flourish of a perfectly manicured hand and a smile that dimpled her cheeks. "One little known fact about Matt is that he still takes his washing home once a week for his mom to do."

Matt choked on his coffee as they all laughed. "Only because I'm saving up for a washing machine. What do you expect me to do? Wash it in the bath with my feet?" He waved his hands around, calling for quiet. He gave up and spoke loudly over the snickering. "Our couple name is Talimat because it sounds like something you should sprinkle on your food to make it taste good."

Jeremy snorted. "Dude, that's *Aromat*."

"Oh, right. Oh well, we like it." He winked at Talia but she wasn't looking. "This little fireball is Talia. She sells makeup at the new department store on Oxford Street, but her dream is to one day own her own spa somewhere just off the beach. One little known fact about Talia is that she lets her leg hair grow super long in between waxing."

Talia smacked him and clucked her tongue.

Dom pointed at Cliff and Tammy. "Let's have our multi-national, or should that be *international*, couple next. An Asian and an African, you could go by A.A."

Cliff coughed into his hand. "Er, no thanks. We're good." His voice was deep with a leftover trace of an accent. "The two obvious options for our couple name are Clammy or Tiff. Strangely, we aren't really keen on either of those. So we're going with Clamiff."

Tammy raised an eyebrow at him, but he grinned and ignored her.

"Tammy is a preschool teacher. I don't know how she does it, but she spends her days herding small people—a skill I don't have and, frankly, don't want. An obscure fact about Tammy is that she has a deep fear of goats." He patted her knee as she shuddered.

"Goats *are* creepy, though. You can't argue. Cliff here, works in an accounting firm with Reg. He basically has a scientific calculator for a brain, in other words—he's very bright. One little known fact about Cliff is that even though he's an Asian, he hates sweet and sour anything." She waved the spotlight over to Alison and Jeremy.

Jeremy tilted his head at Alison and she took the cue.

She had a peace and gentleness about her that soaked through how she spoke, even how she moved. "We are Jelison." She paused for a moment, nodding suavely at their collective genius. "Jeremy makes things pretty for a living, although he would call it being a graphic designer. Whatever. A little known fact ... hmm, picking one is hard." She tapped her lip. "He is the biggest softy. If you want to see a grown man melt like a marshmallow near a fire, just bring out a baby. Jeremy-puddle, just like that." She clicked her fingers.

Jeremy kept his eyes on Alison as he spoke. "Alison runs a coffee shop. She bakes all the cakes and stuff that they serve there. She is really good at baking. A little know fact about

Alison is that she likes to play matchmaker and is personally responsible for at least three happy couples over the last year."

The smug little grin on Alison's face said it was all true.

Gina poked Reg with a long red fingernail.

He dodged her poking good-naturedly.

"Gina, as we all know, runs the studio for Dom. One little known fact about Gina is ..." He scratched his chin while thinking.

It was all Meg could do not to yell out *she's having Dom's baby*. She clamped her jaw shut and held it there through sheer willpower. Enough willpower to make beads of sweat pop out on her temples. Maybe if she knew for sure, she could say something. But even then, was it her place?

Meg sat staring at Gina's nose in an attempt not to stare at her stomach.

Reg scratched his head.

Gina huffed and rolled her eyes. "A little know fact about me is that I'm not a very patient person." Her eyebrow challenged anyone in the room to disagree, and Dom knew better than to take on that eyebrow even though her lack of patience was a well-known fact.

Gina waved a thumb towards Reg. "Reg is a partner in an accounting firm. He's known to hold money with a tight fist. A little known fact about Reg is that he has a birthmark in the shape of a dolphin just over his spine on the small of his back. Your turn, Dom."

Dom slipped his arm around Meg's shoulders. "Our couple name is DoMog, although it might be breaking the rules a bit. Meg, you go first."

Meg sat very still, supremely conscious of Dom's arm around her shoulders. "Dom runs a dance studio and a little known fact about him is that he does it to run away from being an architect in his dad's company."

Dom snorted back a laugh. "Well said. A little known fact about Meg is that she has a big-O birthday coming up that she'd rather avoid. Oh, I nearly forgot. She works in a lab, so if any of you are pregnant, she can confirm it for you."

Gina choked on her apple juice.

· · · · ●·●· · · ·

It was only after everyone had helped clean up and left did Dom remember he had presents to open. Salted caramel chocolate from Talia and Matt, his latest favorite. A new deep blue beach towel from Gina and Reg. His other one was getting a bit shabby, this one was nice. Sunglasses from Cliff and Tammy. They'd been with him the day he accidentally rolled his chair over his old pair. Comfy sheepskin slippers came out the bag labeled *from Alison and Jeremy*. Only Meg's present waited for him.

The others knew him well by now. It would be interesting to see what Meg had come up with. He peeled back the sticky tape, wondering if the girl would get it right or not. Buying presents for people, especially new ones, was hard.

He unfolded the two sides of paper, turned the canvas over and stopped breathing for a moment. Of all the things he'd seen her snap photos of, this place burned like fire in his belly. It was the hole in the roof back at the house. The moon was just peeping past the edge of the broken tiles on the roof, softening and blurring the image. It was his motivation, his drive, his purpose. The contrast of the image itself spoke to him, too. How dark brokenness can feel, and the incredible power of light to transform it.

And this girl had nailed it in one image, wrapped it up and given it to him for a birthday she wasn't even supposed to know about.

Jesus, what are You saying?

Chapter Eighteen

MEG'S THROAT WOKE HER up. It was raw and stinging enough to be a sign of impending sickness. She swallowed with difficulty as she shuffled to the kitchen to make honey and lemon tea. She hated honey and lemon tea, but it was apparently good for sore throats according to Chad.

Chad.

She moved the honey and lemon aside, took a new cup and threw in a regular teabag. Ebb hung around the surface as he did when he was hungry. A few crushed fish flakes for breakfast and his life was back on track for the morning. Meg watched him do gymnastics to eat and wondered if she should try eat her breakfast upside down in solidarity. She'd probably choke, which would leave nobody to feed Ebb. Bad idea.

Last night had been fascinating, but apart from Gina choking on her apple juice, Meg was nowhere closer to solving the mysteries. She'd watched Gina and Dom as much as she could without being creepy, but saw nothing to add fuel to her suspicions. These two had taken pretending to the next level. They were experts.

Her phone rang, it was Sandy.

"Meg, do you know that it's a month until B-day?"

"Thirty-three days to be specific; but yes, I do know."

"Well ..." Sandy's impatience flowed through the phone, an almost tangible thing. "Have you got a plan? You are not letting this one slip by in obscurity. This is a big-O and should be celebrated."

Mourned, more likely. "I know. I haven't quite decided yet."

"Girl! You have to book a venue, decide on a theme, draw up a budget and invitation list. Decide on catering, decor. There are a million things to be done. Wait. Give me a moment."

Meg walked through to the living room and sank into the corner of a couch. The phone in her ear beeped and clicked and she could picture Sandy searching for a "10 step guide to party planning," calling Xan to remind her how to screen-shot, ranting in between as she pushed the back button one too many times. Usually Meg would have laughed, but her head was splitting sore.

Her phone beeped and Sandy was back, buzzing in her ear like a hornet. "I've sent a checklist for you. As you'll see, you're way behind."

"But that's why I have you, Sandy. You're good at all this stuff." Meg's nose started to run and she grabbed a tissue off the box on the coffee table.

The silence from Sandy was so thick, Meg thought the call had dropped.

"Sandy? Are you there?"

"I won't do this at such late notice. Even for you. You know that, right?"

"I know. Obviously. Don't stress, I'll figure something out."

After a few more surface words, Sandy said good-bye and hung up.

Great. Meg's only hope had bailed.

She had no intention of putting on a big do, but it would be nice to have her friend around on the day. Sandy would probably spend the day moaning about not having a party. That girl was not good at letting things be, not at all. But, Meg had learned to ignore her fussing when she had to.

All she had left was her sorry list. It hung on the fridge now, a mocking reminder of the smallness of her life.

Maybe that's why she hated bonsai trees.

She actually was one.

· · · · · ● ◆ · · · ·

Meg tucked the scarf tighter around her neck. As much as she hadn't wanted to leave her apartment, she had to get something for this cold. She was feeling worse by the minute. The pharmacy was wall-to-wall people, as if they'd all got together on the sly and decided to pack themselves in there to make her day more miserable.

She chose the sports nutrition aisle to get to the dispensary. Usually when the shop was full like this, the sports nutrition aisle was the easiest to navigate as most the people were stuck in the other aisles. Today her path was blocked by a toddler flat on his back, bawling at the top of his lungs. His harassed mom stood next to him, dodging his flailing arms and legs with her arms full of a newborn baby. She looked ready to cry as much as the boy on the floor.

Meg checked her escape route. A body builder blocked her way out and she had no desire to squeeze past those unnatural lumps of muscle. She turned back to the mom who was now trying to cradle the newborn in one arm and bend down (without dropping the baby) to peel her son off the floor.

Meg braved the swinging appendages. "Here, let me help you."

The lady eyed her, must have decided she looked safe, and handed over the newborn. Meg cradled the swaddled bundle and hoped she wouldn't manage to break it somehow. Her cold! She turned her head to the side to avoid sharing germs.

The mom leaned close to her boy's face and spoke in a loud, calm voice. "I'm leaving now. You can come with, or you can stay here." She managed to fake a gentle smile, turned and walked. The toddler kept screaming, but the moment she disappeared around the end of the aisle, his tears dried up instantly. He rolled over and pushed himself to his knees. He still had tears all down his face and he drew a shuddery breath.

"Momma?" He blinked a few times and whimpered before toddling down the aisle on wobbly legs. He pushed past the body builder. Clearly no big muscles would get between him and his momma.

Meg had no choice but to follow him, trying not to breathe on the baby in her arms. She contorted to get past Muscles and swung around the corner to find Momma on her knees with a tearful boy wrapped up close to her. His stubby arms barely reached all the way around her neck, but he squeezed her as best he could and her arms held him tight. She whispered calming words in his ear.

The baby in Meg's arms peeped at her through a half open eye, wriggled and started crying. The mom gave her boy an extra tight squeeze, kissed his head and retrieved the baby from Meg. With a quick thank you, she took her tiny family back to the prescription queue.

Meg stood glued to the spot. The image of the mom around the corner waiting for her little guy replayed in her mind. She didn't yell at him, she just waited until he'd calmed himself down and was ready, then she'd hugged him. It turned Meg's insides to smoosh and she couldn't move. There was something about the whole scene that *felt* like God. Muscles attempted to squeeze past her and asked her to excuse him in a high voice that was so unexpected, Meg nearly laughed. It was all too much; she panicked and left the shop.

Halfway home she realized she hadn't got any meds. If she'd had any energy left, she'd have been kicking herself and going back, but she'd used it all up and all she wanted was to take her pounding head to bed.

· · · ♦ · ♦ · ♦ · ·

Dom clicked Meg's number for the fifth time. The four previous times, he'd ended the call before it could actually ring on her side. This time he was determined to stay strong. He leaned his forehead on the glass and focused on a wave breaking onto the rocks below, not the fact that the phone was ringing.

His hesitancy came from not having a clue why he was actually calling. Usually there'd be a purpose, but could you call unease in your gut a reason? The present! He could thank her. That was a good reason, right there.

Meg answered after the eighth ring. She croaked more than spoke.

"Meg, are you sick?"

Loud sniff. "Maybe."

"Have you got vitamin C?"

Long pause. "No. I don't."

"I'm coming over." He ended the call before she could object.

· · · · ● · ● · · · ·

The bell buzzed in its samba tune and Meg groaned at the thought of getting up. She knew it was Dom. On the same night they'd changed the locks, he'd picked out this tune so that she'd always know it was him.

Meg threw her robe on over her clothes and shuffled to the door. Dom came in with a full bag in his arms.

"You look awful. Go back to bed, I'll bring you what you need."

Meg shuffled down the hallway without arguing. Her feet shoveled through the graveyard of tissue carcasses at her feet and she flopped into bed. Her body ached now, too, and she was shivering. She shouldn't let Dom come in like this. She pulled her duvet up to her ears and buried her head in her pillow.

He cleared his throat and held out a hand full of pills of different colors and shapes, his other hand carried a glass of water.

"That's half the drug store. What are they all?"

"The white one is vitamin C, the orange one is an immune system booster, and the round yellow one is a decongestant. Is your throat sore?"

Meg swallowed the pills one at a time followed by sips of water. Her throat ached each time she swallowed. She pressed the cool glass to her hot forehead.

"I can see it is by the look on your face when you swallow. Never fear, the magic cold fighting dude is here. Look, nothing in my hands." He flourished them the way a magician would, then tucked them behind his back and fiddled. "And … er, wait for it."

The man must have lost his mind. He started humming a mysterious tune all the while, fiddling in his back pocket. Meg would have laughed if she weren't in such pain.

"Ta-da!" He whipped out pink throat spray and held it up for her approval. "Look! Like magic."

She all but snatched it and sprayed the fire in her throat. The relief was instant. She sank back into her pillows and felt drowsiness roll over her. Maybe she wasn't dying just yet.

· · · · ·· · · · ·

Dom watched Meg drift off to sleep. Her nose was red against the paleness of the rest of her skin and the dark circles under her eyes made her look fragile.

It would be a stupid move to lose his heart to this girl. Then again, he was known for being stupid sometimes. He watched her breathing deepen and whispered, "Well, God, You do keep telling me that she's important. I wouldn't be listening to You properly if I didn't look after her, right?"

Gina would have his head. On a plate with a salad. What was he doing?

Chapter Nineteen

MEG WAS BOOKED OFF work. Vashti's exact words had been closer to "don't you dare bring those germs anywhere near me," but the result was a day to herself. Dom had warned her not to come to practice tonight either, even though the concoction of vitamins that he'd left for her to take had already started working.

Maybe today could be a list cross day. If she got going early enough, she might even cross off two things.

Meg pulled on jeans and a sweater, fed Ebb, ate a boiled egg—not because she had any appetite, but because she knew her body needed nutrition—and brushed her teeth. She was ready. She checked the list one more time, though she knew it well enough to recite it backwards at 2 a.m. The only thing she'd managed to cross off was "do something kind." Shocking, really. Was she truly that self-centered?

"Right, God, how about letting me cross one thing off this list today? That would be the kind thing to do." She paused, wondering if that was a bit too cheeky. "And I'm sorry if I'm being cheeky, I just really need this."

Silence.

Right.

She took her list and read through it. The most logical one to tackle was *break a never*. All it would take was to figure out something she'd never do and do it. She was going to take to the streets and walk until something presented itself to her.

She locked her apartment and popped the key in her bag. Her neighbor's cat ran up to her with a meow and rubbed on her legs. She bent down to pet it and realized her mistake as her neighbor's door swung open.

Normally she would either dash down the stairs, or throw herself back inside quickly before the old lady had time to shuffle out.

Wait.

Here it was—her never. Her heart sank as she forced herself to stay put while Mrs. O'Riley hobbled over in her corduroy slippers with the morning sun making her white hair glow like a pale halo.

"What are you doing to my cat?" Her face had a pinched look as if she'd spent the morning sucking lemons.

Meg felt her hackles rising, but she slapped a smile on her face and forced gentleness into her tone. "She's a beautiful cat.

I was just saying good morning. How are you this morning, Mrs. O'Riley?"

"My back is killing me, my teabags are finished, and I didn't sleep a wink last night. Not that anyone cares."

Meg grew really quiet. The nudge inside was unmistakable, though it was the last thing on the planet she actually wanted to do. *For the sake of the list, Meg. Do it for the sake of your stupid, sorry list.*

"Would you like to come and have some tea with me?"

Mrs. O'Riley stared at her as if she'd just offered to cook her cat for supper. "Oh, no. I couldn't possibly." She hobbled off back towards her apartment, shuffling as quickly as her old bones would allow. The door clicked behind her so firmly it might as well have slammed.

Meg blew her nose and sniffed. *I tried. You saw that, right?*

Well, as grumpy as the old duck was, nobody should be without tea. Meg fetched some from her kitchen, tied it into a pretty muslin gift bag and deposited it on Mrs. O'Riley's doorstep. She rang the doorbell and left quickly before the old lady spotted her through the peephole.

She hid in her apartment until she heard the door open and shut again. When she went to look, the teabags were gone.

· · · ● ● · ● · · ·

Meg had intended to go past a shop for some softer tissues; fresh orange juice for the vitamin C content; and some lotion for her sore, cracked nose. This cold made her feel like absolute rubbish.

On the way to the shop she drove past the bushes where Dom had stopped to deliver groceries. A slight breeze raised gooseflesh all down her arms and she pulled the car over onto the verge. *What are you doing, Meg?*

She closed her eyes. That's what people do when they pray, right? But then she didn't feel safe because what if she were sitting here, trying to figure out God with her eyes closed, and someone decided she was a soft target? "God, it would be great if you could just show me what my next list-cross thing is. I don't even think it would be cheating, not really." That still sounded quite cheeky. "I'm sorry, God. I'm not used to doing this. If You wouldn't mind, I'd like to cross something off my list today. That would help me feel better, I think." She paused for a moment wondering how to end her little speech. "Thank You."

She waited for a break in the traffic and crossed the road. Her heart thumped in her chest the way it always did when she broke routine. Anything out of the ordinary made her heart pound so fast like it was trying to climb right out of her chest and knock some sense back into her.

Meg ignored the cold chills running down her back and scouted the bushes for a gap. The path was a skinny thing that timidly broke through the thick bushes lining the road. Meg's mouth was so dry her tongue stuck to the roof of her mouth. She couldn't come this far to back out. She just couldn't.

The first step onto the path felt like a step of a cliff. She left scared-Meg behind and pushed through the overgrown pathway quickly. The smell of smoke hit her nose before she came out the other side. It hung thick in the air over the shacks. She stayed in the bushes hoping nobody saw her.

The shacks spread as far as she could see in every direction—a sea of patched-together boxes held together by wire and a prayer. Some were made from corrugated iron, rusted and holey, others from old packing crates lashed together with bits of tattered rope. Barefoot kids played in the dirt street with an empty two-liter bottle as their ball.

One of the boys looked familiar. She'd have recognized his holey pants anywhere. He waved to his friends and jogged down a dirt road deeper into the informal settlement.

She ignored the part of her that wanted to stay hidden in the bushes and followed him, walking as fast as she could without looking suspicious, though being the only white person in the settlement, she couldn't have stuck out more if she'd tried.

Ernest jogged up to a shack that stood with the front door wide open. Meg watched as he slipped inside and banged the door shut behind him. She was suddenly aware of the attention she was drawing.

She snapped a quick photo on her phone and turned to leave. A group of men were hanging around on the street corner and whistled as she hurried past. Of all the bad ideas she'd ever had, this one was way up there.

If Chad could have seen her then, he'd have been rolling his eyes and shaking his head so hard he'd have given himself a headache.

She made it back to the cover of the bushes, and checked behind to see if she were being followed. The group of men watched her, but hadn't moved from where they sat drinking.

Meg didn't want to leave, she wanted to see more. This was Ernest and Buntu's world and it was so far out of her comfortable life that she was fascinated. A plan slipped through her brain, quick and quiet. Maybe with some help, she could come back.

Incognito.

Chapter Twenty

MEG EYED HERSELF IN the mirror. She'd known that Talia's makeup skills were good, but the girl had surpassed herself this time.

Talia dabbed at her temple with a damp sponge and stepped back to see the full effect. "Well, if I didn't know better, I'd have thought you're a granny." She tucked in a stray strand of hair under the curly gray wig she'd borrowed from her hairdresser. "What did you say this was for again?"

Meg breezed over her question by asking one of her own. "How long have you been doing makeup? This looks incredible."

"Your eyes are a dead give-away, though."

"I'm going to keep my shades on and wear some gloves for my hands; it's perfect."

"What is all this for, anyway?" Talia's eyes sparkled with curiosity. She packed her makeup back into her makeup box and shut the lid. "That's okay, you can keep your secrets."

Meg grimaced. It's not that she didn't want Talia knowing. She just thought that somehow saying it out loud might make her lose her courage.

· · · ● · ● · ● · · ·

Dom pushed his Bible aside and propped his feet up on his desk. He leaned back as far as the chair would tilt and tucked his hands behind his head. His thoughts tangled like spaghetti and nothing he read would stick. Praying might be easier.

He sang a simple worship song. Usually that was enough to round up his thoughts and aim them upwards, but not today. He whispered a few thank yous and got stuck on the image of his parents. It was hard to thank God for them sometimes. Who was he kidding—often. Believing in God should be a common ground that created a safe place to have differences and still love deeply. In the case of his folks, it was as if the God they believed in was not the same being who'd won Dom's heart. They saw everything cut and dried, black and white.

Literally black and white.

His connection with Buntu was something they couldn't make peace with, convinced that all she wanted was his money. They judged her as poor and black, and wrote her off without meeting her. It shredded him. They favored Gina and would remind him of their loyalty to her at every opportunity. He choked the words out anyway. "Thank you for my parents, though You know how I feel."

Feel. Such a tiny word. The last four weeks had thrown feelings at him he'd never had to deal with before and they all bubbled up round about the time he met the stubborn, delightful, impossibly complicated yet as simple-as-a-daisy, red-headed Meg. Taking her to the house the other night had been a risk and it had tangled things in a way he hadn't expected. So tangled.

"I feel alive around Meg." There, he'd said it. Out loud and to God. "I don't think I've ever felt quite so alive. Is this You? Did You bring her to me?" He'd seen God work in ways that were simple and quick. A breath of a word from God's lips was enough to turn any circumstance on its head. To even think of Meg in this way was beyond foolish. Both of them were caught up in messy knots of real life that would take a lifetime of miracles to undo.

It was all quite impossible.

Except that with God, nothing was impossible. He said it Himself. Maybe it was time for a heart-to-heart with this girl.

• • • • •• • • • •

Meg's heart was beating so fast she thought she might just pass out. She studied the people around her through the tint of her shades and felt a wave of mental face-palming shiver through her. She couldn't really do it for fear of messing her makeup. The clouds rolling in were not on her side, either. Talia's makeup may or may not be waterproof.

Stop it, Meg. This is not about you.

Right. She shoved her hands into her coat pockets and copied the weariness she saw all around her. The ladies shuffled along, chatting to each other, not in any particular hurry. The only ones with energy seemed to be the kids. They ran, laughed, shrieked, shouted, and danced in a loop that carried on regardless.

Meg tired-shuffled back towards the house Ernest had led her to last time. She had no idea what she intended to do when she got there.

God, help?

She found the right one and sat across the street in what looked like an old cement bus stop. The shack was a patchwork of metal sheets that looked like it might topple if the wind picked up. Eight little kids came out the front door eating dry bread. Their feet were bare and their clothes holey and dirty. They waved towards the house and skipped down the road looking too happy for their circumstances. Buntu came out carrying bucket of laundry which she proceeded to drape over a wire rigged up between two poles. Meg recognized her from the grocery store.

Meg resisted the urge to run over and tell her it was going to rain, but by the way Buntu squinted at the clouds, Meg thought she probably knew already. The small African lady shook her head and carried on hanging items of clothing over the wire. Meg sat watching her, mesmerized by the strength in her slender hands.

A fat raindrop plopped down and landed on her knee, followed in quick succession by three others. Wherever the drops fell, the fabric soaked through and stuck to her skin. Meg felt a drop on her nose and panicked. All she needed was for her disguise to wash off in a downpour. She shot to her feet and scurried to get back to the pathway to her car. The rain was pelting down harder now, smacking into her with meaning.

Buntu's washing was not going to dry anytime soon. If Meg had known her disguise wasn't about to run off her face, she'd have gone back and offered to tumble it dry, but Buntu wouldn't know or trust her and it would all be weird. That was the thing about being kind—it often made things weird.

Meg ran through the small alleyway between the trees and slowed down to walk to where her car was parked a few parking spaces down. Maybe that's what stopped God doing kind things all the time—the weirdness.

But could the God of the universe possibly be scared of a little weirdness? If she could have just figured that out, she could have crossed another thing off the list.

Chapter Twenty-One

MEG HAD HER SHOES off. Rain pattered softly on the window, but inside her apartment was warm and dry. She'd washed off her disguise, slipped into her soft, warm sweatpants, and blow-dried her hair.

The coffee table that usually sat in the middle of her living room had been pushed up against the wall and the couch against the other. There was no official practice tonight, but she wanted to work through some of the parts she was a bit shaky on. The soft rug beneath her bare feet warmed her and contentment settled over her like an invisible hug.

Contentment was so foreign, part of her wanted to stop and unpick it. Pull it apart to see what it was made from so she could construct it again for herself. Even as she thought that, a deep sense of *other* came over her and she knew without a doubt that this was not from within herself.

Her scalp prickled. It was on her list after all—figure out God. What if He decided to arrive in her apartment to help her? Her heart pounded, but not with fear. More like deli-cious anticipation. She stood, breathless, almost too scared to move in case the moment lifted.

The door buzzed loudly, followed by impatient knocks like a machine gun that popped the moment.

She opened without thinking and Chad stood on the threshold with a key in his hand and a basket in the other. "You changed the locks." His tone was flat, accusing.

"Safety first; a girl can't be too careful living on her own. Why are you here?"

He held up the basket. "I brought some of your favorite things. I thought we could have a picnic."

"In this weather?"

He pushed past her and walked straight into the living room. "Looks like you're all ready for me. We can sit on the carpet."

She padded after him, deeply aware of her bare feet. Chad didn't like bare feet. "I'm sorry, I've already eaten."

Chad spread out the mustard-colored blanket that always made Meg think of baby poop. She stood on the edge of it and her insides deflated. She could have saved herself all this by checking the peephole before opening, but the moment (encounter?) she'd had made her drop her guard. Now it was back up, but it was too late.

She watched as he unpacked olives, three varieties of cheeses, and even a tub of caviar. Meg wasn't fussy when it came to food, but she preferred simple things. The only thing on this blanket that she'd happily eat were the dry crackers.

"Sit, Meg. You hovering like that makes me anxious." His eyes flicked over her feet.

"You know that I only eat cheddar, don't you?" She stayed standing with her arms crossed tight.

He waved as if swatting flies. "Nonsense. Everybody loves a good spread of cheese."

She sat on the couch and tucked her feet in underneath her. Another thing that Chad hated. Her heart wasn't pounding, her palms weren't sweaty. In fact, she was calm. "Why are you here?"

Chad had a cheese-topped cracker halfway to his mouth. He put it down with a sigh. "When are you going to stop this nonsense and come back? I've been patient with you, Meg, but this is pushing it. Even I have my limits."

Despite being calm, the words in her head still tripped over each other and face-planted before reaching her lips. *I don't want this. You don't want me. Not really. You want me to be someone else. Maybe you should find someone else.*

Chad frowned. "Aren't you even going to say anything?" His face softened and he rubbed his temple before holding out both hands. "The thing is, I miss my friend."

She heard him swallow hard and the sudden shift made a part of her ache. She saw it in her head—the moment that had cemented their lives together like a concrete block around their feet that would sink them if they carried on. She slipped off the couch onto her knees and took both his hands in hers. They were icy between her warm fingers. She leaned close, holding eye contact to make sure he was hearing her.

"We are friends and we have been for most our lives."

"Exactly! Which is why I don't—"

She laid a finger on his lips. "Shh. Listen. Your sister"—she swallowed hard—"... drowning was a terrible accident and all along we've blamed ourselves. It's been the glue of tragedy that kept us so mangled up in each other all these years. If you imagine two flat sheets of aluminum foil being crunched up together, that's us. You've spent all these years dictating to me, not hearing me, and I've gone along with it because I felt guilty."

Chad's anger burned hot, but there were tears in his eyes. Meg kept going before he could speak.

"But do you know what I remember? I remember your mom and dad drinking and fighting. I remember a counter-top covered in empty bottles. They were too drunk to look after your baby sister. You were five and I was four. It wasn't our fault."

"But—"

"It wasn't."

"I need to think about this."

Meg started packing the food and putting it all back into the basket. Her hands were shaking and she wanted to weep, but for the first time since that awful day, her heart was light.

· · · ● ● ● ● ● · · ·

Dom arrived at Meg's apartment and thought about messaging first, but his resolve was already waning so he chose not to think but took the stairs two at a time. He reached her door and was about to knock when he heard voices from inside.

He checked the window to the living room, the blinds were open for once. Meg usually kept them closed to stop people in the hallway doing exactly what he was doing now—looking in.

A man sat on the floor and Meg knelt in front of him holding both his hands. Queasiness rocked Dom's stomach. Chad.

He pulled away quickly before Meg saw him and doubled over. He *had* asked for a sign, after all. It didn't get clearer than this.

Chapter Twenty -Two

GINA WAS RED IN the face by the time they got her zipped into her competition dress. Meg dug in her bag for a tissue and blew her nose, dabbed at it with a tissue, and wondered if cutting it right off would help. Dom's doctoring skills had worked, she felt human again except for her nose that insisted on impersonating a waterfall.

Dressing Gina had been a team effort that made Meg think of those Grand Prix pit stops. This kind of dancing was a team sport, but Meg had never realized that it would take a team to dress one of them. Alison pulled down, two others pulled the two sides of the zip closer and Meg got the unenviable job of zip-puller. She cringed each time she nearly caught Gina's skin in the zipper, but it went up and now they were ready. Except for Gina's shoes. She stood barefoot. Meg thought about offering help, took one look at the scowl on Gina's face, and didn't.

A knock on the door. "Ten minutes. You all need to get out here." It was Dom, with the carefully controlled tone he used when he was stressed out.

"Do you need help with your shoes?" Meg braced herself for the explosion. This could be her selfless thing for the list. Take one for the team—bear the brunt of the wrath of Gina so the team could be ready in time. But her heart wasn't racing, there was no rush of blood to her eardrums, no pounding emotion. Probably not.

There was also no shouting. Puzzled, she looked up to see Gina blinking tears from wide, false-lash-framed eyes.

"Hold those tears! You'll wreck your make-up! Talia, let's do the left first."

Between them, they wrestled Gina's sparkly shoes onto her feet, while she balanced with her nails digging into their backs. Tammy carefully dabbed the dampness from her eyes with a tissue.

"Done. Let's go before Dom pops something."

They made their way into the glittering hall as the announcer called for them on the floor. As Meg navigated between the crush of chairs and people, she tried to focus on the steps she was about to do, but seeing a soft side to Gina had thrown her. It would have been better if she'd let rip in her normal way.

Everyone seemed a bit rattled. Talia lined up on the left instead of the right (she crossed the floor with a red face), Meg faced the back and spun around quick. Before she could breathe or center herself, music flooded the room. She missed the first two counts, but picked up by count three. Her blank brain responded to the music and the steps she'd worked so hard to remember came back to her muscles. This might just work. They wove through each other in two circles traveling in opposite directions.

The music built to a crescendo and the girls lined up opposite their guys, ready for an assisted jump. This move either made them look like they'd been dancing together for years when it worked, or crash and burned so badly when it flopped that it seemed like a mass-improvisation gone wrong.

Meg's tummy knotted in suspense in the build-up. Step-together-step-hop and they jumped as one. The guys caught them, spun around, placed them carefully back on their feet and prepared to spin them out for a partner swap that would last two counts of eight.

Meg felt steady on her feet. She took the gap and spun out with a quick swish of her skirt. It swirled around her ankles and for a moment, they nailed it. The girls moved as one, arms perfectly matched, moving to the music as if it were a living, breathing thing.

It happened in slow-mo. One moment the girls were twirling past each other, the next Gina was falling. She went down gracefully, her hand trailing through the air like a ribbon floating on the breeze. The expression on her face would have been perfect for floating on clouds. No shock, no surprise, just peace. She hit the floor and bounced, Reg tripped over her and landed hard on his knee with a crack that made Meg cringe. His face was not peaceful.

This was not an ordinary fall. Gina had fainted.

· · · ● · ● ● · · · ·

"Was she fine in the dressing room?" A dull ache settled into Dom's head as if he had an elephant napping between his ears. The light in the hospital waiting area was slowly giving up on life and flickered on and off like a low budget disco. "It doesn't seem logical that she could go from fine to passed out within minutes. Did she complain of anything? Pain, dizziness?"

Meg hesitated. "Getting her dress on was a struggle. I think it might be too tight. It could just be that." She went back to studying her nails.

"That doesn't make sense. Her dress fit perfectly. She's been ironing-board-skinny since I've known her."

Meg cleared her throat and stared out the window.

"Is there something you're not telling me, Meg?"

Meg stared right at him now, her eyes icy. "Maybe the two of you need to have an honest conversation."

Before Dom could respond, a doctor walked in.

"Hi, folks, your friend is resting now. She probably shouldn't be wearing such tight clothing in her condition and she'd do well to avoid high stress situations. Other than that, she's fine. You can go see her now. I'm going to check in on her partner's knee. I suspect he's broken his knee cap."

Dom ran through what the doctor had said. Her *condition*? "Er, excuse me, doctor? What—"

Meg grabbed him by the arm and pulled. "Come on, chop-chop. Let's go see how she's doing."

"But I want to—"

"There'll be time later. The doc needs to see to Reg. Come now, Gina is probably worried sick. She needs us."

The girl was pulling him down the hallway, not letting him get a word in with the doctor. "What is up with you? I just want to ask a few things."

"Gina is more important. Come on."

She pulled so hard, Dom nearly fell flat on his face. "I'm coming, relax."

Gina sat propped up on the stiff, white, hospital pillows, dressed in a stiff, white, hospital gown looking pale and fragile.

Dom had seen her cry in anger before, but never this lost tearfulness. It made him feel weird.

"Hey, girl. How are you feeling?"

"Where's Reg? How is he?" Gina's eyes were wide. "He hasn't been in to see me." If worry and anger had a baby, it would look exactly as her face did in that moment.

"He may have broken a knee. We're going to check on him after you."

Gina blinked twice and rubbed her temples. Her usual stubbornness came right back. "I've been better, thanks." She sighed. "And I'm sorry." She spat out the words as if they stung her tongue. "I ruined our chances at getting through."

Dom sat on the bed next to her. "Stop, don't even say that. You can't control your *condition*." He really needed to find the doctor and ask.

Meg poked his arm. "Gina is thirsty. You should go get her something."

"But I don't want to ..."

"That's so kind of you, thank you."

"But—"

Dom left with a backward glance and watched as Meg moved right into Gina's space. Their heads dropped and they whispered furiously, too soft for Dom to hear. He stood at the doorway with a queasy feeling settling into his belly. There was more going on here than what these girls were telling him. He'd just have to do some sleuthing of his own.

· · · · ● ● ● ● · · ·

Gina sat brewing, an odd mix of fragile and feisty. "I know. I'll tell him. Just don't push me."

Meg leaned on the bedpost, arms crossed. "You can't hide this. I mean, literally—you cannot hide this. Your clothes aren't fitting anymore."

Gina grimaced. "Have you ever had a nightmare of being trapped in a tiny space, one so real that you freak out so much in your dream that you wake yourself up? This feels like that. Only I'm awake and I'm still trapped and nothing can fix this."

"It's a baby, not a death sentence."

"Don't call it that. I'm not ready to think ... like that."

"Like what?" Dom strolled in with three tins of soda which he handed out. "What did I miss?"

Meg raised an eyebrow at Gina. "You two have some things to talk about. I'll let you get on with it."

She left the hospital room and resisted the urge to hang around the door and listen. *Come on, Meg. None of your business, girl.*

None at all.

Meg thought of calling a cab but chose to walk home instead. Maybe the fresh air would clear her thoughts, but her heart stayed heavy enough to kick along the sidewalk as she walked. Only then did she realize—this was the end. Not qualifying meant no more rounds of competition. It was over.

So many things she'd miss. Actually having calf muscles, the sore abs. The blisters that blossomed all over her feet after every practice. Okay, maybe not the blisters, but the rest of it had crept up on her in a way that surprised her.

And the people. Even Gina. They'd become her family as they'd sweated together. No more of that, just back to her lab and her flat and her broken goldfish and her list.

Now what?

There was an old man struggling to lift his groceries into the car in the parking lot she had to cross to get to her apartment. Meg ran over, boosted the bag from the bottom and guided it into the trunk of the car.

His world ran at a slower pace than hers, and he was still turning around to thank her when she flitted off into the dark with a wave. She had no desire to be applauded or thanked.

Was that worthy of a list cross?

One little bag of groceries. Hardly.

This was going to take a miracle.

Chapter Twenty-Three

IT WAS MONDAY—USUALLY THEIR formation team music would be pumping through the studio. Dom lay flat on his back in the middle of the studio floor with his arms and legs spread out like a starfish. He felt like one too, though more like one stranded on a beach above the waterline with no hope of getting back to water, with the sun baking the sand to cook him. They hadn't qualified for finals. It was over. Phoenix was doomed.

The lights were off, but bright moonlight poured in through the high windows, making patterns on the parquet. The sound system hummed quietly in the background though he hadn't decided on music yet.

"What now, Jesus?"

His thoughts rushed through his mind at a speed and he caught them one by one and quieted them.

"I need to hear from You. What is the plan? I know what you want me to do, but I don't know how."

Logically, he could go work for his dad. The salary might be enough for Project Phoenix. But going that route meant stepping into the complicated morass of minefield relationships. A lifetime of reading unspoken clues and hints, trying to gauge expressions and pick up on what everybody was *not* saying had used up all his capacity. He'd rather pluck his toenails out with pliers than willingly step back into that.

"Here's the thing, I know you say I need to lay down my life. I get it. But what about abundant life? You've promised that, too. Phoenix is not for my benefit, You know that. I don't understand why this didn't work."

Gina. Why did the girl have to relapse into her eating disorder now? The timing couldn't have been worse. He'd even mailed the organizers to see if they could make an allowance for them to go through to the next round. But even if they did, there were no guarantees that Gina would be up to it and Reg's broken knee wouldn't be healed in time.

His brain kept turning the situation over, poking at it, looking for a plan B. But all he kept seeing in his head was Meg. The girl was intriguing, delightful. But she was also fast on her way back to being Chad's fiancée and he had more important issues to solve. He mentally shoved her aside, but she bobbed right back. Seriously?

He tried again, focusing his thoughts on how to solve the Phoenix dilemma. Whichever mental path his brain wandered down, it always seemed to loop back to Meg.

"Oh, all right. Meg. What about her?"

The strangest sensation stole over him. It started as a tingling in his belly and shot through him like a belly laugh. Only he wasn't laughing.

"So this girl is crucial to your secret plan, and you're not letting me in on the secret. God, I hope You are factoring Chad into Your plans."

Maybe he should casually pop in anyway. He'd have to figure out a good excuse and an even better one if Chad were there. Well, his mom was forever commenting on his wild imagination. He had the length of the drive from there to her to figure something out.

His phone buzzed and he swiped the lock screen away. It was a voice message from Buntu. He pressed play and felt the hair stand up all down his arms.

"Fire. Please come."

· · · • · • • · · ·

Meg brushed her teeth using circular movements, careful to spend extra time on those at the back. She gave the front ones another once over and spat. The doorbell buzzed and Meg ran through people that she'd like to see at 11:23 p.m. on a week night and decided there was no one. She hummed loud enough to drown out a second round of buzzing. When the buzzer went for a third time, her calm ignoring flipped and she marched to the peephole, ready to yell at whoever was on the other side.

Dom.

Of course.

Who else would rock up this time of night uninvited?

She opened the door to find Dom and a group of kids on the doorstep. The smell of smoke hung thick around them and their clothing. A tiny African lady fussed over them like a mother hen. It was the lady from the grocery store, the one she'd gone undercover to spy on—Ernest's mom. A hot blush flashed through her face. Ernest poked his head out from behind her leg with tears pooling in his wide eyes. His cheek was slashed and bleeding.

"Dom. What's going on?"

Dom leaned in close, soot caked his skin. "This is Buntu and the kids she looks after. Her home ... there was a fire. I need some time to make arrangements. They need a place to spend the night. And maybe something to eat and drink."

Meg froze. She stared at them all wondering if she was awake. This was exactly the kind of bizarre situation her brain would cook up for her to squirm through while she slept.

Ernest rubbed his eyes, either from tiredness or because blood from his cut was getting into them.

The bright red blood shook Meg. This was no dream and Ernest needed his face washed. She stepped back and waved a hand. "Come in."

Dom hugged her as he squeezed past, he still wore his Meg-friendly deodorant. Buntu stopped in front of Meg, her eyes wide and wild. "I need to clean their wounds."

"First left down the hall."

Buntu herded her brood in the direction of the bathroom and Meg heard water running.

Dom looked gray in the face. He ran his fingers through his ash-covered hair.

"What happened?" Meg had never seen him like this, shattered but resolute.

"Buntu doesn't know. She woke up to flames, only just managed to get them all out. Let me go check on them."

Meg watched him leave, more puzzled than ever. He genuinely cared for Buntu, she could tell that by the way his whole face softened when he spoke to her. And yet Gina was carrying his baby. The biggest rub was that she'd been fooled by his charm. She actually liked the guy. That was not clever.

What about Buntu? She'd helped her out in the grocery store for her own selfish purpose of list-crossing. Having them all invade her private space, that was something else entirely. Something she wasn't sure she was ready to do. Surely not even her sorry list called for this.

Except that they were here, bathing in her bath, with nowhere else to go.

"Meg, do you have spare towels?" Dom's arms were wet up to his elbows. Clearly, he was doing more than just checking on them.

And now they needed towels. A small part of her backed into a corner inside and shivered. But the Meg on the outside shuffled down the hallway to the linen cupboard and dug in the back for her supply. She passed them on to Dom, added a spare bar of soap, and followed him to the bathroom to peep over his shoulder. Buntu had all the kids in the bath, and was washing them in a conveyor belt system then handing them over to Dom to wash their hair.

Meg retreated to the kitchen and sat on the chair closest to Ebb. Ebb had no advice for her on what to do with a house full of strangers. She nibbled on her thumb nail and considered her options. Surely there must be a shelter that could take them in? For a moment she imagined what they'd been through. She tried to pretend she'd lost her own home and everything else she owned, but her brain squirmed and refused to go there.

Dom popped around the corner, his shirt water-glued to his stomach, wet and soapy.

"I don't suppose you have some small, old clothes that you wouldn't mind parting with?"

Meg pushed off the chair and shuffled to the cupboard in the hall. She had some old painting shirts and shorts that might do for the night. Adding some blankets to the pile, she shoved it all into Dom's hands and retreated back into the kitchen and tried to make herself feel useful by putting the kettle on.

It took half an hour (the kettle had re-boiled three times and Meg had done nothing with it) for Dom to settle Buntu and her clean boys in the living room. He walked into the kitchen, half-soggy, still covered in ash himself, and switched the kettle on. His mind seemed to be elsewhere as he went about taking cups out of the cupboard and making up a batch of hot chocolate for the boys and three cups of coffee.

Meg watched him with quiet panic building inside like a pregnant storm cloud.

"Um, why me?"

Dom flinched as if he'd forgotten she was there. With a quick glance at her, he shrugged and tapped her broken list. Without a word he loaded the steaming cups onto a tray and took them through to the living room.

Meg stared at her list, sitting smugly on the fridge like some untouchable princess. Dom didn't get it. Right now she wasn't feeling particularly kind or brave or selfless. More like self-centered, panicky, and a bit sick.

He came back and settled opposite her with his hands clasped around his mug. The ash had settled into his hair and the creases across his forehead, giving him a fake old person look. He glanced at her list, caught her eye with a look on his face she couldn't read. "I thought this would tick some of those off for you." He sipped coffee and asked, "Why are you looking at me like that?"

Words crashed from Meg's brain to her mouth. *That's not how it works. You can't create situations to cross off my list. A list doesn't mean the neighborhood can move in.* What came out was a strangled whimper.

Dom sighed and reached for her hand across the counter top, he stopped short of touching her, rubbed the dirt still lingering in the creases of his fingers even after the bath water and grimaced. "I have to go. I'll be back."

Meg locked the door behind him and tip-toed to the living room door. Muffled through the door came the faintest strains of a gentle Xhosa song. She couldn't understand the words, but it made her heart small and sore. She hurried past, shut herself in the bedroom, and hid in her bed with the cover pulled up all the way over her ears. Furry teeth reminded her that she hadn't brushed, but not even that could get her out of the safety of her bedroom. Nope.

Chapter Twenty-Four

A FAMILY OF WEAVERS twittered in the tree outside Meg's window, squabbling with each other loud enough to wake her. The grumpy birds returned to her tree every year, and every year she watched the same drama unfold.

The boys carefully constructed their intricately woven hanging nests and the girls judged their handiwork. Sometimes they were good enough and the happy couple moved in and started their family. But if the boy's work was judged inferior, the girl would reject the nest and throw it to the ground.

Meg couldn't help but admire the tenacity of weaver-boys. They didn't mope or throw tantrums, they just started again. As much as their bickering annoyed her, she envied the girls. To be pursued with such determination must be nice.

Dappled sunlight played through her curtains, dancing on the ceiling. Meg watched the play of light through eyes still blurry from sleep.

There were people in her apartment.

Shock flicked through her as she remembered, quick and cold. She could stay in the safety of her bed all day. That was an option. Except for the fact that she was hungry and thirsty and needed the loo. Her mouth tasted like old cheese. Drat.

Meg slid out from under her duvet still wearing yesterday's clothes. She slipped her feet into slippers—stealth slippers—and eased the bedroom door open.

All seemed quiet. Maybe it had been a dream? But the scent of burned things that lingered in the hall told her otherwise. She tip-toed down the hallway, cringing each time her knees clicked. What was she so afraid of?

No noise came from the living room, maybe she could sneak a quick cup of tea before retreating to the safety of her bedroom. The kettle had never been this loud before and her mug clinked three others despite her best attempt at silence.

"*Molo.*"

Meg nearly dropped her mug in fright. She spun around to see Buntu on a chair in the corner, tightly composed with her feet and legs pressed together, hands clasped on her lap.

"Hi! Did you manage to sleep?"

Buntu's slight smile and shake of her head tugged at Meg's heart. "I've been praying."

"I'll make you some tea. Regular or *rooibos*?" Meg held the two boxes out and Buntu pointed at regular. Meg got out another cup while her mind flew through a hundred different things she could say. All of them seemed inappropriate for someone who didn't have much to start with and had just lost it all.

"Are they all still sleeping?"

Buntu nodded. "Our house was cold and damp always. They are warm and dry here."

Meg slid the cup of tea across the counter top and eased onto a stool, sipping her own. Buntu had both hands clasped around her mug and she breathed in the steam. There was something about her that fascinated Meg, something she couldn't quite put her finger on. Buntu's skin gleamed in the faint light, its smoothness interrupted by a myriad of faint scars—telltale signs of a life that hadn't been kind.

"What are you going to do?" Meg's cheeks grew hot. What an insensitive thing to ask, though it was probably better than most of the other things she could have said that involved weather or the petrol price.

Buntu shrugged bony shoulders with a hint of a frown on her brow. Her forehead smoothed and she shrugged again—though this seemed to be a movement of surrender. "I pray. God knows."

What kinds of prayers would Meg have prayed under those circumstances? Would kicking over furniture count as a prayer?

"Are you angry?"

Buntu fiddled with the edge of Meg's t-shirt that she wore. "I don't think so. Hard things are a ticket to front row seats of miracles. I don't know what to do." She paused to swallow. "But I know Him."

They sipped tea at the same time and as they put their cups down, Meg saw Buntu's chest rising and falling at the same time as hers. Breathing together. The same. In a breath, it fell off her—the need to be polite and say the right thing. The fear of getting it wrong. Buntu was a woman with nothing, but here she sat, clothed in Meg's shirt, but covered by a serenity and dignity more priceless than anything Meg could offer.

"Was it an accident? The fire?"

"Maybe." Buntu held her cup in a hand that shook, staring out the window. "I don't think so." She put the cup down and looked Meg in the eye for the first time. "I know who did it."

"We should go to the police! I'll take you now."

"No. It won't help."

"But whoever it was could have ... it could have been so much worse. We can't do nothing."

"They would go after my family. I have no proof. I'd rather stay quiet."

Meg was raging. The unfairness of it all, the injustice, burned in her chest like a firebrand.

"You're not going to do anything. So you are telling me that you have no desire to kick things right now? Scream perhaps? Throw something?"

Buntu stared at her as if she'd taken leave of her senses. "Is that what white ladies do?"

· · · · ● · ● · · · ·

Dom left his apartment, stowed two suitcases into the trunk of his car, and wished for a strong cup of coffee. Running on no sleep was nothing unusual for him, but last night had been brutal.

He dropped the suitcases off at the studio and drove to Meg's with the sun warming his arm through the window. It was later than he'd hoped and he wasn't sure what to expect. The plan was to get Buntu and her brood out of there as quickly as possible. Meg hadn't looked like she was coping too well last night. A call came through as he reached the bottom of the stairs.

"Dom? Melody here from the competition office. Just to let you know, we are reviewing your request to move on to the next round as you were unable to complete the competition round. The board will be discussing it tonight and we'll let you know as soon as they make a decision."

Dom fumbled his way through the platitudes of thank yous while taking the stairs two at a time and wondering if Gina and Reg would even be able to take part if they got through. He should probably call back and tell them not to bother, but the hopeful streak in him just didn't want to budge.

Before he knocked on Meg's door, he stopped to listen. Someone was giggling inside. Not just one of them, two at least. It didn't sound like the kids at all. He stretched up to see if he could peep in the kitchen window. His toe snagged on a boxed planter filled with ferns and pain shot up his leg, but he clenched his jaw and peeped. The curtains were closed and he saw nothing.

He rang the doorbell and the giggling cut off. Meg opened the door wearing the same clothes she'd worn yesterday, slippers, and holding a steaming cup of tea in her other hand. Her hair poked in all directions and she seemed to be wiping away tears.

"Is everything all right here?"

Buntu giggled in the kitchen and Meg hid behind her cup. Not crying, laughing. She stood back and waved him through.

"What's so funny?"

Buntu appeared around the corner and shook her head. "You wouldn't get it." She caught eyes with Meg who grinned at her.

Ernest came through from the living room, rubbing the sleep from his semi-closed eyes. He shuffled straight to Dom and wrapped his arms around Dom's legs.

"Hey, buddy." He reached down and hoisted the skinny boy up into his arms. Ernest tucked his head onto Dom's shoulder and yawned the biggest yawn. With Dom's arms around him, he seemed to be drifting straight back to sleep.

Dom checked his watch. "Buntu, get the boys. I've got a place where you can stay for now."

Meg pushed off the partition. "They don't have to leave right now."

"You're due at work in half an hour. You know that, right?"

Meg's face paled. "I guess you should all leave now."

· · ·˙· ●·●· ● · ·

Meg pushed away from her desk and stood to stretch. Her body felt stiff. It had only been three days of not dancing, but she could feel the lack of moving. Every muscle felt old and stabby.

All morning long, she'd been processing test samples with a tiny section of her mind, but the rest had all been taken up with the fascinating conundrum of what was going on.

Dom was clearly trouble with a capital T, but that didn't stop her wanting to unravel the mystery unfolding around the man. Correction, mysteries. Many of them. Gina's baby, Buntu and her boys, the folder in the drawer with Meg's face on it. His obsession with winning the competition. She rubbed her arms and stared longingly at the sun outside the lab window. Anyone with a shred of common sense would run and not stop. "Don't forget the moonlit house. That's another story, right there."

Vashti spun around from her desk to frown at Meg. "Girl, I worry about you. What moonlit house? What are you on about now?"

Meg waved her off. "Just thinking out loud."

"Well, it all sounded very dodgy to me. You should be careful."

"Oh, you know me. Careful is my middle name."

Chapter Twenty-Five

MEG SAT IN HER car outside the dark studio, watching the glowing hands on her watch tick closer to midnight. She felt a little queasy from the butterflies in her belly, just as she did every time she did anything out of the ordinary or broke her routine. It was enough to make her physically ill. She sipped water from her bottle and told herself to grow up.

Nothing had moved upstairs since she'd arrived at 11:30 p.m., but she decided to wait until 12:00 p.m. to make sure she wasn't caught. The keys felt cold and heavy in her palm. For the fiftieth time tonight, she wondered about going home. Talia had left them at her place when she'd come to do makeup. Up until this moment, she'd taken it as a sign. But sitting here in the dark, it was very clearly just Talia's forgetfulness and no sign from above.

Curiosity stone-walled her though. She'd come this far, she couldn't back out now. *Well, God, maybe You can help me out here.*

Twenty seconds ticked by and she slid out of the car, locked it, and bounced the studio keys in her palm. Checking left and right, she crossed the deserted street, slipped the key into the lock, and turned it. The door swooshed open with a well-oiled hush and she shut it behind her, letting her eyes get used to the dimness.

She tiptoed upstairs, holding her breath at every creak. Her mission was simple: retrieve the folder with her name on it, and get out.

A grunt cut through the silence and real fear slid through her like cold. She froze and waited.

Two minutes.

Silence.

This was pure insanity.

Come on, Meg. You've just got to keep going. Fear made her feet heavy. She dared not shine any light yet because it would have been visible from the street outside. She stepped off the top step into thick carpet and almost felt relieved.

Using both hands, she inched along the wall until she came to the door that led to Dom's office. Hardly breathing, she slipped into Dom's office and shoved the door almost closed. A sliver of moonlight fell across his desk and Meg's resolve slipped.

She forced herself across the room, slid the drawer open and stopped. The contents of the drawer were in shadow, it was time for some light. She dug out her phone and got the flashlight working. Her palms were clammy and she realized that maybe she didn't want to look inside.

Well. Whether she looked or not, right now was her time to confront this thing head on. She'd come so far, to give up now would be dumb.

She felt around in the drawer until her fingers closed on the worn edge of a pile of cardboard files. She propped her phone up precariously on Dom's dirty coffee mug—he should really take that to the kitchen—and eased the pile out of the drawer. Her file was third from the top and she pulled it out and dropped it on the desk as a wave of heat flashed through her. She'd been wondering if she'd seen wrong and imagined her photo stapled to a file. But now here it was and it was in her hands.

She shoved the others back and slid the draw closed with a bit too much force. It banged and she cringed. Something grunted outside the door. Meg panicked. She grabbed her phone and shoved it up against her chest, hiding the light. She sank down behind the desk hardly daring to breathe.

Someone was in the studio. There was no mistaking it. She had to get out.

Meg shoved the file under her t-shirt next to her skin, and tucked the t-shirt into her jeans. The silence buzzed loudly in Meg's ears as she strained to hear any sign of movement. Hearing nothing, she dropped to her hands and knees and inched forward. As she squeezed out the door, the hinge squeaked and her heart nearly stopped.

"Who's there?"

It was Dom. Relief flooded through Meg, followed quickly by dismay. He couldn't catch her here. What would she say?

She scuttled forward on her knees, got around the corner and stopped. She could hear him shuffling towards her, bumping things in the dark.

"I can hear you. Who are you—" A loud *thunk* and his words cut off in a yelp of pain.

Meg took the gap. She shot to her feet and bolted. She flew down the stairs at top speed, and slammed into the door at the bottom with both hands. It swung open and she was out. She didn't dare look back. Her feet pounded the tar to her car parked across the street. She threw herself into the driver's seat and only checked her mirror as she pulled off. No sign of Dom.

By the time she pulled into her parking bay in the garage below her apartment, her hands shook so badly she dropped the keys twice before locking the car. Only once she was safely in her apartment did she take the folder out from under her shirt. It was buckled from the trip but whatever was inside would still be legible. She popped it down on the counter next to Ebb. Honestly, she was nervous to read what was inside. So nervous in fact, that she felt like throwing up.

· · · · •· • · · · ·

Dom reached the light switch as the door banged shut at the bottom of the stars. The lack of sleep over the past few nights had caught up with him and stuffed his head full of bubbles. Thinking made them pop. His toe throbbed.

Should he run after the thief, or should he check what had been stolen?

A car engine cranked down on the street and he ran down the stairs two at a time. He slammed through the door in time to catch a few digits of the car's registration plate before it pulled out of sight. FXS.

He repeated the three letters on a loop as he hobbled up the stairs. Pain shot up his leg every second step. Stupid stubbed toe.

Dom did a quick check through the two studios to see what had been taken, as quick as his injured toe would let him. As far as he could tell, nothing had been disturbed. He pushed back the door to his office and hit the light switch. The laptop sat on the desk, undisturbed. Studio petty cash still sat in the cupboard where it always was.

Why would someone break in and not take anything? Clearly they hadn't expected someone to be sleeping here. Maybe his presence had scared them off.

The thieves he read about in the news wouldn't have bolted without a fight, though. They would have knocked him out (or worse) and then helped themselves to what they wanted.

He pulled the drawer open and took out the project Phoenix folders. Meg's was gone. It all made sense now.

The girl was onto him, but not brave enough to ask him to his face.

· · • • • • • • • · ·

Meg sipped her tea at 3:00 a.m., even though the liquid was technically too hot and she ran the risk of blistering her top lip. Open the folder, read the contents. Easy.

If she read anything that told her Dom was a crook, she'd have to report him. There was nothing else for it. He should know better than to do illegal things.

She sniffed once and pulled the file closer and quickly opened it before she could change her mind.

There was a photograph of her. The lighting made her hair look dark brown instead of red and there were rings under her eyes. She clicked her tongue and moved the offending photo aside. The next page seemed to be all her vital statistics. Measurements, height, shoe size. Standard for ordering costumes, though knowing Dom knew all this about her made Meg squirm a little inside.

The next page listed all the practices she'd been to and what she'd struggled with. Nothing illegal here unless making someone feel like a lost cause was against the law. The only other things in the file were two newspaper clippings, carefully folded in half twice.

Meg opened up the first and frowned. "Kingston Breaks Ground on New High-rise on the Esplanade. Looking for Next Prime Location." She scanned through the article, it had nothing to do with her at all. Just a report on a new apartment block going up on the beachfront, probably by Dom's dad's company. The other was an auction notice on an old property. The date was set before her birthday. She held the empty folder and shook it to see if anything else fell out. Nothing did and Meg couldn't help feeling cheated.

All that trouble to break in, the bruises on her knees, wasted adrenalin, and nearly getting caught for this?

"No, Ebb, I don't believe this is it. There has to be more going on that isn't in this folder."

But then she remembered the phone call where she'd overheard Dom talking about tearing down to build the new. The article confirmed her suspicions. The house he'd taken her to, the one she'd fallen in love with—he was going to tear it down to build an ugly apartment building.

• • • • • • • • • •

Dom slid the drawer open, took out the pile of folders, and set them aside. Using his pocket knife, he inserted the tip into a groove in the base of the drawer. The false bottom slid back and he sighed, relieved. The actual contents of Meg's folder sat safely nestled inside the hidden compartment where he'd stashed it only a few days back either by a hunch or a Holy Spirit prompting. He whispered a silent thank you heavenward. Meg was probably not ready to see this. Not at all.

Chapter Twenty-Six

SANDY HAD ARRIVED AT Meg's and demanded she come with her to the beach. Meg, sick of her own thoughts going round and round like a dog trying to catch its tail, had agreed. The wind on the beach came in gusts that sand-blasted their legs, but Xan and his buddy didn't care. They headed straight for the waves with shrieks that made Meg want to stuff her fingers in her ears.

Sandy settled onto her round beach towel, painted like a giant slice of watermelon. Meg's towel was a standard rectangle that used to be a bright emerald, but had dulled over time to an insipid shade of mint. Meg stretched out, enjoying the warmth of the sun on one side and the chill from the sand below. An African lady and her son walked past and for a moment, Meg thought it was Buntu and Ernest. But this lady was relaxed and well-cared for and the little boy's shorts had no holes. They still had that stiff, haven't-been-washed-yet look to them.

Sandy poked at Meg's washed out towel with a perfectly manicured fingernail. "Maybe I'll get you a new towel for your birthday. By the way, how is your list thing coming along?"

"Moving along, I suppose."

"You want some help?"

"That's not how these things work. I've got to figure this out and do it all by myself."

Sandy lifted her shades and squinted to check on the boys. She settled back down on her elbows. "I can be your accountability buddy."

Accountability buddy. Meg would rather be chained to a lamppost in the middle of the North Pole in her bikini than have Sandy checking in on her all the time. Meg had to get her off this trail and fast. "I've been thinking about my birthday party." There, that should do it. Not strictly true, but it *was* always lurking at the back of her mind.

Sandy sat up straight as if a crab had pinched her bottom. "Do tell. I want to know everything." She shoved her glasses up onto the top of her head and stared at Meg with eyes that sparkled.

"Well, I've been thinking ... I know you said you wouldn't help me at such late notice, but I was wondering ..." Meg frowned at her feet buried in the cool sand as a thought blipped across her mind. A quick, insignificant flitter. A thought that came from elsewhere, not from her own synapses. It carried the same tummy-fluttering intimacy of that moment in her living room. What if …

She thought about Buntu who'd never had very much but had nothing now after the fire. Meg thought about her and the kids with no home. Maybe there was something she could do to help.

"What if the party was the thing that crossed off everything on my list?"

Sandy's face crumpled. "Huh?"

"What if I make it a fundraiser for a good cause?"

"But it's your birthday. *Your* special day."

"Exactly. That means I can do whatever I want."

Sandy was not convinced. "I suppose so, but—"

Meg's mind ran at full speed. Sandy could handle the logistics of venue, food, and advertising. She could auction off her photos. Even if they only brought in a few hundred rand, it would buy Buntu some groceries.

Now that was a thought.

She stopped Sandy's *but* with a hand on her shoulder. "And you can help me. It will be your birthday gift to me. You're always moaning that I'm impossible to buy for, so this is the perfect solution."

Sandy had nothing to say to that, nothing at all.

· · · · ● · ● · · · ·

Dom sat at the dinner table biting his tongue. Mom had out-done herself with a roast lamb shank and all the trimmings, but Dom had lost his appetite. As he'd suspected, this dinner in-vitation was like everything else involving Dad—it came with strings and an agenda.

"Son, I'm not saying you aren't free to pursue your little ... hobby, I just think you are wasting your talent. Do I need to remind you that you graduated as the most promising archi-tect of your class? All that is being squandered while you fritter away your time at that dance studio." The tone of his father's voice cut deeper than the words.

Mom cleared her throat and handed the carving knife over. Dom's dad took it and proceeded to dissect the lamb with cal-culated movements that filled Dom with morbid fascination. He didn't skip a beat with his tongue.

"Is it money? You know that you just need to say the word and I'll deposit into your account."

Dom knew better than to fall into this trap. It was a Catch-22 no-win situation. They'd been here before, many times. Whatever he answered at this point would lead to an-other string of arguments that would vary according to his answer. The only answer that would shut his dad up would be to say yes. Yes, Dad, I will come at work at your heartless organization. Yes, I will be paid your money that comes with so many strings I might as well be Pinocchio.

He'd spend the rest of his years spouting, "I'm not a puppet, I'm a real boy."

Rather not, thank you very much.

Dom made it through the main course without arguing and decided to forego the mousse that was chilling in the fridge for the same reason. More than anything, he wanted to see Meg again. All he needed was a good excuse.

After all, she hadn't said anything to him about getting back together with Chad, so he technically didn't know anything. Technically.

He drained the last bit of cappuccino froth made so lovingly by his mom and mumbled some excuse about an early night. By the time he reached the car, he had a plan. If Meg's struggling goldfish was anything to go by, this girl's heart ran on pure compassion. That would give him the perfect reason to pop in. He shot off a quick message.

Hey, I want to pop in and check on Reg and his knee. Can I come fetch you?

• • • • •• • • • •

They took the elevator to the fifth floor of Reg's apartment block in an uneasy silence. Meg had been about to climb into her PJs when Dom's message came through. She'd quickly responded *yes*, before her brain could get to work on complicating the simple message. Bottom line—she wanted to be around Dom to figure out the mysteries. With no more dance competition to work towards, this was as good an excuse as any.

Now in the quiet elevator, she couldn't think of anything to say, let alone the right questions that would give her the answers she wanted.

Dom wiggled the bag in his hand. "Snacks. I'm sure he doesn't get out much."

"How long have you known each other?"

"We're old school buddies. Went to the same varsity, though I did architecture and he went into commerce."

Meg frowned. "So you're a qualified architect, right?"

Dom leaned back on the side of the elevator and studied his fingernails. "I am."

"Why are you running a dance studio?"

"Why does it bother you?"

Meg hunted for the right words. "If you have a gift like that, surely you should be using it?"

"Actually, if things pan out as I'm hoping, I will. Just need a few things to fall into place."

The house! He was talking about the house. More evidence. He was going to tear it down and put up a monster.

The elevator bumped to a stop on Reg's floor and she was saved from having to choke out any more polite conversation.

They rang the bell and Meg was surprised to hear normal footsteps on the other side, and not a hobble mixed with the clomping of crutches.

The door swung open and there stood Gina. She was wiping her hands on the florally apron she wore over a loose-fitting pink shift dress. Her hair was clipped up into a tiny fountain ponytail, there wasn't a scrap of make-up on her face and her feet were bare.

· · · · • · • · · ·

Dom blinked twice to make sure his eyes were working properly. "Gina?"

Deep within the flat Reg called out, "Who is it, babe?"

Gina flushed bright red. She cleared her throat. "Don't be an idiot. Of course it's me. What are you two doing here?"

Meg jabbed Dom in the ribs and he shut his mouth and held up the bag. "Snacks. For the wounded."

"Of course. Come in. He's in the living room." Gina stepped aside and waved them through.

Reg sat propped up in an armchair with his plaster-casted leg out on a footrest. The table next to him was a mess of empty bowls and cups, a sudoko puzzle book, and a bottle of pain tablets.

Dom slapped him on the back. "We've come to check on the wounded. How are you?"

Reg grimaced as he tried to push himself up on the chair. "I'm great. This is just what I was hoping for right now, what can I say?"

Dom guided Meg to the couch and sat down next to her. "What does the doc say?"

Gina hovered, fiddling with the apron. "I'll go put the kettle on."

Reg patted his injured leg. "The kneecap is cracked. Nothing is out of place, but it needs time to heal. I won't be dancing for some time."

"I got a call from the competition office, they've provisionally put us through. We could still compete."

"Except for the fact that I can't dance, that's great. Just great." Frustration seemed to come out of Reg as sarcasm.

"There's got to be a way of getting Phoenix back on track."

Meg sat forward and asked, "What is Phoenix?"

Dom quietly yelled at himself. The girl didn't know. He'd been thinking it might be time. Now after this slip of the tongue, it would have to be. He turned to her, she sat close enough he could feel the warmth from her. "How about I tell you over supper?"

Meg pulled up her nose but didn't say a flat-out *no*.

Gina came back into the room at that point, carrying a tray of steaming mugs. "I think that's a great idea. We should all go. Then we can figure out what to do now."

Chapter Twenty-Seven

IT WAS TIME. AFTER her spate of failed list crossing attempts, wasted break-in, and the awkward visit with Reg and Gina, she decided it would be safer to stay home and practice gluing on false eyelashes.

At this stage, the dance team thing was all over, but you never know when you'd need to wear falsies. She'd bought them on a whim after buying groceries (not the *natural* ones, she'd chosen *flirty*) and hidden them in her drawer. Thinking of them made her want to giggle.

She took a deep breath and opened the drawer. She had to fish around near the back before she found them. Holding the box in her hand, she avoided the urge to go clean the kitchen, do a load of laundry, sweep the apartment and water the potted plants. Twice.

There were no instructions on the back, so she opened the box and slid out the small plastic tray that they were attached to. No instructions there either.

That meant one of two things. Either it was so easy that no instructions were needed, or it was only for professionals who knew what they were doing. There was only one way to find out. She pressed the glue out of the tray and picked up one eyelash. So far so good. She opened the glue and squeezed out a fat worm of it onto the eyelash. It was runnier than expected. Holding it between two fingers, she held down her lid with the other hand and jabbed the eyelash towards her skin. Simple.

Except the lash was still attached to her finger.

She pulled it off and tried again, holding with the tips of her fingers and aiming more carefully. The eyelash stuck and her hand was free. Success.

Except she couldn't open her eye. The doorbell rang and she got up to answer it without thinking, panicking about her glued-shut eyelid.

Her neighbor stood on the mat holding out a small plate of fudge. Her face, through Meg's one working eye, was still all lemony-puckered, and she shoved the plate into Meg's hand the moment the door opened.

"In exchange for the teabags." Without another word she turned and hobbled off, only to turn back and squint at Meg. "What's going on?" She wiggled a knuckled finger towards Meg's face.

"Falsies. I'm trying to teach myself to put them on. It's not going too well, as you can see."

"Aah." The ancient lady turned away, sighed, and turned back, muttering. She herded Meg back inside the apartment and followed her in, shutting the door behind them. "Bring the glue."

Meg, too shocked to argue, retrieved the glue from the bedroom and put it in the old lady's hand. She examined the glue first at arm's length, then up close and nodded once.

"Kitchen. Sit, sit."

The lighting was better in the kitchen. Meg dutifully popped her bottom on a chair and surrendered to the bizarreness of the moment.

Mrs. O'Riley made short work of removing the offending lash, cleaning off the glue and restoring Meg's sight.

"I was beginning to worry that I'd never see out of that eye again. How do you know about all this kind of thing?"

Mrs. O'Riley tsk tsk'd while she cleaned off all traces of the old glue. "I wore them on stage all the time."

"You were a performer?" Meg looked at the crinkled lady in front of her and suddenly saw things she'd never noticed before. How straight she held her back, the way she moved her hands, hands that hadn't taken kindly to the passing of time.

Deep beneath the wrinkles carved into her skin, hints of beauty lingered. "Dancer or singer?"

"I sang. Pay attention, now." Her shaky hands steadied as she applied the thinnest line of glue to the lash. She waited, blowing gently on the lash twice. "Close."

Meg felt the cold glue and gentle pressure as Mrs. O'Riley pressed the lash to her skin, working from the inside of her eye outwards.

"Keep closed. I'm doing the other side."

Meg sat with her eyes shut, listening to the wheezy breathing of her neighbor who she'd been avoiding up until now. Could she be the one who sang sometimes in the midnight hour while the rest of the world slept? Probably not.

"Mrs. O'Riley, do you know anything about God?"

Mrs. O'Riley didn't answer and Meg wondered if she'd heard.

"All right, open slowly."

Meg braced herself for the panic of another glued eye, but they both opened without any trouble. Her eyelids felt heavy, but other than that, she couldn't really feel that she was wearing them.

"Go look."

Meg blinked her way to the bathroom and braced herself. Ha! Something about long, silky lashes darkened the shade of her eyes. "They look amazing!" Meg swished back to the kitchen blinking and preening. "I feel so exotic! But you put them on for me. That doesn't count."

Mrs. O'Riley dipped her chin. "Small line of glue, wait, then start from the inside. You practice, you get it right. Don't steal my plate."

Meg nearly laughed but bit her tongue to stop. She couldn't tell whether the old lady was serious or not. "I will bring it back. I love fudge, thank you."

On her way out the door Mrs. O'Riley paused. "God? I don't know much about Him. If you ever figure Him out, you can fill me in." She shuffled out of Meg's apartment and back to her place without a backward glance, a wave, or another word.

· · · · ·· · ·· ·

It was getting close to 2:00 a.m. Dom sat on the floor in the studio with a laptop balanced on his legs. *There has to be a way. Come on, Jesus. Show me.*

He searched for dancing competitions and the only site that came up was the one he already knew about, the one they couldn't take part in now that Reg was out. He changed the search keywords slightly and hit enter. Again, the same competition came up.

There had to be something else. He kept trying different search criteria and came up blank. There had to be a better way. *Any time now, Jesus.*

He opened up the competition website and was about to click on the Ballroom and Latin American category, as he always did, when something caught his eye. It was a category he'd never paid much attention to before.

He clicked to enter this new section with a fluttering in his belly. It was time to dust off their dancing shoes again; this might just work, Reg's broken leg and all.

Chapter Twenty-Eight

IT TOOK REG A long time to navigate his way up the stairs to the studio on crutches. Meg was stuck behind him for every agonizing second of it, hoping he wouldn't lose his balance and topple backwards and she'd have to catch him and be the only thing stopping them both making more broken bones.

He was sweating as he made it off the last stair, breathing heavily as if he'd just run a marathon. Gina was nowhere to be seen, and it seemed like Meg and Reg were the first two to make it in. The studio was deserted.

"I can't believe how much fitness I've lost since being in this thing." He tapped his cast with a crutch. "And everything takes so long. I'm starting to wonder whether all the one-legged pirates in the old days were wicked because they were so frustrated at how hard life was." He peered around and dropped his voice low. "Between you and me? Dom is dreaming if he thinks I'm going to be able to do anything close to what I could before. His desperation is clouding his judgment."

Meg saw the gap. She was proud of the fact that her voice came out even, without a quiver. "Why is he so desperate to win this anyway? Is it all for the glory?"

Reg flopped into an armchair in the waiting room and shut his eyes as he leaned his head back. "Project Phoenix is all he's been living and breathing for months now. How much has he told you?"

Meg sat on the sofa closest to the armchair so she wouldn't miss a thing. She chose her words carefully. "He's shown me the house."

Reg's head popped up. "You've seen the house. None of us have seen the house."

Before Meg could respond, the rest of the team arrived, chatting and bantering as they came up the stairs. Dom directed them all to the waiting room, not the studio.

Matt had his arm around Talia and they had their heads down over her phone. Gina barely said a word, but sat stiffly in a chair furthest away from Reg. Her make-up was immaculate, hair swept back off her face in a gelled bun. The girl was all business again to the point that Meg wondered if she'd dreamed up the barefoot home-maker she'd seen at Reg's apartment. She wore a loosely fitted spaghetti string top rather than the skin-tight gym clothes she usually wore.

Dom squeezed in next to Meg and she shuffled up to make room for him. He was so close that she was in danger of being elbowed in the face if he got too excited.

He grinned at her. "Hey, Megnificent. I've missed you."

"Are you slaughtering my name?"

"Upgrading. Trust me." He winked at her and turned his attention to the rest of the group.

"Guys, I'm glad you're here. This is where we're at. The urgency of Project Phoenix has been ramped up. Now more than ever, we have to make it work. We've qualified for the finals, but we no longer have a team with the numbers we need to take part in the section we signed up for."

Reg stuck up his hand. "You could get someone to take my part? There are guys who could pick up the routine and do without breaking a sweat. Unlike me who currently can't even get up the stairs without being drenched." He trailed off quietly, looking bleak.

Gina glared at him from across the room. "What a stupid idea."

Dom held up a hand to keep the peace. "Reg, to be honest, I've considered that. But"—he shook his head at Gina and she shut her mouth and crossed her arms—"I'm just not going to go there. But I found something last night, something that might be a way we get to compete."

Cliff, true to his accountant nature asked, "Prize money?"

"Enough for the Project."

That seemed to be all Cliff needed. "I'm in."

Tammy sat forward in the chair to get in Cliff's face. "Hold on, you don't even know what it is yet."

Reg patted the leg he had propped up on the coffee table. "If you are serious about including me and this disaster, you should probably tell us what we'll be doing."

Dom took a deep breath. "Musical theatre."

Meg blurted, "I can't sing." Her voice came out low and husky. She should have cleared her throat first but she'd been listening to it all, ready for most anything. But not this. Not singing.

Everybody was throwing their opinion into the air like confetti and nobody was listening to anybody else. It was hard to tell who was excited and who, like Meg, was horrified.

Dom steadied her with a hand on her arm. "You won't have to sing. Guys, wait. Hear me out." He paused like a school teacher who was used to being in charge and having everyone listen. One at a time, they all fell quiet until they sat blinking at Dom like owls.

"So for this particular competition, the musical theatre genre is way open. The only requirement is that your piece must tell a story. I reckon we can create a story around Reg and

254

his leg. Maybe he's a soldier returning home after fighting in a war."

Talia giggled. "So one of us has to be preggers. Who is volunteering?"

Meg watched Gina's face pale. She excused herself and hurried down the hallway to the bathroom.

Talia thumbed in Gina's direction. "What's up with blondie?"

Meg leapt in. "Do you have music for this thing? Maybe listening to it will inspire us."

"Well, I have some, but I'm going to need a whole lot more. I was wondering if you'd help me pick out a few more tracks and storyboard the idea? What do you say, Meg?"

He'd put her on the spot. There was no way out of this gracefully, not with the entire dance team staring at her. "Sure. Why not?"

Dom fist-pumped the air. "Great. Well, folks. It seems like Project Phoenix is back on. Let's get together on Wednesday for practice. Hopefully, by then we'll have some music and ideas."

Reg got up and awkwardly hobbled across the floor. "I'm going to check on Gina."

Tammy popped up. "I'll go with you, I'll get to her a bit quicker."

Talia tapped Meg's leg. "I got some ideas while Dom was talking. If you guys get stuck, give me a shout."

"You should come, too."

Talia giggled and shot Meg a sideways look. "No, I'm busy. Sorry."

"Text me your idea at least?"

"That, I can do!" Matt dragged Talia off the couch and the two of them left chatting and laughing.

Watching them poked at the hollow place inside of Meg. She hung around and waited for the others to leave. She nearly chickened out and left with them all a few times, but her curiosity got the better of her and she stayed.

When it was finally just her and Dom, she faced him with her arms folded to pump up her bravado.

"So we're going to do some brainstorming."

Meg pitched her voice low, you-can't-mess-with-me low. "I have one condition. You have to tell me what Project Phoenix is."

· · · · ● · ● · · ·

Dom opened the sliding door to let some fresh air in. His apartment was cold inside and opening the door took the edge off the chill. Buntu and the boys were out and he took the gap to have Meg over. Buntu kept the place spotless; it was as clean as if nobody were living there.

He was having a hard time staying calm. Meg was coming over to brainstorm. The girl had a way of making his heart happy. Even the fact that she seemed to be getting back together with Chad couldn't completely squish the feeling.

He frowned at the thought. Meg and Chad getting back together made his insides twist like that time he'd eaten funky lasagna and spent the next few days in agonizing cramps.

Apart from that though, whenever he thought of her—which was more often than he'd care to admit—the word *catalyst* kept coming up. Meg the catalyst.

"Jesus, is that word from you? What do You even mean?" He carried dirty cups and the bowl he'd eaten cereal out of through to the kitchen. "It would be great if You could just tell me what's going on. I know, I know ... she's important."

Dom walked out onto the balcony and leaned on the rails, breathing deeply of the fresh air. That was the other question—how much to tell Meg. Part of him wanted to tell her everything, but what if she didn't agree? Growing up with that family of his had skewed his trust of people. They believed the exact opposite of what he did. He loved God. They supposedly did, too, but not in any way that seemed real to him. He wanted to make a difference in the lives of those around him but they were all about looking out for themselves.

Where did Meg fall? Chad aside, he couldn't afford to lose his heart to someone whose heart didn't match his.

He walked back inside. "Jesus, will you show me this girl's heart?"

The doorbell rang and there she stood, wearing the same pink trainers as the first day they'd met. Her hair was pulled back into a high pony that bounced when she moved. He just wanted to run his fingers through it and see if it was as soft as it looked. She handed over a pack of cookies.

"I'm a bit early. Do you have company? I heard you talking."

"Oh, that! No, nobody is here. Come on in. I'm all ready for you."

Dom sat on one end of the couch and patted the seat next to him.

Meg sat on the opposite edge of the same couch, slipped off her shoes and drew her legs up under her. "What are you thinking?"

Dom connected his phone to the speaker system and scrolled through his music. He dimmed the lights, he preferred listening to music without the intrusion of brightness.

"Okay, listen to this." He pressed play and music flooded the lounge. A light, breezy piece, carried by the pianist.

Meg chewed her lip, tapping a finger in time.

"It gets a bit boring in the middle, but I liked the start of that one. Then there's this piece." A brooding swell of sound filled the room carried by low pounding drums. This piece never failed to shoot up pictures in his mind. He watched Meg's face as music filled the room. Her eyes slipped closed and a pulse beat in her throat. Only when the music finished did she open them.

"Anything else?"

"Were those two not enough for you?"

"I'm missing something." She rubbed her fingers together as if feeling fabric.

"Maybe this." Soulful, slow pan flute, joined by an orchestra. Full strings took the music to a crescendo.

Dom waited for images to fill his mind as they usually did when he got lost in the music. But no images came, only the strongest urging from heaven that he'd felt in a long time. Only once before had he felt it this strongly.

Dance with Meg.

God? But that's weird, she's going to think I'm a psycho.
Silence.

Seriously, Lord. I know we dance together at the studio, but this is different. You don't understand. She will bolt. Run a mile so fast I'll never catch her.

••••••••••

The silence in his spirit was deafening, he could almost hear a heavenly foot tap.

Dom sat very still and slipped a quick glance at Meg. The girl was lost in the music as it soared and dipped. Resting on the backrest of her chair with her eyes closed, Dom had never seen her with her guard down, so vulnerable. It made a deep part of his soul ache.

He mentally scrambled to make sense of what he'd heard. *Lord, was that You? I'm supposed to just go over there, grab her hand and dance with her?*

Silence.

It made Dom want to laugh. God had been a father long enough to know better than to argue with his kids. The silence spoke volumes.

He slipped off the sofa and out of his shoes, padded across the soft rug to Meg on bare feet. He didn't want to interrupt the music, so he whispered as he reached for her hand.

"Meg, come dance with me."

She kept her eyes shut and allowed him to take her hand and lead her to the middle of the open space.

· · · · ● · ● · · · ·

As the music filled the room, Meg shut her eyes and allowed herself to go with it. One moment she was in Dom's living room, aware of the couch beneath her, the soft carpet under her feet and the fine layer of dust on the coffee table. The next moment heaven was there. The feeling was so strong, she dare not open her eyes in case Jesus was actually standing in front of her. She thought she might just die of fright.

As the music swirled around her and through her, a sense of being known washed over her. Known completely, inside and out. All the bits she wasn't so proud of, all those things she'd rather hide, right there, unpacked and in the open. But there was no shame. This was being known and being loved *anyway*. Through and through, top to bottom and back again.

Someone spoke and she knew it was Dom, but his words flowed seamlessly with the overwhelming feelings washing through her and she didn't fight it. He took her in his arms and she kept her eyes closed and let him move her. She was dancing with Dom in his living room, yet she was in the arms of the God who loved her. He loved her surrender. He loved how she resisted brushing off crumbs, He loved how she loved her broken goldfish, He loved that she'd seen Ernest (not with her eyes, but with her soul and spirit). He loved that she wanted to figure Him out.

Really, God?

The music soared and Dom lifted her and spun around and she knew God's answer.

Oh yes, my girl.

God felt so close, she opened her eyes to see. Cold shot through her. Through a gap in the door to his bedroom, Meg spotted it. A red jacket lay across a corner of the bed. She'd seen it before—Buntu's.

Meg shivered as reality slammed back into place and all the warm fuzzies snapped back with a sting. She moved with Dom, but felt more wooden by the moment. Dom was full of secrets. A secret project. Buntu and Gina. He was supposedly marrying Gina and all the signs said they had a baby on the way. And yet Buntu's jacket was in his bedroom.

She pushed away from him and the music smacked into her ears with a shattering force.

"Meg, what's going on?"

"We should do some planning." Leaving seemed like a great idea. She coughed and forced herself to sit in the single chair.

Dom picked up his phone and paused the music. "Well, those are the main ones. I'd wondered whether we start somewhere darker and build towards that."

Meg mentally shoved all the enormous feelings buzzing through her body into a tiny suitcase in the center of her being and sat on it to lock it. She took a deep breath, and as she exhaled she let calm return. Well, it sort of clawed its way back by the fingernails, but it was as close as she was going to get.

Focus, Meg.

Her thoughts squirreled and she lost it. Too many conflicting things burned in her. There was no way she could stay here. "You know what? Talia actually had a brilliant idea." She dug around in her bag for her car keys. "Maybe you should chat with her."

Chapter Twenty-Nine

TALIA HAD THEM ALL sitting cross-legged on the dance floor in a big circle. Her eyes sparkled. "What if ..."

She seemed to see it all in her head but was struggling to put it into words.

Dom sat way forward, as if Talia were about to sprout the secret to eternal life. The man was desperate, no doubt about that.

Talia held up her slim, tanned, hands. Her nails were beauty therapist short, but beautifully manicured. "I'm thinking of isolation. Each dancer alone, separate from each other. Dom, I like that piece of music you played with the clock ticking. We move on each tick. Then we bring in Reg. We could even put him in a wheelchair but he must have a crutch with him."

She paused to catch her breath, she'd been speaking so fast she looked a bit dizzy. She gathered her thoughts and carried on. "As he gets to the first person, he circles them and they do a move that relies on the wheelchair. Some kind of horizontal cartwheel, leaning on the armrests. Is there someone who can do that?"

Dom thought for a moment. "Probably you, Talia."

"Okay, fine. Then it continues to the next person, and so on. It all builds into one unified movement with Reg in the wheelchair as the catalyst. Then we pick up on the routine we've been rehearsing, but adapt it for Reg."

She scrunched up her nose at Dom. "I can see it all in my head, it doesn't sound great coming out of my mouth. And it's probably not really narrative."

Dom was staring into the air in front of him rubbing his chin. "No, no. I like it. I think it has potential. It's better than my idea of a war hero coming home to his pregnant wife."

He shrugged and Meg didn't know whether to cry or laugh.

"Reg, you will have to learn to maneuver that wheelchair as if you're dancing. But I think we can find interesting ways to include the chair into our choreography. Where does that leave Gina, though?"

"And will Gina still fit into her costume by then. That's the big question." Meg bit her lips. Of all the times to let her thoughts spill out of her mouth ...

Gina sat glaring burning holes through Meg.

"Sorry, it's just that your costume has been causing some issues. I shouldn't have said that." She trailed off, wishing for a hole to open up under her and suck her in.

Tammy shrugged. "You're not wrong, Meg. What is going on, Gina? Has your sweet tooth come back?" Tammy had a frank way about her that meant she could say absolutely anything and people would seldom get offended.

"I have things under control." Gina spat out the words through thin lips. "I'd appreciate it if you could all stop meddling in my business."

Dom waved them all down. "Guys, let's focus, please. Gina, you are part of the team. That does give us some rights to your business, especially when it affects what we do as a team." He held up both hands to stop the fierce argument that was about to fly out of her mouth. "But we aren't here to discuss whether or not your costume fits. We can always make a plan."

"Talia, show us what you have in mind."

Talia paced, getting her thoughts together. She called Matt over and the two of them conferred in quiet voices.

Dom leaned close to Meg and whispered in her ear, "Is there something you aren't telling me? What do you know about Gina that I don't?"

Meg could have kicked herself. "Let me just say this, you need to have an honest conversation with her. The sooner, the better."

Chapter Thirty

THE SUN WASN'T UP yet when Meg settled on her balcony with her blanket wrapped around her. She pulled up a second chair and patted it as she would when inviting someone to sit down. Talking to God felt less strange if she imagined Him sitting here next to her. This was a weird thing to be doing—talking to a deity who may, or may not exist and may, or may not be interested in listening to her, anyway. But it was on the list and it had to be done.

Also, she couldn't deny that she'd encountered something real in Dom's apartment. A tingle shot through her at the memory.

Should she say *good morning?* But she'd read somewhere that God never sleeps, so good morning seemed a bit pointless.

Er, I'm just going to start talking, if that's okay? I was wondering what I could do for Buntu. You know I have this list? She mentally face-palmed. God knew everything. *Well, my list. I feel like I want to do something to help her.*

She fell silent while thoughts flittered through her mind. The house that Dom had his eye on, it was clear that he intended to demolish it and put up some high-rise monstrosity. The very thought of it made her feel off. How could he not see the charm of the place? It was a perfect home for a family. It would take some fixing up, actually a lot of fixing up, but it was gorgeous.

Imagine setting Buntu up in a place like that. She could take all the kids that she's looking after and keep them safe there. She'd be so much better off than where she is now. Don't You agree?

There was no voice in her ears or head to answer but a stirring inside that felt like butterflies in her tummy. The same sensation came over her that had when she'd danced at Dom's apartment.

She took a deep breath and stayed there, goose bumps raised down her arms.

He was here, He was listening.

The thought fell as soft as a feather. If Dom were going to bid on the house at the auction, maybe she could raise enough to outbid him.

The very idea twisted her belly in a knot, but it was possible and it was right. The feather-light thought came with a steely resolution in her gut and she knew.

It was ludicrous, completely deliciously out there. But she was going to do it.

Okay, God, let's do this.

Chapter Thirty-One

PRACTICE WAS NOT GOING well. Reg objected to feeling like an invalid, Gina kept sitting down. Talia kept trying to place them but the others couldn't quite see what she was getting at. Frustration built to the point of leaking out of her eyes.

Dom took Talia to the foyer and Meg followed. She'd grown to love this girl.

Dom's voice was gentle. "Hey, kid, believe it or not, first practices usually go like this."

Talia stared at the ceiling, blinking furiously to stop the tears. "I can see it so clearly in my head, but it just won't come out of my mouth. I can't get them to do what I want. I feel like I'm going to disappoint you." Her face crumpled and she let out a strangled yell.

Meg crossed her arms. "Tell us the floor pattern. Maybe between us we can pull it together." Dom wanted to kiss her serious face.

Talia cleared her throat. "I need paper and pen."

They gathered around the reception desk and Talia swiftly sketched out a five-step action plan.

"I think we can do this. It's a good plan." Meg nodded at Talia.

"You think so?" Talia looked worried, but hopeful.

"What do you think, Dom?" Meg asked.

Dom was having trouble focusing. "I like it. Let's go try."

Talia scooped her papers together and shuffled back to the studio chewing on her lip.

"You still haven't explained Project Phoenix to me."

Dom shot a glance at the team who all stood staring at them through the open doors. "Not here, not now. Come with me after practice and I'll tell you."

"You'd better."

"Let's go finish, Talia needs us."

Meg gritted her teeth and went back inside.

She sat on the floor with her legs crossed, and held out her hand for Talia's papers. "Guys, come sit."

Gina was huffing. "I'm not going to sit on the floor. Are you mad?"

"Pull up a chair, suit yourself."

Dom was fascinated by this side of Meg. He fetched a chair for Gina and sat himself down next to Meg. She'd spread out Talia's plan and sat looking at him.

Dom reminded himself to breathe, this girl took his breath away. She tapped the papers and he took the cue.

"So this is the picture Talia has in her head."

· · · • · • • · · · ·

Meg washed her plate and stacked it. She'd been antsy at work, going for a jog (she hated jogging) hadn't helped either. The only reason she jogged sometimes was because her pink trainers had cost so much, not using them for their purpose didn't seem right. So she sometimes took them for a spin around the block and that cleared her conscience for approximately 3.5 shopping trips in them.

She'd been trying to get to the bottom of her restlessness and usually washing dishes helped. As the last bubble disappeared down the drain, she knew.

Buntu.

Whatever her involvement with Dom, Meg couldn't ignore the fact that she'd connected with Buntu that morning right here in her kitchen. Their worlds couldn't be more different.

Honestly, she made Meg's world feel small and plastic. Buntu had so little, yet she spent her life for the kids she took in.

Meg wouldn't even blame her for being involved with Dom, especially if he helped provide for them. Having hungry kids to feed blurred the lines between right and wrong somehow.

Meg sprinkled fish flakes for Ebb. *So, God, this wild plan of Yours. Will it actually work?* It was one thing to get an idea like that while sitting on the balcony sipping tea. It was quite another to actually make it happen.

A voice lifted, clear and pure, singing "Moon River." Not God, but her neighbor.

Meg stopped breathing. Sound was deceiving sometimes, it was hard to tell where it came from, but she could have sworn this was her false-eyelash neighbor. The voice was sweet and rich, but the song had a sadness to it that made her heart ache.

Focus, Meg.

She ignored the song as best she could. The question remained. Could she actually do this thing and help Buntu? Part of her envied the woman. Her life counted. If she disappeared, she'd leave a hole. Meg wouldn't leave a hole. She was more like a bit of a hole already. A vacuum.

It would be nice to make a difference. After all, it was on the daft list. The list that she was regretting making, more and more with each passing day.

Buntu.

It was time. Meg slid her phone closer and opened up her chat with Sandy. Sandy's display picture had her in sunglasses and a bright yellow strapless top, sunshine gleaming on her tanned shoulders. She had a cold drink in one hand and was holding her hat with the other, mouth open wide, laughing.

Right, sunshine friend. You are going to help me spread some of that joy. She typed out a message and hit send. Her message was simple:

Party planning tonight, my house, 7pm. Yes?

· · · · ● · ● · · ·

Dom washed the shaving cream from the studio basin and stretched out the crick in his back. Sleeping on the studio couch was not doing his back any good. But he was grateful that the studio had a shower and a small kitchen. With Buntu and her boys living in his apartment for now, at least he had a roof over his head.

The fact that they'd been out while he had Meg over was a good thing. His folks would never have understood why he'd let a family from *that* side of town stay in his home. Would Meg have gotten it? He wasn't ready to find out.

He poured himself a cup of coffee from the brewing machine in the studio kitchen. The tiles were cold under his bare feet and it helped clear the fuzz from his mind.

He checked in with the seamstress, their costumes were being adapted. Particularly Reg's. He was tempted to send Gina for a fresh fitting after the trouble they'd been having, but he wasn't quite brave enough to make her go.

There were seven days between them and the competition and he'd already warned everyone that their evenings this week would be spent at the studio.

He loved the thought of having seven built-in excuses to see Meg. She couldn't even pull out or run away. If he knew one thing about the girl by now, it was that she was reliable and wouldn't let the team down, regardless of what issues she may have with him.

The property auction was happening two weeks after the competition. The timing was tight but do-able.

He should tell Meg.

Chapter Thirty-Two

SANDY CAME WITH A picnic basket full of snacks. She unpacked a bowl of chilled strawberries, a second one with chips and a *biltong*-flavored dip, and a bag of chocolates individually wrapped in shiny colors. She ripped open the bag with her teeth and sent chocolates flying.

"Whoops." She sat perched on the edge of the couch and made no move to pick up any of them.

"Finders, keepers." Meg threw herself down and started scooping.

"No!" That got Sandy off the couch and she grabbed a purple nutty one out of Meg's hand. She sat on the carpet and leaned back on the couch, unwrapped the sweet, and popped it in her mouth.

"Those are my favorites, you know."

"Sorry." Sandy mumbled around her full mouth. "So. What are you thinking?"

Meg unwrapped a red one, nibbled a corner. "Turkish delight, yuck."

Sandy took it from her and popped it in her mouth, too.

Meg gathered her thoughts, unsure of where to start. "We need the biggest venue we can reasonably get."

"The badminton hall?"

"Where they did the bonsai thing?" Meg shuddered.

"You can't argue, it's a nice hall. Meg, without being rude … No, actually this is rude, but I'll ask anyway. Do you even have enough friends to fill the badminton hall?"

The doorbell rang. It was Talia squeezing the top of her nose and blinking to stop herself crying. She was carrying a basket. Meg knew better than to ask what was wrong, though she did wonder if the basket had more snacks.

"Come, I have chocolates." Meg led her into the living room. "Sandy, this is Talia. We dance together."

"Oh, honey! You look like you want to cry. What's going on?" Sandy cranked herself off the floor with her knees popping and her back creaking. She swooped over to hug Talia. Her kindness opened the floodgates and Talia sobbed.

Meg shoved a tissue in one hand and a chocolate in the other.

Talia sobbed the tissue soggy and Meg swapped it out for a fresh one. Sandy cooed and rubbed her back and Meg couldn't help but be grateful that her friend was there for this crying girl. She would've felt lost by herself.

Three big nose blows later, Talia had stopped sobbing.

"You want to tell us what's wrong?" Sandy had a comforting hand on Talia's jean-clad leg.

Talia sniffed, an injured little sound that pained Meg. "They say I can't have him. He can't be mine." Tears swelled and she broke down again.

Sandy caught Meg's eye and she shrugged.

"Who, Matt? Is Gina being a cow again?"

Talia blinked and looked at Meg as if she were two raisins short of a fruitcake. "Not Matt. Gina? What are you talking about? No, the owners of the apartment block I'm staying in. They said no." She shook her head, reached into the basket and brought out a tiny gray kitten. "I found this little scrap all lost and cold near where I work. He would have died if I'd left him there."

Meg's nose twitched. "I have allergies. I couldn't possibly—"

Talia shoved the kitten at her and Meg's hands took it without permission from her brain. Her fingers closed around fuzzy fur and the little thing starting purring so hard she could feel vibrations in its ribs. It was small enough to sit comfortably in both her hands with room to spare. She sneezed but the kitten didn't flinch, it rubbed against her thumbs, turned in a circle, curled up and fell asleep.

Meg thought her heart might burst. Her eyes itched.

Talia had another little cry, dabbed at her eyes and smiled through her tears. "He likes you."

Sandy leaned in closer for a better look. "I don't think it's old enough to be weaned yet. Do you know what that means, Meg? You'll be up feeding every two hours. Wiping its nether regions after each feed. It will be like having a newborn. How fun for you."

The sarcasm in Sandy's voice was lost on Talia. She reached into the basket and hauled out a syringe full of milk. "I've been using this. It's some stuff I got from the vet."

"Every two hours? How am I going to do that? I have work and a party to plan and we're dancing." The kitten in Meg's hands had fallen so fast asleep that its head lolled back and its mouth fell open.

Talia reached down and stroked the tiny thing with one finger. "Look, he knows he's safe. What party are you planning?"

Sandy tilted her head towards Meg. "Someone here is throwing a huge splashy fundraiser for her birthday party for the hundreds of friends she doesn't have."

Talia grimaced but Meg nodded.

"It's true, I don't have friends. But I have a ..." She struggled to find the words.

Sandy rolled her eyes. "A list. She has a list of things she wants to accomplish before eating her birthday cake and apparently this event will tick off every box."

Talia's eyes, still red from crying, lit up. "That is the best thing. I wish I'd thought of it!" Her nose crinkled. "How, though?"

Meg still sat with her hands up, holding the kitten as if it might break if she moved. "There is someone I know who is in desperate need of a home. I want to help her." There, she'd said it out loud. It really was that simple.

Sandy grabbed a strawberry and settled back on a chair. "You didn't tell me that part."

"It could work, though. Right?"

· · · · ● · ● · · · ·

The kitten was asleep in the basket and they were onto their second round of snacks and planning when Meg's phone rang. She answered without checking who it was. The voice on the other end was panicked.

"I'm bleeding. I don't know what to do."

"Gina?"

"No, the Queen Mother. Of course it's me. What do I do?"

"Where are you?"

"I'll send my location. What do I do?"

Meg had never heard Gina like this before. Meg had also never been pregnant before. "I don't know, lie down flat or something. I'm coming."

"Okay, I'm lying down. Get here already."

Meg ended the call. Gina would be furious if the others knew, but there was no way Meg was handling this by herself.

She looked at her two friends who hadn't known each other half an hour ago but were deep in conversation over nougat versus turkish delight as a chocolate filling. Yup, she was not going to do this by herself.

"Girls, are you two up for a rescue mission?"

· · · · • · • · · ·

Dom was finalizing the music cut when his phone rang. His teeth felt like they were wearing socks and his mouth tasted like metal. Cooking at the studio while pretending not to live there would be too tricky and he'd been living on take-out. It was Meg.

"Dom, it's Gina. You have to come now. I'll send a location."

"What's going on?"

"Have you had that chat I keep telling you to have yet?"

"Uh, it's been hectic. A lot going on."

There was an edge to her words that Dom hadn't heard before. "Well, you should've made time. Anyway, it's too late. Just come."

She ended the call and Dom stared at his phone, speechless.

Another beep, a message from Meg with the location. The girl had him spooked, it would have been better if she'd just told him what was wrong.

He checked the location Meg had sent. The address was Gina's home. What were those girls up to now?

He hibernated his laptop and grabbed his car keys. There was a tone to Meg's voice that he couldn't ignore.

•••••••••••

The door stood open at Gina's house. They found her on the couch in the living room, flat on her back with her feet propped up on the back of the couch. Her face was paler than Meg had ever seen.

"What are they doing here?"

"They were visiting when you phoned. They came with to help. How are things here?"

Gina clucked her tongue. "By which you mean am I still bleeding? Yes, yes I am. I phoned my doc and he says I need to come in for a shot." Her bravado slipped and her voice cracked on the word "shot." She grabbed Meg's hand and pulled her closer. "You better not have told them what's going on."

Meg patted her shoulder, though it was more than a little condescending. "Let's get you downstairs. The sooner you have that shot, the better."

"I need to stay horizontal. I can't walk." Gina was red in the face.

Meg could happily have tranquilized her. "Are you nuts? Fine. Don't walk, we'll carry you. Have you packed a bag? You might need to go to the hospital."

"I'm not being admitted. That's not happening." The tremble in Gina's voice contradicted her words.

Meg forced gentleness into her voice. "Stop fussing. Let's go see what the doc can do for you."

"Fine, whatever."

Meg had her by the armpits, the other two each took an ankle. As hard as they tried, they couldn't stop her swinging.

Gina squirmed in their hands. "I'm supposed to be flat. You're all doing it wrong." She fought until her feet touched the ground, then she pushed them all away. "Just leave me."

They trooped down to Sandy's car like bodyguards around a diva. Sandy drove faster than usual, muttering under her breath at any driver who even looked like they might to do something stupid in the traffic.

The doctor's rooms were walking distance from the hospital. Meg made a mental note in case Gina needed to be admitted. Meg panicked as they pulled up outside. Should she tell the other two to stay in the car, or was that rude? Should she ask Gina? Did she want to get her head bitten off?

Sandy made it simple in her usual, unflappable way.

"Off you go, you two. I'm going to get to know my new friend Talia. Shout if you need us."

Meg threw her a grateful glance, but Sandy was already completely focused on Talia. Her hands were firmly and deliberately on her lap. Meg walked through the doors next to Gina, not sure whether to offer a running commentary of helpful noises, or simply be a strong, silent, supportive type of friend. Friend wasn't quite the right word.

They got her signed in with the receptionist and as they took their seats Gina's eyes welled up. "I'm scared."

"I know."

Gina nodded, it was enough. She grimaced and doubled over in pain. Her face was suddenly pale and she stared at Meg, wild-eyed.

Meg's phone buzzed. "Dom's here, he's just finding parking."

"Why did you call Dom? What is wrong with you?"

Meg flinched. "He needs to know what's going on. You can't keep him in the dark forever. Surely you know this?"

"It's not your business to go around telling people." Angry Gina was back and her pale skin made her even more scary.

Meg was beginning to feel a bit annoyed. "The only thing I've told him is that he needs to have an honest conversation with you because apparently you don't have the guts to be honest with him."

Gina was about to speak when Meg shoved a hand up, millimeters from Gina's nose. "Don't start with me. I'm right and you know it." Gina's lip twitched and Meg waggled a finger. "Uh-uh. No. Nothing more from you."

"But ..."

"No!"

"You're sitting on my sweater. I'm cold."

"Oh, sorry." Meg fished out Gina's jersey and gave it to her.

Gina pulled the soft wool over her head and fussed with the hem until it was tucked under just right. A slim man in a shirt and jeans poked his head in the room and smiled when he saw Gina.

"Your turn, let's go."

Gina left Meg sitting in the waiting room feeling awkward. Many ladies were obviously expecting, some waddled with bellies that looked bigger than a belly should ever be. Others just looked thick around the middle. To think that she'd likely been the one who'd processed the positive tests on most of these. It was entirely possible that she could lean over, ask a name, and remember that story she'd spun in her head.

Dom appeared at the door and came straight to Meg who waved towards the hallway Gina had disappeared down.

"She's down there with the doctor."

Dom collapsed into the chair next to her. "What's going on?"

Meg frowned. "Why are you still here? You should be with her right now."

"I can't just barge in on Gina's doctor's appointment. That would be weird. Possibly even rude."

"You should be in there supporting her. Honestly, you men are clueless." Meg clicked her tongue in frustration. "Listen, you hold the fort. I have friends in the car and I can't just leave them there."

"Why don't they come in?"

"Gina didn't want them to."

"You see! Exactly. Gina won't want me to barge in on her appointment like that."

Meg stood up with meaning and shook her head. "You're absolutely clueless. Do you know that? You stay here and see to Gina. She needs you right now."

· · · · ●· ●· · ·

Dom watched Meg stomp off with tiny, furious, steps. If he was absolutely clueless, she was completely bewildering. He'd obviously done something to make her mad, but he had no idea what.

A medical person poked her head around the corner and scanned the room. "I'm looking for the family of Ms. Gina MacMillan."

Dom stuck up his hand. "That would be me. Is everything all right?"

"Come with me, please."

She led the way down the closed-in olive-colored hallway. The roof felt too low, too close to Dom's head. He hated this place. It even smelled like a hospital. She waved him through a door and shut it behind him.

Gina lay on a stretcher bed with a drip pumping fluid into her arm.

"Hey, kid. What's up?"

"Where is Meg? What did she tell you?"

"She told me her friends are in the car so she couldn't stay long. How are you feeling?"

"About me, what did she tell you about me?" She waved towards the drip with her free hand. "About this?"

"It was all very urgent, so I'm here now. Do you mind telling me what's going on?"

Gina shrugged. She wouldn't look him in the eye.

"Gina?"

"I want to go home. Where is Reg?"

"I can phone him for you if you want. You are making me worry. Are you sick?"

Gina blushed bright red and choked out, "Let's just call it lady problems."

"Oh. Oh! It's better if you don't tell me, then. Let me get Reg."

Chapter Thirty-Three

MEG WAS FEEDING THE kitten when Talia phoned. The tiny fuzz ball squirmed off her lap onto the couch and proceeded to hunt the cushion tassel, complete with the pre-charge bum wiggle and pounce.

"Meg, I just want to confirm a few things for your party." She sounded breathless as if she'd been jogging.

"Have you been out running? What's up with your breathing?"

"Oh, I get breathless when I'm excited. I'm excited about your party."

"Really? Why?" Meg wasn't even excited about her party. She would probably identify closer to terrified.

Talia sighed. "Well, I've been talking to some people and they're happy to get on board."

"How on earth did you get that right?"

"I know good people." Meg could *hear* the big grin on her face.

"So, the guys have got the social media side all zipped up and ready to go. Once you've given them the go-ahead, it will all go live. Tickets will be going on sale at midnight tonight. I think you have a good shot at getting in the money you need for your friend. So do you think we can pop around tonight and show you everything?"

Meg's hand shook as she held the phone to her ear. Gooseflesh raised cold bumps all down her arms. She'd had a wild idea that she'd dare open her mouth about, and now somehow it was happening with the momentum of a bull rolling downhill and picking up speed as it went.

"Meg? Tonight?"

"Sure, why not?"

• • • • • • • • • •

Meg didn't know who to expect, but Talia knocked on her door with all the males from the dance team in tow except Dom and Reg.

Talia came in first and shoved a full shopping bag into Meg's hands. The guys trooped in after her.

They were all tall and took up more space than she was used to sharing in her foyer. Talia went straight to the kettle and switched it on. The boys followed her into the kitchen and settled in around the table.

Matt tapped on Ebb's bowl. "Er, Meg? I think there's something wrong with your fish."

Jeremy studied the little orange fish as he wriggled and squirmed to get to the food. "Don't judge. He's just got some fish issues."

Matt snorted. "He's got fishues. Wahaha!"

Meg blinked at the room full of males and scuttled over to help Talia make tea. Talia was happily digging through Meg's drawers to find spoons.

"Where's your sugar?"

Meg tapped the sugar that sat squarely in front of Talia, right under her nose.

"Oh, silly me. Reg is visiting Gina to help her if she needs anything. Personally, I think that's ridiculous because he can barely look after himself with that broken knee, but who am I to judge?" She circled a pointed finger around her face. Her skin glowed even under artificial light. "See? No judging."

Talia chatted away while effortlessly whipping up a round of coffee, tea, and frothy hot chocolate for Matt who was basically the equivalent of a big kid. A really smart kid, but a kid, nonetheless. Talia patted the chair next to her for Meg to sit.

"Right, guys. Show us your magic." Talia's eyes sparkled. She sipped her milky rooibos with honey and Meg couldn't help thinking she was the most unexpected gift of a friend in this strange season she found herself in.

"There's just one thing." Meg floundered. They couldn't tell Dom, he'd ask too many questions. How could she expect this of them?

"What?" Talia's face glowed even under the harsh kitchen lights.

"You can't tell Dom. It's a surprise." She slapped a smile on, though it felt fake and she was sure they'd call her out for being conniving and sneaky.

"Aah, that's sweet. Our lips are sealed. Right, guys?" Talia might as well be a conductor of an orchestra. The guys followed her lead without hesitation, gruffly muttering variations of *sure*.

· · · · ·•· • · · ·

Dom buzzed Gina's doorbell and crossed his fingers that she wasn't actually in. He had to check in on her as her dance team leader and her friend, but he didn't relish the idea of tiptoeing through the scattered gunpowder of her whims and feelings. She could be exhausting. With the competition so close, he had to know if she was up to it. She'd ignored all fifteen of his messages. Things weren't looking good.

Reg opened up. His face flushed red at the sight of Dom.

"Hey, Reg. How is she?"

Reg hobbled backwards to wave Dom in and shrugged. "You can never really tell. I think she's feeling better. She's been sleeping a lot."

"I don't want to pry, it's none of my business, but the competition is next weekend ..." He trailed off, feeling awkward.

"She's on meds." He shrugged. "This is all way above my pay grade. She's awake now, you can go see her yourself." Reg aimed him at the hallway, relief all over his face.

Gina lay on her side on a crisply made bed, legs tucked up, clutching a pillow to her chest.

"Hey, kid. What's up?"

Her eyes flicked to him for a second before settling back to staring out the window. Dirty gray clouds skidded past, low and hurried.

"How are things with the, uh, lady problems?"

"If you're asking if I can perform, I'll be there." Her eyes reflected the clouds outside, gray and stormy.

"You don't have to if you're not well enough."

"I said I'll be there."

Dom could see the muscles in her jaw working as her teeth clenched. In all the years he'd known her, he'd never seen her in this state. He didn't know what to say without risking a full meltdown. Reg hovered at the door looking as nervous as Dom felt.

· · · · ● · ● · · · ·

It was tea-break at work. Meg and Vashti usually ignored the fact and worked straight through, but Meg had been obsessing over how many tickets had been sold to her party and thought she might just log on and have a peep.

Vashti checked her phone too, smacked it with the back of her hand and frowned hard. "He keeps messaging me to ask how you are. What should I say?"

Meg clicked the link to the members' area of the ticket site and watched the circle spin as the site loaded. "Who?" *C'mon, circle.*

"Your ex. Who do you think?"

"Chad?"

Vashti's long fingernail tapped on her desk. "Do you have another ex you're not telling me about? Yes, Chad. He keeps asking about you."

"What do you tell him?" The website still wasn't loading.

"I've taken to having fat chats with the man." Vashti settled back in her chair and waved her hands across the empty space in front of her. "I chat about things I've read in the news, how my day's been. It's great."

"I can't believe what I'm hearing. What does he say?"

Vashti grinned and her teeth flashed white against her tanned skin. "He chats back and eventually forgets that he asked about you."

"That's genius. I think?" Meg shook her head and made a firm decision to stop asking questions. It was all too weird. The circle on her internet browser disappeared with a blip and the ticket sales page popped up, all yellow and proud. Meg felt her heart rate dip. "One hundred and eighteen tickets sold. What?"

Vashti hurried over and squinted at Meg's phone. "To your event?"

"My party, yes. This is crazy, I didn't think we'd make it past twenty!"

Vashti took the phone and scrolled. "This looks fun, I'm going to get some tickets."

Cold washed through Meg. The guys had done their part brilliantly and they were gathering an audience. Meg had thought about getting them all in and making money, what she hadn't thought of was how to keep them all entertained for an entire evening. For that price, her entertainment had better be worth watching. Ugh.

Chapter Thirty-Four

20 Days And Counting—The Competition

MEG TUGGED GENTLY ON her false eyelash to make sure it wouldn't come off while they were dancing. The lash stayed on and she could still see out of both eyes. Apparently, her eyelash-gluing skills were improving.

Dom knocked on the girls' dressing room door. "Is it safe?" At the chorus of yeses, he came in bringing his jittery nerves and the other guys with him.

"The audience is packed, completely sold out. It's a long shot, but we might just do this." He caught Meg's eye and winked at her.

Meg did an odd eyebrow-raise nod-thing in response and quickly looked away. Knowing what he wanted to do with the money, she toyed with the idea of doing badly to sabotage their attempt at winning, but it was as impossible as ignoring crumbs on the crouch.

Gina's costume sat snug around her new fluffiness, but it was on. She'd showed up on Meg's door in a flat panic the night before and Meg had called on Mrs. O'Riley, whose theatre skills apparently stretched as far as knowing all the tricks to making things fit. She'd shuffled off in her slippers and come back twenty minutes later with an insert panel that she'd thrown together that was nothing short of a miracle.

Dom sidled in next to Meg and slipped an arm around her waist. How nice it would be to yield. To soften and fold into his chest, his arm, breathe in the scent of him. But he was everything she opposed and she stiffened.

Dom called them all closer for their pre-competition pep talk. Over the last few months, Meg had come to recognize the signs of a good talk and one that didn't quite inspire the right things. She could feel tension packed like a tight ball of carefully contained throw-up inside Dom. He was more nervous than he'd ever been before.

"You really want to win this, don't you?"

"I do. I have big plans and this win will secure them."

Right. Big plans. Skyscraper-size plans. Not if she could help it.

Dom lifted an eyebrow. "And that face? What's going on in your head, Meg?"

She really needed to master the art of separating her thoughts from her expressions. "Oh, just nerves, I guess."

Reg took up half the open floor of the small dressing room with his wheelchair. He rolled back and forth, practiced his one-handed, on-the-spot turn, causing the dancers to jump back for fear of having their toes driven over.

Gina hissed and clucked. "Reg, stop it. Honestly."

He shrugged. "Honestly? Just trying to nail the dance. It's like learning a whole new routine for me. At least you guys get to adapt something we've been working on already. This is hard for me. Also, I've got calluses on my hands from wheeling this thing around."

Tammy smoothed her skirt over her hips. "It's going to be different to be on stage with lights and everything. We are so used to a dance floor in among everybody."

Meg shrugged. "I like it. We're not at eye-level with any-body."

Talia elbowed her, with a cheeky grin dimpling her face. "And you've got lights in your eyes so you can't see anybody either. It's perfect."

Meg grinned. "Exactly!" Her grin swallowed itself with a knock on the door to warn them it was time.

Dom led his troupe backstage, silently praying. They were so close to making this dream a possibility. He gathered them around in a huddle as the announcer warbled on in a tinny voice about their item.

"Guys, you've made me so proud. It doesn't matter what happens out there today, you are ..." Words failed him.

Matt took the gap. "Top class in my book." He nodded suavely.

"That's not quite where I was going with that." Before he could clarify, the lights went dark. "Right, let's go."

There was just enough light spilling from the side for them to get into their starting positions on the stage.

Competitive dancing was nothing new for Dom, but it was usually on a floor among the audience with lots of opportunity for charming the crowd. Now they were on a stage with one of his dancers in a wheelchair and his most reliable dancer given to fainting spells and temper tantrums. This was sheer lunacy.

Phoenix. Focus on the Phoenix.

He whispered a prayer under his breath. *Jesus, I know all the miracles you did in the Bible. We need one of those now. Maybe*

not the one where you multiply food. Or that other one with
water at the wedding.

The music started and cut him off mid-prayer. He squeaked out a strangled, "Help, Jesus!"

The dancers stood in a semi-circle with their backs to the audience. A lone flute played a mournful tune and Dom felt Reg's wheelchair brush past him. He heard the squeak of the wheels as Reg opened the floor with his solo section.

At just the right moment, the dancers began thumping their heels. The sound magnified on the hollow wooden floor and sounded much louder than it did in the studio. The music grew as a full orchestra came in. Dom started the ripple and turned around, the other dancers followed. Stage lights blinded him and he couldn't see the audience.

Talia cart-wheeled across Reg's wheelchair and led the other girls into an anti-clockwise circle, while the Dom led the guys clockwise. The lines intermingled and they weaved through each other, keeping perfect time.

Drum beat. They all stopped dead-still and let the music wash through them. One track blended seamlessly with the other and they found their partners for a tango section with sharp head flicks and quick-moving feet.

Gina danced through her piece of choreography that started behind Reg's wheelchair with a complicated series of kicks, head-flicks, and dips, all using the wheel chair for balance.

Crescendo and boom, they all froze and the music changed. Reg moved away from Gina and began to weave in and around the dancers, turning his chair in a complicated series of turns and dips. As he reached Meg, there was a moment of connection and Meg softened just as they'd practiced it. She danced with him as they moved on to Talia and Matt. Talia and Matt's piece started with their backs to him as if he were invisible, but they warmed and *saw* him. Two counts of eight passed in a blink as the four of them moved as one, Reg and all.

Dom saw the dancers and in a moment he knew what this was more than just a dance. It was a vivid picture of seeing the invisible ones. Including, not excluding. Love made visible.

This was so much more than a just dance.

· · · · ● · · ● · · ·

Meg felt like a bug under a microscope, a sparkly bug that was sweating enough to feel every drip that ran down her spine. Do bugs even sweat?

Dom's hand grabbed hers and brought her back to the moment. He pulled her close as the music changed, a slow waltz in open hold around Reg in the middle, still seated in his chair. The violins stopped, and the sound of a clock ticking filled the auditorium once again. Gina's solo. Meg checked Dom's face, he was feeling it too, the stress of not knowing if Gina was reliable or not. She danced in from the wings using Reg's crutch as a prop.

On a clock tick, each pair rotated and Meg could see Gina dance in her peripheral vision. She'd always been a stunning dancer, but had moved with a cold calculation that was fascinating to watch but didn't touch Meg. Now, though ... it took all Meg's self-control to keep her head forward. There was a softness to Gina's moves that prodded at a tender spot so deep inside of Meg, she'd forgotten it was there.

Gina reached Reg at the last clock tick and their eyes met. With her back to the audience, her face carried the softness that had been in all her moves and the smile they shared undid Meg. She blinked furiously. Tears and this amount of mascara would trash panda her face.

Dom whispered through his teeth, "You okay?"

She blinked even faster and dipped her chin, a vague nod.

During the crucial moment of the piece, Reg took the crutch from Gina. It was a shiny stainless steel one that they'd chosen for effect under stage lights. He placed it carefully and transferred his weight. As the orchestral piece swept back in, he stood.

The crowd must have been swept into the drama of the piece as they cheered and clapped. As one, Meg, Dom, and the other couples wove around Reg and Gina in the center before spinning off into a wide semi-circle.

Reg and Gina eased into their duet section, which was almost a trio with the crutch thrown in. Apparently they'd been practicing in secret because Meg had never seen them nail this without someone nearly face-planting. Watching them now in between her own moves made her heart swell.

They ended the routine in their final pose and held it. As they stood there, blinded by the spotlight, the sense of presence came over Meg so strongly, she stopped breathing for an eternal moment.

She was probably losing her marbles, but she could have sworn that their dance had delighted God.

· · · · ● · ● · · ·

Dom stood on the podium holding the oversized check and his heart sang. Phoenix wasn't completely in the bag yet, but this amount of money brought him a whole lot closer. He was so proud of his team he'd have had them all up here with him if there had been room. They stood in a bunch together down below, grinning and slapping each other on the back.

Except Meg. Meg's face was a weird combination that he could only describe as panic and frustration. Dom tried to catch her eye, but she had her arms across her chest and was looking everywhere *but* at him.

Chapter Thirty-Five

The Auction

MEG'S HEAD SWEATED UNDER the wig that Talia had jammed on her head to redo the granny look. She was back incognito just in case. If her hunch were right, Dom would be there to bid on the house and she fully intended snatching it out from under his nose. She just couldn't bring herself to face off against him as Meg.

Her bag jiggled and she peeped in to check on her kitten. The tiny, gray, fur-ball was still curled up in the corner of the spacious, and otherwise empty, shopping bag. It yawned before tucking its head back in. She'd tried to leave it with Mrs. O'Riley, but the old lady was out so Meg had no choice but to bring it with. So far, the tiny thing had been no trouble.

Mrs. O'Riley was an amazing kitten-sitter for whenever Meg had to be out. The kitten seemed to be warming her up inside; she smiled when Meg dropped the ball of fuzz off. Together they'd decided to call it Max.

The heat and sweat made her head itchy, but she couldn't scratch anyway with her gloves on so she settled for yanking on her thumb. It was stuffy in the auction room, the kind that made you aware of breathing in air that came from other people's lungs. Meg fidgeted with her bag, wishing this were all over. She'd never been to a property auction before and here she was, all ready to actually bid on a house. Crazy.

It was even crazier that she didn't actually have any of the money in hand yet. Sandy had done a quick calculation of tickets sold—they were well into the 500s—and given her a figure to work with. She'd also guesstimated an amount they could bring in from the sale of Meg's photographs. The auctioneers website stated their terms were payment within three days of winning a bid, which gave her some wiggle room until Monday.

But still.

This was ridiculous and it made the room spin. There she was, about to bid on a property with money she didn't have yet, to give it a woman she didn't know. One quick bark of a laugh shot out her mouth. She mumbled *sorry* to the people around her who glanced her way.

A large man shuffled past her and took the seat next to hers. He wore a threadbare suit that was worn nearly all the way through on the elbows. The smell of old cigar smoke and peppermints hung over him like a cloud.

Meg was busy constructing an emergency contingency plan for in case he decided to strike up a conversation when Dom came into the auction room. He was red in the face and sweating as he pushed through the crowd and found an open chair close to the front.

Swallowing was impossible. Her tongue stuck to the roof of her mouth. A drop of sweat trailed down her spine and she shivered.

The auctioneer took his place behind the podium with his gavel in hand and smacked it down hard to call for order. Meg flinched. This just got real.

· · · · ● · ● · · · ·

Dom felt for his keys in the pocket of his jeans, parking had been ridiculous. He'd had to leave his car on the pavement and run the rest of the way to get in on time. The crowd shifted restlessly and Dom felt the tension as a tight band around his head.

He scanned the sea of faces, half-dreading he'd see someone familiar. One of his dad's golf buddies stood at the back, casually leaning on the wall. A guy from the gym sat in the center block. It was strange to see him in a pressed shirt and not the muscle-hugging t-shirt Dom was used to. Second row from the front, he spotted an elderly lady who didn't fit the mold of the average auction bargain hunter. She wore sunglasses in the dim room. Maybe she was blind? There was something vaguely familiar in her jaw-line, but that's where it stopped. He must have taken her for a dance lesson at some point.

The auctioneer came out of a little side room and settled in behind the podium. With one hard thud of the gavel, the room fell quiet and they were ready to start. With all the properties on offer today, Dom hoped his little run-down gem would be largely ignored. He'd done his best to raise the funding, but what he had was a fraction of what he might need if there was any competition in the room.

Jesus, please help.

· · · · ●· ● · · · ·

Bidding opened low and Meg felt blood rush to her head and buzz in her ears. She sat paralyzed. The auctioneer acknowledged a hand—Dom's. Meg shot up her hand next.

Time ran both slow and fast, blurring into a mess of tension and raised hands. The auctioneer rattled off amounts in a high nasal voice, the vocal equivalent of nails on a chalkboard.

On and on it went, the price creeping higher in small increments.

The next bid would take it out of Meg's price range. She balanced on a precipice. This was the final moment. She saw it with crystal clarity—here was her big thing, her purpose, her destiny. She wasn't made of stuff that could change the world, but she could do this one thing for a woman she barely knew. A woman who was changing the world with every child she rescued. Meg couldn't make a difference, but Buntu could. And this moment could give her a home. A hope. A future.

The auctioneer's hand moved in freeze-frame. Meg could barely breathe. He pointed at her, lifted the gavel. It began its descent, a slow arc that would validate her existence.

But it swung away from her towards Dom, his face contorted as if he was in pain. It was over. She couldn't go higher.

Suddenly her bag leaked warm liquid. She shot up in shock. Max had used her for a sandbox.

The auctioneers hand swung back to her, the gavel fell and he yelled, "Sold!"

Meg felt her insides turn as liquid as what soaked her lap. She didn't have that much.

···•·•••··

Dom felt gutted. He wondered about approaching the old lady and asking her what she intended to do with the property. Maybe she would rent it out to him if he chose his words carefully. Half of him wanted to run from the auction venue and never come back, but he ignored himself and walked over to where the lady sat, in the same spot she'd sat during the auction.

Her eyes were hidden behind the pamphlet and when he got closer, he could see she sat with her eyes shut and her mouth moved wordlessly. It certainly wasn't the look of someone who had just successfully won a bid on a house.

"Hi."

The lady shot him a quick look through her sunglasses.

Dom gestured towards the seat next to her and she nodded once though her body language screamed how uncomfortable she was. He sat down anyway.

"Can I ask you a few things?"

The lady nodded at him but kept her mouth tightly shut. She was fanning herself with a wad of pamphlets. From the moisture collecting at her temples, she was clearly feeling the heat. No wonder—she was horribly overdressed for this hot room, she'd even tucked a scarf tightly round her neck and it covered some of her face, too. Crazy.

Before he could ask a single thing, an auction official came over and tapped the lady on the shoulder. "Ma'am, please follow me. There is some paperwork for you to sign."

Dom watched her leave and felt his heart follow.

Jesus, what now?

He knew the verses and could quote them at himself —*trust in the Lord with all your heart and lean not on your own understanding. In all your ways acknowledge Him and He will make your paths straight.*

This didn't feel like path-straightening—more like a live, lava-spewing volcano erupting in the middle of his plans. *What is going on, Jesus? Should I be doing spiritual warfare? Binding and loosing? I don't get it.*

He hung around for thirty-two minutes, waiting for the lady to come out of the office. Thirty-five minutes later, he realized the office must have a separate exit and the lady was long gone, together with his childhood home and the whole point of Project Phoenix.

Chapter Thirty-Six

The Party Set Up

MEG WATCHED SANDY AS she moved around the badminton hall directing her volunteers. Some were balanced on tall, death-cheating ladders, hanging billowy draping and fairy lights. Others whipped cream and sprinkled chocolate flakes in the kitchen. Meg kept herself busy deciding which pictures should hang where.

Xan was on Max duty and followed the kitten around armed with food and water. He'd set up a cat basket for when the tiny thing got tired, but that didn't seem like it would be anytime soon.

Meg had been determined to help Sandy, but had been shooed off under orders to get some beauty rest, whatever that was. When Sandy saw she wasn't keeping Meg away, she assigned Jeremy to "Meg-duty" and gave him strict orders to do whatever Meg said. Being a graphic designer meant that Jeremy had a genuine artistic edge and they soon found that they worked well together figuring out which picture should go where.

Sorting through the pictures was a bit like opening a present. Meg didn't have a clue which of her photos had been block mounted. With all the extra rehearsals leading up to the competition, Meg had run out of time to pick and choose so she'd dropped off a flash stick and asked for the whole folder to be done. It was a little extravagant, but she'd been feeling gung-ho. Much like when she couldn't leave crumbs without cleaning up, she usually went through her camera roll regularly to delete any that weren't up to scratch. Knowing her meticulous self, she'd taken a risk and had them all done.

They'd been ready in time for her to collect them on the way to the hall to be hung. She'd have preferred to sort through them all by herself first, but there just wasn't time for that.

As each picture went up, she felt a little weirder. It was like inviting a group of strangers to come and have a look through her underwear drawer.

Jeremy held one up and chuckled. It was a portrait of her kitten swatting its reflection in the mirror. The tiny thing had ears that took up more space than ears should. He pointed at the wall just outside the kitchen area. "What if we hung this one up over there?"

Meg was about to answer when Sandy came swishing over with a wild look in her eye that Meg had come to recognize as well-contained panic.

"Meg, darling. I need you backstage quickly. We have an issue with the stage." She blinked at Jeremy, checked the time on her watch and let out a quick *drat*. "Jeremy, carry on. Stick them up all over. I'm sure you'll make it all look amazing."

The stage issue ate up an hour and a half with faulty microphone batteries, a flickering spotlight, and a wonky wheelchair access ramp. Between Sandy, Meg, Matt, and Cliff, they got it all steady and working as Dom arrived.

He seemed a bit taken aback at seeing the others here in her space, but he quickly recovered and headed straight to where Meg stood patiently explaining to the lighting guy the intricacies of the follow-spot timing for the program line-up.

Meg had invited the team to dance at the event and Dom had agreed because it was for her birthday. What he didn't know, was that every scrap of money raised was being used to pay for the bid against him in the house auction.

· · · ● · ● · ● · · ·

Meg had outdone herself. Dom had played a good few friendly badminton matches in the hall and he associated it with squeaky sneakers and sweat. Now the place looked more like a scene from a movie, one of those rom-coms with a leading man and his unbuttoned shirt that had all the ladies swooning and a leading lady who made them weep with jealousy over her perfect eyebrows.

Throughout the space hung large, block-mounted, photographs. He would have happily had any of these in his apartment. He figured all these photos must be Meg's own work.

The photo of the parquet flooring at the studio taken at sunset with the last few rays of light streaming through the window and setting the floor alight just about did him in. Dom reminded himself to breathe.

A little boy from behind in holey shorts caught mid-dance, anonymous but for the fact that Dom knew him. Ernest. The background was blurred and he couldn't tell where the shot had been taken. In a single shot, she'd captured the essence of the boy: free-spirited and light-hearted even though his life was tough.

He moved on to look at the next one and even though the subject matter was less close to home, it prodded him in the feels anyway. Meg's goldfish, swimming upside down in a golden glow of morning sunlight through the bowl. She'd even captured a few rainbow bubbles in the water. Next.

An abstract shot of something he could swear were crumbs on a couch. Odd subject matter, but the result was surprisingly appealing.

On and on he walked, getting glimpses into the soul of this woman who had snuck into his life in pink sneakers.

There was a big guy hanging pictures and Dom did a double-take as he seemed familiar. It was Jeremy. He waved a quick hello to Dom and went back to hanging pictures before Dom could grill him with twenty questions. Why was he here helping?

He wove through the tables and found the other guys from the team on stage helping Meg. All except hop-a-long Reg. He was parked at the sound desk, ticking things off a list. Meg and the guys were in deep discussion with the sound/lighting guy.

Dom stood at the edge of the stage and watched Meg as she spoke. She looked so serious but her eyes sparkled. He'd never seen her look this alive. Sound guy must have said something funny. Meg hid behind her hand and giggled.

Her eye caught his and her expression shifted to something he couldn't read. She patted the sound guy's shoulder and came over.

"Hey. I'm glad you could come."

"Hey, yourself. This is impressive."

Meg scanned the room and shook her head with a dazed look on her face. "I still can't believe it. You have some talented friends."

"So do you, apparently."

Meg laughed, one sharp bark. "Maybe."

"So is there anything you want me to do? I see you've got all the other guys working."

Meg reddened around her ears and squirmed before answering, "No, I think we're fine. Kind of you to offer, though. I better get back to, er,"—she waved behind her—"this."

In a flash, he understood. She was getting back with Chad and didn't know how to tell him. That explained everything—the awkwardness, the fact that she couldn't look him in the eye ... it all made perfect sense.

"Meg, listen. I won't always agree with your life choices, but I would like to think we've become friends at least over the last few months. You don't need to worry about me judging you or anything."

There was no mistaking the expression on her face now. It was pure rage.

Chapter Thirty-Seven

The Party

MEG GLUED ON HER false eyelash in the make-shift dressing room behind the stage. The first one went on without a hitch and Meg felt rather chuffed with herself. Sandy sat on a box next to her, running through a checklist of party things.

"That's been done, and that. So you're happy to go the silent auction route with your pictures?"

Meg bit her tongue to stop her hand shaking as she applied a thin line of glue to the second lash. "Whatever you think will work is fine by me."

"Okay, silent auction it is. And you're happy with the program line-up?"

Meg glued the second lash on askew and ripped it off. "Gah! This is dumb. Look how I'm shaking."

"Jittery nerves. Don't stress about a thing. This is all going to work beautifully." Her phone beeped and she checked the message that came through. "Your first guests have just arrived."

Meg felt the blood drain from her face. "That's terrifying." The amount of money they needed to raise tonight was even more terrifying, but she couldn't bring herself to tell Sandy what had gone down at the auction. She didn't even want to think about it, the thought of admitting it out loud made her throat close up.

"Shall I help you with that eyelash?"

"Your skills are amazing, Sands. But I don't think they stretch as far as eyelashes."

"Oh, thank goodness. I had visions of you dancing in an eye patch because I trashed your eyeball."

Meg snorted a laugh and ran a fresh line of glue and blew on it the way Mrs. O'Riley had taught her. She was about to stick it on when there was a knock on the door. Sandy got up to let the knocker in. It was Mrs. O'Riley in a top-to-toe sequined dress in a deep shade of jade green. Her hair was immaculately done, all curled and pinned up with sparkling diamanté clips that matched her dangly earrings. She carried herself with an effortless grace.

Meg shot up to hug her. "Look at you! You look so beautiful. I'm so happy you can do this for me."

Mrs. O'Riley waved a hand in her face and pointed at the chair. "Sit. I see another thing that I can do for you." In seconds flat, Meg's second eyelash was attached and ready for action.

Sandy took Mrs. O'Riley and led her out of the room. "Come let's go and chat to the sound guy about your backing track."

Meg watched the two of them leave and found herself blinking back tears. Getting emotional over seeing her old neighbor. What was going on with her? *Pull yourself together, Meg.*

She stuck her head into the next dressing room down the hall and found the entire dance team squished into it.

"Hey, guys. Are you ready?"

"As ready as we'll ever be." Reg grinned at her from his wheelchair and waved his plaster-encased leg at her.

Gina had her zip half undone and was waving a paper at her face furiously. "It is so hot in here, good grief."

Meg looked at them all and a wave of fondness washed through her with such force that she felt quite weepy. "You guys, thank you for doing this. I don't even know what to say."

Talia grinned at her in a way that made her eyes twinkle. "Of course we'll do this with you. After all the sweating we've done together, we might as well be family."

Meg nodded, blinked hard, and left the room with the excuse of checking in with the other entertainers. She stood in the dim hallway outside the dressing room, letting the breeze cool her down. The door creaked open and the others filed out. Dom came last and took her hand. She didn't fight it, though logic said she should pull away.

"No tears, remember your make-up. Come on, let's go do this."

· · · · ● · ● · · · ·

Dom watched the emotions play across Meg's face as she fumbled her way through thanking them and he fought the urge to go bear-hug her tight and never let go. Tonight was a huge big deal for her. He had his own suspicions as to what she was raising money for and it involved a snazzy white dress, a six-tier cake, and a first dance with a man that wasn't him. The thought of it made him feel ill.

He waited for the rest of the team to lead out before following, where he found Meg outside blinking back tears. Tears could trash a dancer's make-up and the last thing she needed was to go on stage looking like a panda. He gently reminded her, "No tears, remember your make-up. Come on, let's go do this."

If he couldn't have her, then he was at least going to make the most of this last dance together.

Their competition routine was up first on the program list so they made their way into the auditorium via the stage entrance and took up their places.

It was all going as practiced until he spun around and saw the photo he'd taken of Meg dancing in the moonlight in the room with the holey roof back in the house. Shock tingled through his body, stirring like a big wooden spoon through the pot of his feelings, scooping them all up to the surface. He shoved them all down desperately before they showed on his face. *This girl, dear Jesus, this girl.*

He froze for a full four counts until Meg hissed at him and he picked it up and carried on. The rest of the dance blurred past on autopilot without a single face-plant.

As they held their end position, it took all Dom's self control to stay on the stage and not make his way through the crowds to get a closer look at his photo.

· · · • • · • · · ·

Meg was breathing fast as they held their end position. The hall was packed with people and the irony of herself, the poster child for introverts, throwing a huge birthday bash with hundreds of people she didn't even know made her want to break out in a fit of giggles.

They took their bow and left the stage. Dom shot off as if his bottom was on fire and he needed to find a puddle. Strange man.

Meg disappeared into the wings to find Mrs. O'Riley, standing tall and dignified, waiting for her turn.

"You're going to be amazing. Are you nervous?" Meg stretched out a hand to squeeze her shoulder, threw out that idea, and hugged her.

Mrs. O'Riley patted Meg's back awkwardly and pushed her away. "Nervous? Do I look nervous?"

"You look drop-dead gorgeous, elegant, classy ... spectacularly *not* nervous!"

Mrs. O'Riley said nothing more, but dipped her chin, as regal as a queen. She almost smiled as Meg took her elbow, hooked their arms, and led her out to center stage. Meg left her there, and felt her heart in her throat as grumpy old Mrs. O'Riley melted away under the spotlight, leaving a radiant creature who owned the stage just by standing on it.

Meg couldn't help but stare and hold her breath as she waited for Mrs. O'Riley to start singing.

The backing track started and Mrs. O'Riley closed her eyes, opened her mouth, and Meg thought her heart might burst. "Moon River." One of the nightly songs she was so used to, but coming over a sound system sounded so much larger than life, just like the old lady looked right now. She could easily have had her own show on Broadway. She barely moved, yet her voice lifted effortlessly, filling the vast space with rich sweetness.

Meg hardly breathed until the final note rang out through the air. Mrs. O'Riley bowed as much as her ancient spine would let her and sauntered off stage with the air of a true performer.

As much as a room full of strangers wasn't Meg's favorite thing, this room full was all about getting her closer to her goal. If this worked, she could write a guide on List Ticking 101.

They slipped effortlessly into the rest of the program which ran like clockwork with Sandy doing what she did best.

This might just work.

· · · · ●· ●· ● · · ·

Sandy and Meg sat at Meg's table next to her broken goldfish. Sandy pulled the metal petty cash tin out of her bag and dumped it on the counter, then swung the lid back on creaky hinges.

"I hope you like counting money—there is a lot of it here. There will also be EFTs deposited directly into your bank from the sale of five of your photographs. Alison has offered to hang those that didn't sell in her coffee shop for you."

Meg eyed the piles of money. It sure looked like enough, but they'd only know when they'd counted. Meg opened up her laptop and got her spreadsheet program running and she entered how many notes of each value as they counted.

It took the two of them 45 minutes and two cups of tea each to count the whole pile. Meg added in a column for pictures sold and the EFTs that would be coming. She hit the button to add it all together and wanted to throw up.

They were short by 10K.

It wasn't enough.

· · · · ● ● · · · ·

Monday Morning

Meg had trudged through the weekend under a cloud of worry. Now it was Monday morning. That meant she was due to make payment to the auctioneer and collect house keys.

Ten thousand short and only a few hours to raise it.

Basically impossible.

When lunchtime came, she'd have to go down to the auctioneers, pay the fine, and forfeit every single thing on her list. It sucked, but that was all she could do. With so few days until her actual birthday, leaving her list unticked seemed more and more likely. It all made her feel rather blue.

It was a sweet thought, God. It would have been nice, don't You think? Imagine being able to take someone with a heart of gold and put them where they can truly make a difference. I suppose life isn't like that, even with You involved.

Vashti came in late and stowed her bag in the drawer as she always did. "Let me just say this, I didn't know you had it in you. How the heck did you pull that whole event out of the bag? What a crazy beautiful night. And you, dancing! Wow."

Meg laughed and batted the compliment sideways. "I have some seriously talented friends." They really had grown close, now that she thought about it. All the excitement was over, now she just had to cough up for a fine. Her heart was rather sad as she got started on a batch of pregnancy tests. A text came through from Sandy.

Meg, sit down.

Someone bought one of your photos. They'll be depositing 15K this morning.

Go sign for the house, girl!

Straight after the message, her phone beeped with a message from the bank confirming the deposit. Her vision swam.

"Vashti, can you cover for me? I have a house to go sign for."

Dom wasn't particularly sentimental, but having the house snatched out from under his nose made his blood boil. All those months of planning and now nothing to show for it.

He pulled up outside the house and climbed over the SOLD sign that had been hung across the gate since his last visit. The very thought of it made his scalp itch with frustration. This may well be his last time coming here.

He was usually a good sport about losing, but to lose both the house and his chance with Meg was enough to make him bitter. He pushed open the door and walked straight through to the room with the holey ceiling. His phone buzzed, it was a message from Meg.

Hey you, I need your help. How do I find Ernest's mom? I have a surprise for her.

An excuse to see Meg, he'd take whatever he could get. He'd been praying about his feelings for this girl and if anything, they were stronger now than before. Why would God let this happen while she was still involved with another man? Was it some weird test he had to pass? If it was a test, he was about to fail miserably.

He voice-noted back, "Hey, yourself. If it's a parcel for her, I can come pick it up. I'll come past now."

His phone beeped a couple of times on the drive to Meg's apartment, but he didn't stop to check it. Whatever it was could wait.

· · · ● ● · ● ● · ·

Meg pressed play on the voice-note and quickly messaged back.

It's not something you can pick up, just tell me how to get hold of her.

When she saw her message stayed unread, she sent another.

You'd better not be coming over here.

She peeped out the window and saw his car park downstairs in the street.

And ... you're here. I guess I should get out of my PJs.

When Dom found out she'd bought the house, he was going to be stinking mad. How was she going to tell him? She'd just managed to slip into a t-shirt and some sweatpants when her doorbell rang with their custom samba tune.

She opened the door for him and he came right in and hugged her. She breathed in the Meg-friendly scent of him and sighed. "Why didn't you read my messages?"

"I was driving over here. I don't do that sort of thing."

Just then, Max came to investigate the newcomer with squeaky meows that made him sound like he was malfunctioning.

Dom sank to the floor cross-legged and waited for the tiny cat to come to him. He let it sniff his finger and sat patiently while it scaled his leg and made its way towards his shirt. It was so small it climbed his shirt without breaking a sweat and settled on his shoulder purring like a motorbike engine.

Dom sat frozen with the kitten perched on his shoulder and Meg turned to mush. "Tea?"

The kitten was rubbing on Dom's chin and he seemed to be feeling as mushy as Meg felt.

"Later is fine, I wouldn't be able to drink now anyway."

Meg sat opposite him, split in two. One side reveled in his company and wished for life to be simple. Surrendering to this moment would have been so easy to do.

The other side was permanently guarded, and with good reason. The guarded side slapped the surrendering side hard in the chops.

"Have you spoken to Gina about what's going on with her body?"

"No, I haven't. There are some things she's really private about and this seems to be one of them." He must have seen the look on her face, he quickly added, "I know it seems urgent, but take it from me—she's been struggling with this for a long, long time."

"I don't get it; you can only be pregnant for nine months. What are you talking about?" she blurted. She really needed to stop doing that.

His face. His face looked like he'd just been told aliens were living in his fridge snacking on his milk.

"Pregnant?" The kitten had curled up on his shoulder.

"Yes, Dom. That can happen when you sleep with someone."

"So many things make sense now." He stroked the tiny kitten's head with a single finger, gently tracing circles between its ears. "This can't be happening."

Meg had wondered how she'd feel in this moment, now she knew it was all glum. The beginning of the end of the friendship. She studied his face which she'd come to know so well and a deep, gut-level, loneliness swelled up inside that she didn't know what to do with.

Dom gently pried the kitten off his shoulder, unhooking its claws from his shirt. "I have to go speak to her, we have to do something about this." He handed the kitten to her, collected his keys and wallet, kissed her once on the forehead, and let himself out.

Meg shoved the ache deep down and let out an *ugh* of frustration. He hadn't told her how to find Ernest's mom, plus now she'd lost him to Gina for good.

This called for backup.

Chapter Thirty-Eight

The House

SANDY AND TALIA MET her at the house. Meg figured if she couldn't get Buntu to the house yet, she might as well get the house ready for Buntu.

Sandy took one look at it and scratched her chin. "Erm. This is it?"

Talia had a hand on her hip and her nose crinkled as if there were an open dustbin nearby. "I dunno, Meg. This is a bit beyond help. It looks like there was a fire through here, too."

Meg had only ever seen the house by the soft light of the moon. Moonlight had a way of hiding flaws, which was likely the explanation as to why so many people fell in love at night.

Daylight, however, was not so kind.

"Come on, girls. It can't be that bad on the inside. Let's go see."

Sandy picked her way down the path, frowning at one of the many weeds growing in between the paving stones as if it had committed a crime. "This is going to take an army. Oh, by the way, Meg, you've sold another photograph. The money should be in your bank by morning."

Meg stopped dead. "How is that possible? I mean, I won't say no. We can use all the extra money to get this place habitable."

Sandy shrugged. "Most were sold on the evening, but I took the few that didn't go to Alison's coffee shop. She hung them all over and they're selling. You should get some more of your photos done, they are rather popular."

"That's crazy." The thought of it made Meg feel weird. It had taken so much nerve to put herself out there at the party, the thought of continually doing it was daunting.

Talia was on her tip-toes peering through the window. "I agree, you have talent. You shouldn't hide it." She squinted through the dirty glass pane. "This room is gorgeous inside. Look—bay windows."

Meg unlocked the front door and waved the ladies inside. "Let's see what we can do with this space. It needs to be as kid-friendly as possible."

Together they walked through the house and Meg found her tummy filling with butterflies all over again, even in the harsh light of day.

Talia stood under the hole in the roof and announced, "I know some people."

Sandy grinned at her, nodding. "Me, too."

· · · · ● · ● · · · ·

Meg lay in bed feeling each aching muscle in her body. The past week had been a whirlwind of work on the house. Between Talia and Sandy's connections, all the major repair work had been seen to. While that was happening, the girls mucked in and cleaned. Alison and Sandy agreed that should their regular jobs not work out, they'd just start up a cleaning service of their own.

The four of them had spent hours trawling the secondhand shops to find beds, couches, and other bits and pieces that would make it more comfy for Buntu and the kids. It was after midnight when they'd finished hanging the last few curtains, and all this made Meg rather fond of her duvet.

Now all that remained was to find Buntu and convince her that the house was hers.

She considered asking Dom again, but she couldn't face the possibility of him asking why. The courage to tell him about the house had long gone and probably wouldn't be back. She shuddered at the thought of how mad he'd be.

Ernest. Now there might be her solution.

· · · · ● · ● · · · ·

He was in his usual spot, though the clothes he wore were clean and his feet had the look of a recent brush with soap and water.

"Ernest, do you remember me?"

He turned, ready to bolt, but squinted at her with the morning sun in his eyes. He nodded once.

"I have a surprise for you and your brothers. Can you take me to your mom?"

He balanced on one leg, rubbing his free foot up and down his calf. She could see him processing the request, weighing it up against bad experiences and warnings from his mom not to trust strangers. He planted both feet squarely, looked her in the eye with a frown and nodded once.

Meg breathed again. One tiny step closer. He took the hand she held out and followed her back to the car.

· · · · ● · ● · · · ·

They pulled up at Dom's apartment building. Meg's heart raced. This was the last place she wanted to be. "Are you sure your mom is here?"

Ernest nodded and her disgust at the man doubled. Getting one girlfriend to move in while the other was having his baby? How did he even look himself in the eye to shave? With a rage-fire in her belly, she now almost hoped he was there for her to confront him.

Almost.

"You've been living here?"

Ernest nodded again, though this time a broad grin split his dark face.

She suddenly went cold. What if Buntu didn't want to leave? Why would she?

· · · · ●· ● · · · ·

Buntu was washing the kitchen floor when Ernest brought Meg inside Dom's apartment. He even had her cleaning for him.

"*Molo.*"

Buntu straightened up and rubbed her lower back. "*Molo sissie*. It's good to see you again."

A thousand words of chit-chat flew through Meg's mind at once, but she ignored them all. "Buntu, do you trust me?"

Without a second's hesitation, Buntu dipped her head. She tapped her chest and tapped Meg's. "You are a good person."

It might be enough. "I have a present for you and your boys. Will you come with me?"

Buntu shut her eyes and went absolutely still. Meg was just beginning to wonder if the tiny woman had fallen asleep standing up straight when she answered, "We will come." She rattled off instructions to Ernest in Xhosa and he ran off to do whatever she'd asked him to.

One surreal car ride with too many of them tucked into her car later, they stood outside the house with Meg's tummy doing somersaults.

She'd rehearsed this moment in her head so many times, but all those practiced speeches melted away into a single hug and a key pressed into Buntu's hand.

"This is for you and your kids. We'll need to do some paperwork so that it's yours forever, but you can live here safely."

Buntu's boys were chatting with each other. They seemed to be trying to figure out what was going on. Ernest patted Isaac on the shoulder and he shushed them all.

Ernest waved a thumb at the place and a single word came out. "Home."

Meg grabbed Buntu's hand and dragged her down the path. The African lady followed with her eyes wide. The garden had been quickly tamed, though it was still quite bare and could do with a lot of TLC.

Buntu unlocked the door at Meg's urging and frowned at her as the door swung back. The boys pushed in without hesitation and ran to explore. Buntu hung back, a deep frown-crease across her forehead.

"Why?"

Meg shrugged. How do you explain a deep desire to live a life that makes a difference? She'd have been feeling freaked out in Buntu's shoes, too.

"Your life matters. These boys matter. They deserve hope." She watched Buntu process her words.

"They deserve hope." Buntu nodded.

"Okay, goody. Come look at this!" Meg's trepidation gave way to excitement. "Come see!"

As they strolled through the house together, deep contentment settled into Meg. This was good and right. Buntu took it all in with quiet dignity, but the packed grocery cupboard was too much. Tears rolled freely and her whole body shook.

· · · · ●·●· · · ·

Dom popped home to check on Buntu and the boys. Living at the studio was wearing on him, but he was no closer to a solution than he'd been before the competition hadn't worked out.

Buntu and the boys were out, which was unusual. She usually messaged him when she was going anywhere. He made a cup of coffee and was dragging a chair onto the balcony to drink it in the fresh air when the message arrived.

***Nkosi*, I don't know how to thank you. B.**

For what? Where are you? He quickly texted back.

A minute later a location arrived.

She was at the house.

·· • •·• • • ··

The house looked so different, he did a double-take to make sure he was in the right place. The sold sign was still on the gate, but the hedge had been trimmed and the lawn mowed.

The broken catch on the front door had been replaced and the knocker that hung in the middle was shiny and new. He tapped twice and waited.

Buntu opened and her face lit up when she saw him. She showed him inside and followed him through the house on quiet feet. All the damaged bits had been restored. The hole in the ceiling was no more. His mind flipped back and forth, trying to make sense of it.

"Buntu, why are you here? I don't understand. You should come back to my house before the owner comes back and kicks you out."

Buntu fished around in her pocket and drew out some folded up papers. She shoved them at Dom. "I won't kick us out. You did this for me. Why are you asking such questions?"

"Who brought you here?" Dom opened up the papers and scanned the contents, growing more puzzled as he read, until he saw the name and signature at the bottom.

Doubt crept into her eyes and Buntu folded in on herself. "Was this not you?"

"Not me, but I know who."

Chapter Thirty-Nine

MEG PULLED UP OUTSIDE Dom's apartment and felt like throwing up. She had to tell him that she was the one who'd bought the house out from under his nose and nipped his high-rise plans in the bud.

It took all her courage to keep heading up the stairs and to not bolt back down to the safety of her car.

He answered her knock with a half-full bag in his hand. "Meg, it's you." He stood frozen in the doorway and Meg wanted nothing more than to use that as an excuse for bolting. *He just wouldn't let me in, what was I supposed to do about that?*

As if reading her mind, Dom stood back and waved her inside.

"I'm sorry for barging in, I need to talk to you."

"I've been wanting to talk to you, too. I'm glad you came. Something to drink?"

"No, I'm good, thanks." Meg imagined being halfway through a cup of tea with him when he found at what she'd done. Would she have to leave it half-drunk? Or keep sipping while he raged? Better not to.

She followed him into the living room and sat down on a single-seater. Right in front of her, almost life-size, was the block-mounted photo of her twirling in the moonlight through the hole in the roof of the house.

It was a gorgeous photo, anonymous enough that someone who hadn't been there wouldn't be able to say it was her.

Dom came in with some tea for her in spite of her saying no. She took it from him and sipped gratefully, feeling the sting of the heat all the way down her throat.

"Where did you get that?" Her eyes flicked to the photograph.

· · · • · • • · · ·

Aaah, shoot. He'd forgotten to take the photo down, now it was going to be twenty questions.

"I fell in love with ..." *You, Meg. I fell in love with you.* "... the picture. There's something magical about knowing it was in my house. I saw it at your party and I thought about it for a while. But I had to get it."

"Your house. Dom, I need to speak to you about the house."

"And I need to tell you about Project Phoenix. What do you know about the house?"

Meg braced herself. "How did the auction go?"

Dom shrugged. "I lost the bid to an old lady. I had such big plans for the place and I had to let them all go."

Meg sensed an openness about him that wasn't there before. "Why was the place so special to you?"

Dom's smile was whimsical. "I grew up there."

Meg nearly choked on her sip of tea. He was going to build a sky-scraper over his old home. "You must have some awful memories of the place."

"My parents are stuck in their ways and stubborn enough to make me cry, but they aren't bad people. Dumisani was my best friend at school and I brought him home to play. This was thick in the middle of the *Apartheid* era. They didn't like me having an African boy for a friend but they tolerated it. He came over a few times and each time, they would moan about him for hours after he'd left. On the day of the fire, he'd been over to play, but he left long before the fire started. I think the gardener started it by accident with a stray cigarette butt. To them, it was the excuse they'd been waiting for. They blamed Dumi and forbade me from seeing him again. They wouldn't listen to anything I tried to tell them. Shortly after the fire, we moved out but I kept going back. It stood empty all these years and I've wanted nothing more than to buy the house off them, but they wouldn't hear of it. The auction was my last hope."

Dom fell quiet and his eyes lost focus. "Me and Dumi, we kept in touch secretly all through high school and studying. I remember the night he met Buntu. He came to see me in my dorm and he couldn't sleep. He kept going on and on about her and I knew they were meant for each other. I was best man at their wedding."

"What happened?"

"He was working as a taxi driver between jobs. Do you remember a few years back when the taxi bosses got territorial and things turned violent?"

"The media dubbed it taxi wars. I remember. It was awful."

"It was a full-on bloodbath. Dumi was killed in one of those skirmishes. I was with him in the hospital when he passed and I swore to him I would take care of his family. We suspect the same rival taxi group started the fire at Buntu's home out of sheer spite. We have no way to prove it though."

"So are you and Buntu, er ... involved?"

"If you're asking if I love her, I do. She's been like a sister to me."

Meg absorbed that word. Sister. She allowed it to seep into her and reshape facts. It brought her a sneaky sliver of delight. She quickly changed the subject. "So Project Phoenix is what?"

"Project Phoenix was all about getting that house back."

"So you want the property so that you can put up a sky-scraper?"

Dom frowned at the girl as if her head had been baking in the sun for too long. "What did you want to tell me about the house?"

"The old lady who bid against you? That was me."

Chapter-Forty

MEG PACKED AWAY THE last few dry dishes in her kitchen. Dom had taken the news of her subterfuge quite well, all things considered. Although to be fair, she'd told him and bolted. Left him standing with his mouth gaping like a gold-fish. It wasn't her fault that she wasn't born with bravery in her genes.

She swept the floor and her thoughts tumbled around like dust bunnies. Then there was the whole thing of her photo hanging in Dom's house. Not just a photo she'd taken, but a photo of *her*. Meg couldn't even remember seeing that photo among those she'd selected for block mounting. Curiosity was eating her alive; how much had he paid for it? He was probably one of the one hundred rand donations that had come in.

She shot Sandy a quick text.

Apparently Dom bought one of my pics (the girl danc-ing in moonlight). Do you know what he paid for it?

Sandy was online as Meg clicked send and the message delivered immediately.

The sale of that one brought in 15K.

Shock spiked through Meg, zig-zagging through her in hot and cold flashes.

· · · ● · ● · · ·

The last bit of sorting after a big event always seemed to take the most effort. Meg had packets of things arranged all down her hallway to go back to people. Fairy lights by the ton from Vashti. Meg still hadn't figured out why anyone would need that number of fairy lights but they'd worked beautifully for her party, so she wasn't complaining.

She had Sandy's event toolkit that had been inadvertently stowed in her car instead of Sandy's and needed to go back.

The one thing that simply had to go back today was an enormous disco ball that she'd borrowed from Reg. It seemed like the most fragile thing in her hallway and for this reason alone, had to be returned immediately.

It was tucked up inside a padded bag that Meg only just managed to carry all the way down to the car. Once it was safely buckled in, she took a slow, careful drive to Reg's flat. His car was parked downstairs in its usual spot and it was only when she saw it that she realized it would have been a good idea to let him know she was coming over.

Too late now.

She used the elevator to get up to his floor, resting the bag full of mirror ball at her feet as often as she could. The elevator made it all the way up and Meg was happy to see that the door to Reg's flat stood open. With no free hand to ring the doorbell, she let herself in.

She stowed the bag at the entrance and walked into the living room, about to shout out her name, but there in the middle of the room stood Reg and Gina deeply involved in a smooch.

"What ..."

The two flew apart and Gina turned an instant shade of red, hid behind her hand, muttering under her breath.

Reg grinned at Meg and waved. "Hey, Meg."

Heat flashed through Meg. "Sorry, the door was open."

Gina smacked Reg's belly with the back of her hand. "You left the door open. What is wrong with you?"

Reg took it in his stride, gently holding her hand in his and focusing on Meg. "Can I offer you something to drink?"

Meg's throat pinched tight. "Does Dom know about all this?"

Reg squirmed. "He's a bit weird about this sort of thing, so we have kept a low profile."

"He's a bit weird about being cheated on. It would be *weird* if he weren't." Meg eyeballed Gina's belly which was clearly growing. "And what about the baby?"

Reg tipped his head, looking puzzled. "What's this now?"

Gina rolled her eyes and huffed. It all looked a bit silly on someone with such a red face. "Will you please shut up?"

Reg was still holding Gina's hand, he tapped it a few times. "What baby?"

"I'm pregnant. I haven't decided what to do about it just yet." She glared at Meg. "There, are you happy now?"

Reg's face split in a broad grin. "We're having a baby?"

Meg's insides churned. One small detail sat unmentioned like an ignored crumb on the couch. *Don't get involved, Meg. It's none of your business.* "It's Dom's baby. You need to know that."

"You slept with Dom?" Reg's face wrinkled up. "You don't even like him."

Gina growled in frustration and stamped her small foot. She had no shoes on, so it was completely unimpressive. "No, I didn't. Meg, here, is delusional."

Reg sighed, relieved. "Oh good, because that would be a bit awkward."

This was no longer one crumb. Somebody had tipped the cookie jar. "I'm not delusional. All along you've been very clear that Dom was off limits because he is yours."

"You probably won't believe it, but there's never been anything between Dom and me. We hide us from him. We have our reasons."

Reg stuck up his hand. "Er, one reason actually. Gina here doesn't think it's a good idea to tell him. Me, I have my own opinion." He held up his hands, declaring the peace. "Just saying."

Gina huffed. "I'm right and you know it. He would hound us about the fact that we are living together. We'd never hear the end of it."

Meg eyed them both, trying to figure out if they were being honest. "You said reasons. That's one."

Gina's mouth drew tight. "The whole Rising Stars thing."

Reg cringed. "That was an ugly one. Dom was dating his partner and we were set to take part in a formation team competition, but he did something to annoy her and she left. Flat-out refused to participate. Unfortunately at that stage, I didn't have a broken leg so there wasn't a back-up plan like this time."

Gina frowned at him, but Meg couldn't help grinning.

"Gina has been pretty acid with him since then about dating partners and here we are, getting all cozy. It is quite hypocritical, actually."

"Except for the fact that I'm not a flighty young thing that's going to take off because you say something I don't like. You say things I don't like a hundred times a day and here I am."

"Truly amazing," said Reg, looking pleased.

Meg sifted through what they'd said, weighed it all up.

Gina huffed. "You were new, gorgeous, and had the potential to out-dance me. What would you do in my shoes?" Gina faced Meg, bare-foot and rumpled.

Reg kissed her temple. "*You're* gorgeous, babe."

Meg squinted at Gina (who was swatting at Reg) and tried to figure out if she were being honest. "You think I'm gorgeous?"

Gina rolled her eyes. "I liked being the star and I was ready to throw anything at you to get you to back off."

"Even to the point of ruining Dom's chances at winning?" asked Meg.

"He's been going on about Project Phoenix for ages now. This competition was another stab at supposedly raising the money he needs for that. Trust me, that boy has pots of money. He doesn't need a silly dance competition to solve his problems. I'm not unpacking all that for you, you need to get it from him."

"And the baby?"

Reg nodded. "Yeah, I wanna know about the baby, too."

Gina pressed her hands into her lower back. "Reg, make us some tea. I need to get off my feet."

"He needs to hear this. You've been lying to him." Meg resisted crossing her arms.

"Fine, whatever. I don't care. Both of you sit down and hear me out." Gina waved them both towards a sofa, but Reg kissed her cheek and went to the kitchen.

Their apartment was laid out as an open plan and the sounds of the kettle and clink of cups filtered through. Reg whistled as he took milk out of the fridge. "I can hear you from here, carry on."

Gina checked to see if he was looking and leaned in close, whispering furiously, "He didn't know about this"—she waved over her belly—"because I don't know if I'm keeping it."

Reg called out from the kitchen, "We're keeping it. I want to call him Olly."

Gina rolled her eyes, but something softened in the set of her shoulders that made Meg's heart twinge. The security of being loved so completely changed one.

Gina dropped onto the couch next to Meg. "I hate the name Olly."

"But you love Reg."

"I do."

The softness was back, a visible, tangible thing that fascinated Meg.

Chapter Forty-One

B-Day

DOM RANG THE SAMBA doorbell and waited for the birthday girl to open up. The dance team dancers were all waiting at Alison's coffee shop ready to surprise her. It was Dom's job to get her there.

He hadn't quite nailed a strategy when she opened up the door. She wore a white broderie anglaise shift dress with bows for straps on top of her shoulders.

"Oh, it's you."

He couldn't read her expression. Or maybe he wasn't ready to admit that she wasn't happy to see him.

"Meg, please come with me. It's about Ernest." He hoped she wouldn't ask, because he hadn't thought it all through.

"Is he okay? What's going on?"

"Can you come? I'll explain in the car."

Meg shut her eyes and rested her forehead on the door. When she looked up, her eyes were sadder than he'd ever seen before. "I'm so sorry, Dom. I really can't."

"But ..."

"I'm truly sorry."

And with that, she shut the door in his face.

He messaged the *Meg's Party* group he'd created.

She's not budging. Plan B everybody.

Cliff is typing ...

Righto, be there shortly.

Dom hung around at the bottom of the stairs to Meg's apartment. In his mind, her party hadn't really counted as a true party. It had accomplished the goal that she'd set for it—buying the house for Buntu. He still couldn't get over it.

But a celebration with a group of people that you hardly knew didn't really hit the spot in Dom's book. Also he needed an excuse to see her again.

He led the way upstairs with the dancers trailing behind him. Only when he got to the top of the stairs did it occur to him that Chad might be there. Too late to worry about that now.

Tammy held the cake that Alison had made especially at the coffee shop, an enormous blueberry cheesecake concoction.

They rang the doorbell and the rhythm of samba filled the air. Matt threw him a puzzled look and he was about to explain it all when Meg opened the door with a frown.

"I'm sorry, I told you I can't ..."

They all yelled surprise and Meg looked ready to faint.

"Can we come in, please? Even if it's just for a few minutes."

Meg stood back with eyes that looked suspiciously teary. She waved them in and they trooped in like a rent-a-party. Meg definitely looked sad.

They'd brought everything that had been set up in the coffee shop—a happy birthday banner, the cake, candles, snacks. They moved into the living room to set it all up while Dom steered Meg to the kitchen.

Dom followed her. "Are you okay?"

Meg shook her head and waved at the bowl where Ebb should have been. It was empty.

"Meg, I'm so sorry." He took her and drew her close and she sobbed. Chad should have been there to make her feel better. If that man wasn't careful, Dom fully intended to swoop in and steal Meg out from under his nose.

"On my birthday. There should be a law against that."

He stroked her hair and wished he could take her pain. "There should be a law. That's not right." He kept whispering *I'm sorry* into her hair over and over.

"I knew he wouldn't be around forever, but I just thought
..."

"I know. He's in a better place now." Did that really just come out of his mouth?

"Did you honestly just say that?"

"It seemed like a good idea at the time." Dom shrugged and hugged her gently. "Come on, you have to blow out candles."

· · • • • • • • · ·

Meg followed him through to the living room and into the hugs of the rest of the group. Alison had Max on her lap and was cooing over him.

Dom quieted them down. "Meg's goldfish is no longer with us. She's a bit sad."

Talia pushed through the others to get to Meg and wrapped her tanned arms around her. "You were such a great mom to him while he was here." Her hair smelled of flowers and made Meg's nose itch despite the antihistamine she'd taken to be around Max.

Meg was passed around the room, getting love and hugs from each one as she passed. Someone had fetched Mrs. O'Riley from next door and she stood among the others looking a bit spare but happy, nonetheless. She gave Meg a quick lavender-scented hug and shoved a small packet of home-baked shortbread into her hands.

Sandy and Xan were hiding out in a corner with a basket full of pampering goodies. "Happy birthday, dear girl."

"No, Sandy. My party was my present, you didn't have to."

"Oh, hush. You're the only friend who puts up with all my nonsense. Don't even think about it."

The doorbell rang and Dom went to answer it. He came back with Vashti and Chad in tow. The two were holding hands and Chad's usual egotistical swagger seemed to be toned down by a shade.

"Vashti, Chad. How are things going?" Meg's focus slid off Chad and homed in on Vashti. The girl was glowing and Chad seemed to hang on her every word.

"A better question is, how are you?" Vashti eyebrowed towards Dom and she winked.

Meg shrugged. Gina and Buntu were no longer between them, but it wasn't as simple as that.

"Can we chat in the kitchen? It won't take long," Chad asked.

Meg saw him looking at the empty fishbowl as they walked in and she shoved a finger under his nose. "Don't say a word."

"But—"

"Not a word about my fish."

Chad held a finger to his mouth. "I just wanted to check if you're okay with me and Vashti."

"You're asking for my opinion? Are you feeling sick?"

"C'mon, Meg. I know what we had hasn't always been easy."

"And?"

"And I know that what we had wasn't always good for us, but it feels different with Ti."

Meg saw in him the closest thing to vulnerability she'd ever seen. "If you hurt her ..."

Chad shook his head. "Never intentionally." He twiddled his thumbs—something Meg had never seen before. "You know, Meg, what you said that day about us, about that thing that happened ... you were right."

"I know. You don't have to say anything else."

"I still think you're giving up one of the best things that ever happened to you, but, you know ..."

Meg felt hot indignation rise until she saw the corners of his mouth lifting. "You're making a joke. That's a first."

"Yeah, I'm funny now. Ask Ti."

· · • • • · • · • · ·

Dom stood outside the kitchen trying to keep it together. The last obstacle holding him back from pursuing Meg had just been removed.

· · • • • · • · • · ·

Reg and Gina were the last to leave. He openly doted on her now, and she made a half-hearted attempt to keep up the appearance of being annoyed, though the hand that rested on her belly sported a sparkly ring on a tell-tale finger.

Meg waved them all off feeling better than when they'd arrived. Dom was stacking dishes into the dishwasher and Meg's belly fluttered at the sight of him.

"Gina is softening. It's sweet."

Dom wiggled a plate into the dishwasher even though Meg doubted there was any room left. The man had skills.

"I can't believe I didn't see what was going on. But then again,"—his gaze slid her way—"I did have a lot on my mind." He smiled as he said it.

"And you didn't pick up that she was pregnant?"

Dom set the timer and shut the dishwasher. "I've known Gina a long time. She's had many, many issues over the years.

Eating disorders, mental struggles. I'm not going to go into it all, but it's not the first time her weight has fluctuated drastically. Or that she's fainted. Or thrown-up, for that matter."

"But still."

"You're right, I should probably have figured it out. You thought it was my baby?"

"She gave me every reason to."

"Yeah, but me? You thought that of me?"

"You're a handsome guy. How was I supposed to know?" said Meg, trying not to laugh.

"You think I'm handsome?" Dom's eyebrows flicked up and down as he slid across the room in his most come-hither manner, making Meg screech and run.

"Oh, wait! I still have a present for you." He fetched a present bag from the hallway, hauled her back to the kitchen, and handed it over.

Meg reached into the bag and her insides deflated. "A bonsai. How quaint." This man knew nothing about her. Absolutely nothing.

"Do you like it?" He looked so chuffed with himself.

Meg didn't have the heart to be a downer, but she couldn't lie, so she settled for avoiding eye contact and nodding.

"Oh, wait! That's only half the present." He held out a hand. "Come. Bring it with you."

They drove out of town and turned onto the road that led to Buntu's new home. Meg panicked when she realized that they'd be seeing Buntu's home together for the first time.

Dom led her through the gate and to a bare patch in the front yard. There was a hole dug, ready and waiting. "Here is where you set that little guy free."

"Wait, I don't understand."

Dom took the little bonsai out of the present bag and held it up to the light. Sunlight glimmered through the leaves. "This little thing has been clipped and contained long enough. It's time to let it grow wild and free. Don't you agree?"

Hot tears pricked at her eyelids. He got it. He understood. Meg hugged him hard. He didn't let go as the hug ended, but kept an arm around her shoulders.

"I'm sorry about your apartment block. I know this isn't what you intended."

He pulled her so close she felt his heart speed up through the fabric of his t-shirt.

"Meg, I don't know where you got the high-rise idea from. All I ever wanted is exactly what you've done—a home for my best friend's family as I promised."

"There were newspaper clippings ..." Meg realized that she'd just admitted to breaking in and stealing her file. "Whoops."

Dom laughed. "So that *was* you. You could have asked, you know. I would have told you."

She back-handed his belly. "I did ask and you wouldn't tell me anything!"

He grabbed her hand and chuckled. "I can't actually argue. I didn't know if it would all make sense to you. But now? This is so much beyond what I ever imagined. You've no idea. Do you know about the myth of the phoenix, the fire bird?" He watched her as she shrugged. "It's just a myth, but I like it. A phoenix dies by going up in flames, but then out of the ashes, a new phoenix is born. Our home nearly burned down, but out of the ashes of suffering, Buntu and her boys have a new life."

"Destruction turned on its head. Full circle."

"Exactly. And you, dear girl, made it happen."

"So are you sure you and Buntu don't want to,"—she struggled over the words and wiggled her fingers to get her point across—"get together?"

"I love her. I do. But not like that. I will, however, always look out for her and all the kids she's looking after." He frowned at her with his nose all crinkled. "But then, apparently so will you. I still can't believe you pulled this off." He stared at the house with a grin on his face before his attention snapped back to Meg. "What about you and Chad?"

"That mess is mostly detangled. Tragedy glued us together and we brought out the worst in each other for far too many years. We had an honest conversation though, and I think he *heard* me. That's nothing short of a miracle, believe me. He and Vashti seem to be getting along."

"Does that worry you?"

"Vashti is a lot tougher than me, he won't get away with treating her the way he treated me. I think she'll be good for him." Chad and Vashti drifted from her thoughts as she realized Dom's arm hadn't moved. In fact, he stood so close, his breath warmed her cheek. If she tilted her head ... Meg felt heat wash through her.

She stretched up quickly to take the plant from him and hunkered down to hide her blush. Tapping the outside of the pot, she removed it and loosened the potting soil around the small tree's roots before placing it in the hole and scooping the soil back in.

Dom got down on the ground with her and they patted the soil into place around the stunted stem. Ernest ran out of the house with a watering can and hugged Meg before watering the plant, while Buntu watched from where she leaned on the doorframe.

Dom wiped the dirt off his hands on the back of his jeans before he helped her up. He kept her hand in his and rubbed Ernest's close-cropped head with his other hand.

Ernest ducked out and skipped-ran to the house. "Come see!"

"So, *Meg*nificent ..." He drew her towards the house. "Do you want to show me your handiwork?"

Chapter Forty-Two

THE SUN WAS RISING on the morning after her big-O birthday. Tattered clouds skidded across the lazy sky, each one turned fiery orange as they caught newborn sunrays.

Meg sat cross-legged on the cold stone of the high cliffs of Morgan Bay. Waves crashed against the rocks far beneath her, filling the air with tiny drops of moisture that made rainbows in the light.

She held her list in her hands, as flimsy as the clouds.

Dom shivered and inched closer. "I should have brought a hoodie."

She wriggled back to nestle against him. She could feel the heat from his skin through her shorts. "Are you getting soft in your old age?"

"Pfft, I'm not the one who has just clocked over a big-O birthday." He leaned across her to tap the List. "How's it looking? Did you manage?"

"That was totally an excuse to put your arm around me."

"Who me?" Dom looked suitably mortified. "Oh, I don't need an excuse." With that, he wrapped both arms around her and cuddled her close. "Besides, this is not about me, this is about you. You and your list. Stop changing the subject."

Meg surrendered to the heady feelings that swirled through her when this man was close. "Okay, then. Here we go. Do something brave, do something kind, do something selfless, break a never, stop an always. Figure out God."

"Breaking in to my studio, that was brave."

"You're never going to let me forget that one, are you?"

Dom picked up a pebble and tossed it over the edge. "Let's just say our grandkids will be telling their friends the story." He snorted at his own joke, but then grew quiet. "Seriously though, in this short time we've know each other, you have nailed every one of those many times over. In fact, I think you are missing the point entirely."

"Excuse me?"

"This list is all about doing something once. But here's the thing, Meg: I've come to know that these are *who you are*." He kissed the frown between her brows. "You are brave, you are kind, and selfless. You've done nothing but push your own boundaries since I met you and you said no to something that would have destroyed you if you hadn't. This isn't about what you have or haven't done. Meg, it's who you are."

"You're not wrong, Mr. Kingston." With a quick rip, she tore the top of her list free and let it float off in the breeze. A gust of wind took the strip of paper and it plummeted down towards the crashing waves. Only one remained. Figure Out God.

She tapped the last line. "This one. This one is tricky."

Dom leaned in close and kissed her cheek. "Oh, I dunno. You've taught me many things about Him."

"Oh, please. What?" Meg rolled the edges of the last bit of paper shreds between her fingers.

"I always thought that when He gave me a promise, it was up to me to make it happen."

"Like Phoenix."

"Correct. But when you got involved, I realized miracles and promises are His territory, not mine. My job is to believe and watch Him work." He hugged her close. "Obviously we do the bits He gives us to, but the bigger picture? It's all Him. What about you?"

Meg fiddled with what was left of the List. "I used to think I had Him all figured out. He was the mean one who set you up to fail. The one who stood with arms crossed while you floundered."

"And now?"

"Now ... I know He can't be figured out. He's so far beyond what our minds can grasp. But what I do know, is that He's good. Whether it looks like He's bailed on the disaster that is my life, or not—He won't leave. He's altogether too good. Here's the clincher—I will probably never understand what He's up to."

Meg breathed in the salty air, felt the warmth of Dom's arms and the rising sun on her face, and knew she could trust him. And Him.

"Uh-oh. So does that mean you're leaving something on your list *un*ticked?"

"I guess it does."

"You failed."

Meg shrugged, closed her eyes and rested against him. Her head fit perfectly into the hollow of his shoulder, much like it was made to. "I did."

"How does that make you feel?" His voice was husky in her ear and sent a shiver through her that had nothing to do with how numb her rear was from the cold rock.

She let the last strip of the List go. The wind took it and billowed it up so high, she had to squint to see it and then it was gone.

A failure; a crumb on the couch.

And yet failure had never felt this right before.

"I am perfectly okay with that."

Epilogue

A TINY NIGGLE HAD been bothering Meg all day. Like a mosquito at midnight, it went quiet whenever she tried to catch it. It pricked at her subconscious again now, as she glided down the aisle to where Dom waited at the end.

It was like a sharp pebble in her shoe on an otherwise perfect day.

Sandy had outdone herself. Bunches of wild cosmos caught up in translucent organza bows adorned the ends of each pew. Billowy silk draping framed tall windows that let in the golden glow of the setting sun.

Xan walked down the aisle in front of Meg. He carried the rings tied to a white satin pillow and frowned at it so hard, she thought he might burn holes through the fabric. He took his job as *ring-bearer* most seriously. Meg suspected Sandy had finally relented and read *Lord of the Rings* with him which would explain his fierce determination to live up to his title.

Dom waited for her at the end of the aisle, looking misty-eyed and beaming.

The day had come at last.

Dom's family sat together, all smiles. Meg had finally replaced Gina as mom's favorite and Dom's dad couldn't get enough of the story of how Meg had outbid Dom to buy their old house.

Buntu and all her boys (there were over thirteen of them now) sat together all clean and smart for the occasion. Vashti and Chad sat close to the front, holding hands and whispering to each other.

The dance team took up a row all by themselves. Talia held a hand to her chest as if her heart may well stop beating and Matt stood next her, patting her back in an effort to contain his own emotions. Tammy and Alison dabbed at their eyes as Meg walked past. Gina and Reg stood on the far end of a pew with a stroller parked neatly next to them. Reg flashed Meg a big grin, but Gina barely looked up. She cradled their baby in her arms awkwardly and looked flustered even though Olly was fast asleep and not bothering anybody.

There it was again, a nagging suspicion that Meg was missing something crucial.

Underwear? Check.

Dom shifted from one foot to the other, like the floor was cooking his toes. She reached the end of the aisle as the song finished. Dom reached for her hand and it hit her …

"Dearly beloved, we are gathered here today to unite—"

Meg coughed and stuck her hand in the air. The minister glared at her for a split second before regaining his composure. "Er, yes?"

Heat flooded through Meg. Even her neck was on fire. "I just need to have a word with"—she pointed at Dom—"if you don't mind. It won't take long."

Dom took her cold hands in his and warmth seeped into her. "What's going on?"

Meg cleared her throat and leaned close to his ear to whisper, "I need to ask you something."

Dom frowned at the small church packed with people. "And it can't wait?"

Meg grabbed his arm and pulled him down the aisle towards the vestry. She pulled the door shut behind them and spun around to face him, nearly bouncing off his chest in the small space.

"You look beautiful, my Meg."

She frowned at him. "Focus, Dom. We're not here for all that."

Her hair was swept up and clipped with sparkling diamante clips and Dom curled a lock of her hair around his finger and stared at it as if it was the most beautiful thing he'd ever seen.

Meg pulled her hair away and grabbed his cheeks between her palms. "I need to know something and you'd better tell me."

Dom had the goofiest grin on his face and Meg hoped she could get something serious out of him.

"Anything."

"You had a folder of me in your desk drawer. You even had my photo clipped on the front."

He snapped out of goofy and took the tiniest step back. "And?"

"You didn't have a photo of anybody else. Well, Gina obviously. But she's staff. Of all the other dancers, it was just me with a photo. I also don't understand what the point of the folder was and why there were newspaper clippings and ..."—she bit her lip—"I feel like you're hiding something from me."

Dom straightened up and fiddled with the neck of his shirt. "The picture of you was just for me to stare at. I've been smitten since day one." He cleared his throat. "But here's where it gets bad. You haven't seen the actual contents of the folder."

Tiny hairs stood up all across her scalp. "What are you saying?"

Dom fished around in his pocket. "I was going to do this later, but I think now might be more appropriate." He held a gift in his hands, wrapped in silver and tied with a ribbon that matched her dancing outfit.

"Your folder started out as if you were just another potential dance team member, but then God started highlighting you. He began showing me how important you were and I didn't know what He was on about so I just collected everything and hoped it would all make sense later. And look at us now."

"But what else was in there that I supposedly haven't seen?" Meg's heart was pounding. How do you prepare for the carpet to be pulled out from under you?

Dom fidgeted. "This is a little embarrassing for me, but here you go." He put the present into her hands.

Meg's hands shook so hard, she removed the bow and nearly dropped it. Dom held the gift for her and together they peeled off the wrapping.

It was a white notebook with a single feather on the front.

"Open it." Dom's ears were red again.

Meg felt like she was stepping off a cliff. The first page was simply titled "Promises for Meg," handwritten in Dom's slanted style. The rest of the book was filled with page after page of meticulously hand-written Bible verses.

Dom's ears were practically glowing. "I've been praying them over you since we met, adding to the list as I went along."

Meg's eyes blurred. "You've been talking to God about me?"

"Oh, yes. We've had some fabulous conversations about you. Is that weird?"

"A little." Meg's mind flew, filtering the last few months through this new information.

Dom took the book. "Look, this is my favorite. Psalm eighteen, verse nineteen." He flipped to a page and shoved it back at her.

Meg read it and thought her legs might fail. "He brought me out into a spacious place; he rescued me because he delighted in me." She tapped the page. "No more bonsai?"

Dom grinned and there were tears in his eyes, too. "Meg Davies, your bonsai days are officially over." He drew her to his chest and hugged her and it felt like coming home. "Now please can we go do something about that surname of yours?"

He took her hand and led her out of the tiny room, out of a tiny life and into everything that was on God's heavenly list for her.

THE END

Glossary

Here are some of the 'South Africanisms' used in Cake List:

biltong

Lean meat which is salted and dried in strips.

boetie

Informally used in conversation to mean: buddy, pal. Traditionally *boetie* is an Afrikaans word meaning brother.

doek

A square of cloth worn mainly by African woman to cover the head.

jersey

Jumper, sweater

molo

Used when greeting a single person, hello

rooibos

An infusion of leaves of the *rooibos* plant drunk as tea, affectionately referred to as 'bush tea'.

Acknowledgements

Rob

My alpha reader extraordinaire!

If I could pay you what your feedback is worth,

you could retire comfortably tomorrow.

Paula

My eagle-eyed friend, who knows more than I ever will.

You are a gift to me, I am more grateful than I have words to

express. Working with you is both humbling and delightful.

Marion

You share your vast expertise so freely and made

the impossible, possible for me.

Shirley

You are a constant source of encouragement to me.

I'm so grateful that our paths crossed!

About the Author

Dianne J. Wilson writes across genres including women's fiction, humor, romantic suspense, and YA fantasy.

Weaving Invisible into words, she explores spiritual truth, woven through ordinary life with equal dashes of breathless adventure, delicious romance and tongue-in-cheek humor, all soaked in God's Grace.

Her early books were written in stolen moments, usually in the back seat of her tiny car (see the pic for proof). Then she graduated to a couch or the bed. Now, at last, she has a desk of her own that she occasionally has to share with a cat or two.

Her home is in Makhanda, a South African university town, where she lives with her hubby and three daughters who all take turns at being home.

Her love-language is tea and taking long drives to listen to new songs with her girls. When she's not stuck in her car writing, you can find her feeding all the hungry people in her house who gaze at her expectantly around mealtimes.

Please visit Dianne's website for more of her books:

www.diannejwilson.com

Find Dianne on:

Amazon | BookBub | Instagram | Facebook | Goodreads

Also by Dianne J. Wilson

CONTEMPORARY ROMANCE & MYSTERY
feel-good, faith-filled and funny

THE LIST BOOKS
The Cake List
The Never List
The Paper List

RIVER VALLEY ROMANCE
Inheriting Ubomi
Running Ubomi
Raising Ubomi (releasing 2024)

ROMANTIC SUSPENSE

romance on the run ... suspense, mystery and faith

SUNSHINE COAST MYSTERIES

Shackles

Undertow (releasing 2023)

STAND ALONE

Finding Mia

YA URBAN FANTASY

What if we could see into the spiritual realm?

THE SPIRIT WALKER TRILOGY

Affinity

Resonance

Cadence

DEVOTIONAL

for when you need a hug from Heaven

When God's Dreams Meet Your Reality
(previously released as 'Messy Life')

In All Things - 13 Weeks of Devotions from Africa
(11 Author Collaboration)

PURCHASE LINK TO ALL TITLES

A Gift For You

Thank you for reading The Cake List! I hope you enjoyed it. May you discover more and more joy in adventuring with the God who loves you so much!

Here's a little gift for you...

Claim your free quick-read when you sign up for my newsletter at www.diannejwilson.com.

The Hairy Godfather

Because sometimes love needs a little help.

Samantha loves Max. He's finally noticed her and invited her to a ball. But what's a jeans-and-t-shirt girl with zero budget going to do when fairy godmothers don't exist?

The Never List Excerpt

A grieving daughter, her ex-best friend & a truckload of secrets

THE LIST BOOKS
~ 2 ~

DIANNE J. WILSON

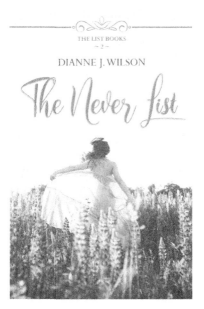

Chapter One

There's no manual on losing your mom with a handy chapter on dealing with your departed mom's secrets.

Isla-Skye Whittaker had the worst timing in the world. She stared at the slim, white, laptop she'd found in the linen chest at the end of Mom's bed. She'd been looking for blankets to give to charity and instead, she'd found this.

Naughty lingerie couldn't have surprised her more. It made her doubt everything she thought she knew about Mom.

Her dear old mom wouldn't even get a touch-screen cell phone. She needed buttons and would take five minutes to carefully tap out a five-word message, using one finger and muttering to herself the whole way through. How would she have coped with this?

If Isla had found this a week ago, she could have asked her technophobe mom. But the funeral was yesterday and there was no hotline to heaven that you could use to ask awkward questions.

Honestly, though, would Mom even have told her if she'd asked?

The laptop sat smugly on the rose-patterned duvet now, hugging its secrets close and mocking her ignorance. It defied all three of the *nevers* Isla chose to live by.

"Never surprise me, never keep secrets, and never have expectations. Really, Mom. This secret of yours is quite a surprise, a bit of a double whammy."

Expectations? That was all on Isla herself. She'd expected Mom to be her usual, predictable self. Who would have thought that would have been a colossal mistake?

Isla knew about the half-knitted jersey-carcass in the cupboard. Isla had been skeptical when Mom had come home from shopping with a packet of wool, a set of size 4.5mm knitting needles, and a pattern. But Mom had insisted that she would finish it. Within a few days, she'd quietly stashed it at the back of her cupboard behind her undies and never mentioned it again.

Isla knew about the stalled mosaic bird bath that cluttered up the dining room table. It had sat untouched throughout Mom's illness that dragged on for months, all twenty-four of them.

This laptop, though. This was a complete surprise and it made Isla doubt everything.

Isla fiddled with the nebulizer cable that dangled from the machine on Mom's bedside table and dialed her big brother. Maybe Craig would know about the laptop. Maybe he'd bought it for Mom.

With four small people under the age of eight, he worked hard at the office to provide, and hard at home to keep his Jasmine sane. He didn't always have the luxury of time to chat with his baby sister but—knowing him—he would make time for her right now. Yep, she was right—he picked up after one ring.

"Mom has a laptop." She spat out the words as if they tasted bad.

"Hey, Squishy, nice to hear from you. Repeat that, I don't think I heard you right?"

"It's not even an old-fashioned thing." Isla poked at it much like you would an animal to see if it were dead or sleeping. "It's all sleek, silver, and white. Did you buy it for her?"

"I'm innocent. What's on it?" Craig sounded remarkably unfazed by this news.

"I haven't looked. Do you think I should? This kind of thing is private. You shouldn't really go poking around on someone else's laptop."

"Isles, Ma is probably having a personal tour of Heaven right now by the Archangel Gabriel himself. I don't think she'd mind if you took a look."

"Well, it's snooping and it still feels wrong. I didn't mean to find the stupid thing anyway, I was just sorting blankets."

"Exactly. You're doing nothing wrong. Just open it up and see. It might not even be hers. You'll only know when you investigate."

Isla could hear two kids fighting in the background, some *uber*-happy nursery rhyme playing (probably on repeat), and Jasmine telling the dog off for barking. Happy chaos.

"But that's even more reason not to go snooping. I'm not going to do it."

"Drat, my small person is yelling from the bath. I'd better go see what Madi-Pops is up to. Be brave Isla-Skye. Check out the laptop. Do it. Chat later!"

He hung up to go save Madison from the bath, or the bath from Madison. With that three-year-old live-wire, it could go either way. The silence seemed tripled after getting an earful of the family noise at Craig's house. It made her brain hurt and stabbed her heart a little too.

She carried the laptop through to her bedroom and avoided the living room with the recliner they'd bought for Mom thinking it would be more comfortable for her cancer-riddled, aching, body. She'd never sat in it once. Stubborn, stubborn woman.

Being reminded of Mom's stubbornness provoked a miniature rebellion in Isla. She settled on her bed, opened the laptop, and turned it on.

It hummed and lit up and Isla watched a blue circle turning on the screen. This was all so out of character for Mom that it made her heart flutter.

Dad had died when Isla was barely a teenager. He'd left behind dotted memories of the few times he'd actually been home, an investment that paid enough each month that Mom didn't have to work, but little else.

Mom had been a steady ship for them since: always a home-body, content to be around her family and make sure they all ate their greens. Her world was small and colorless.

In short, a lifestyle that Isla wanted to avoid more than a vegan dodged a pork chop.

The circling stopped and the screen blipped to life and Isla stared at herself. The background was a photo of her and Craig taken at Christmas the year before he got married. They were both tanned, relaxed, and happy, caught in a frozen moment of laughing at one of his lame jokes.

"So, I guess this means the laptop is yours, Mom. Nobody else in their right mind would have us as their background."

With a loud buzz that made Isla jump, a countdown timer popped up, covering the whole screen with its ominous ticking. Isla panicked and clicked to get rid of it. The best she could do was to minimize it, but it carried right on reminding her that there were thirty days and three hours until ... something.

It was like a hot poker to her anxiety levels.

She clicked *start*, hoping to find a way to turn it off. A menu popped up. Pretty standard stuff for a laptop, word processor, spreadsheet program, and social media icons dotted across the desktop haphazardly. Apparently, Mom didn't know about auto-arrange.

She glanced at the bottom of the screen, avoiding the countdown timer. Forty-nine unread messages. Who would she be getting that many emails from? It all made her more uncomfortable than the unused recliner in the lounge. Probably spam and marketing.

Isla slid off the bed, rinsed her face in the en-suite basin, and eyeballed herself in the mirror. "You are a big girl, you have power of attorney. You need to check these emails." Right. It *would* probably be a whole lot of spam and marketing anyway.

Spam and marketing.

The mailbox loaded much quicker than Isla's old dinosaur of a laptop did. The screen blipped and sprang to life with the enthusiasm of an '80s aerobics instructor in a headband and leg warmers.

Isla scanned the inbox. There was a sub-folder simply named AEA. She clicked on it and a password request popped up on the screen.

Isla closed the box with an annoyed click. "Really, Mom? What would be in there that would need a password?"

Back in the regular inbox, she found an overdue telephone account. Isla forwarded that to herself to be dealt with later. The subject of the next one down was *Good News!* and it came from Shelly who was *pregnant at last!*

"I'm happy for you, Shelly. But why are you telling my mom?"

The countdown timer kept ticking down as she scanned through Mom's inbox which was full of random strangers telling her how they were getting on with various problems.

There were at least ten from someone named Eli. Isla clucked her tongue and clicked to open them expecting a promise of some staggering fortune that just needed a valid bank account and I.D. number to claim. Mom had always been too trusting with things like that.

The conversation slid open, and Isla scanned through it, reading without really wanting to read.

My Elle,

I think it's about time you make good on our bet.

I'll be waiting for you on the corner of 14th and 7th.

I know you don't always agree with the life I'm living, but circumstances have left me with little choice.

I live in hope.
Always yours,
E.
P.S. Here is the link to some memories for you.

The word "link" was in blue and underlined—hyperlinked. Isla's finger hovered over it as the room turned strangely chilly.

Should she look? Isla couldn't imagine that any of these would be worth looking at. Mom's life had been a small peach pip of inflexible routines that all revolved around making it through one more day. Medicines, food chosen carefully that wouldn't make her nauseated, doctor's trips. Chemo. Strict bedtimes and pain. So much pain.

They certainly hadn't taken many photos over the last two years. Maybe it would be easier to look if she distanced herself a little. Not her mom, but some lady called Eleanor.

"Right, Eleanor. I'm going to look through your photos now if that's okay?"

She held her breath, clicked the button, and peered at the screen through her fingers. After two years of excruciating routines, the appearance of a laptop was so out of character for her mom, it had rattled Isla more deeply than she cared to admit.

Folders appeared, neatly arranged, and carefully labeled. She scanned the album names and found one called Golden Oldies. It seemed like a safe choice.

The laptop whirred to life as a slideshow loaded. Isla plumped the pillow behind her back and winced as pain stabbed through her. It was a bad time for her back to be acting up, she had a whole house stuffed full of a lifetime of memories to pack up.

The first image loaded. Mom as a teenager, laughing as she flew through the air on a swing in some park Isla had never seen before. Her hair was long and wavy, catching the sunlight in the long strands. Her long skirt caught the air and hung forever suspended like a soft butterfly wing. The second image must have been edited as it showed Mom twice.

Another one, this time, there was no mistaking that there were two of them. Either that or Mom had a body double.

By the fifth picture of Mom and her look-alike, Isla was a little freaked out. There was no way they had access to photo editing software back then. Smartphones would do it now, but back then? Sure, it could have been edited recently. But this didn't *look* edited.

Was it possible that her mom had had a twin sister? One she'd never mentioned or even hinted at? Surely not. There had to be another explanation.

"Oh, Mom, I can't believe you kept all these secrets from me. These people loved you." Isla tapped her lip and combed through all the emotions bubbling in her belly. One thing was sure, she needed to get away for a while and these mystery people—that hadn't existed in her world until moments ago—needed to know that their friend had passed.

And maybe this Eli man could shed some light on whatever was happening in 30 days and who Mom's body double was.

"Right, Mom. I don't know if you'd agree, but the way I see it—there's only one thing for me to do. I need to go on a road trip."

· · · · · · · · · · ·

Chapter Two

The GPS lady sing-songed cheerfully in her high-pitched voice about taking the second exit at the next roundabout.

"You could just say *go straight*. You know that, right?" Arguing with her was completely pointless, but Isla did it anyway. The lady never, ever answered. She never got frustrated or raised her voice. She didn't sound put out in the slightest.

Conflict-less conflict. It was all rather unsatisfying.

Isla drove into her old hometown, feeling every one of the 200 kms she'd driven in all the screaming muscles down her back.

She'd worked through all of Mom's emails carefully and flagged those who appeared more than once. The handful that seemed to have had close relationships went on Isla's road trip list. The least she could do was let them know of Mom's passing in person.

The very thought of these strangers knowing her mom so well made her a bit breathless. Why hadn't she even mentioned them?

A flutter in her belly reminded her that she'd grown up in this neighborhood. Their old next-door neighbor was first on the list.

Ignoring the GPS lady who told her to go straight, she took the first left down a windy road lined with old trees whose tops intermingled high above the road. She loved this road. How many hours had she and Griffin spent skateboarding up and down it? They'd competed to see who could clock up the most injuries. If you could have bought property with shed blood, this road would have been theirs.

Isla found her old house, though someone had painted it pumpkin orange. She pulled to a stop and stretched her neck. It looked just as she remembered, yet completely different at the same time. The eucalyptus tree she'd climbed still stretched up high, arching over the roof in a smooth curve. The driveway had been redone with pale paving stones.

Curtains moved in a window; someone was watching her. A smooth u-turn and she headed down the street along the side of the house. Her belly flipped at the sight of her old neighbor's house. Griffin Stewart.

Just his name was enough to stain her cheeks red. The incident in high school had been enough to make her change schools. The sight of his house filled her with an uncomfortable flurry of emotions that left her slightly queasy.

Mom had never been friends with Griffin's mom, Poppy Stewart. On the odd occasion, they'd passed recipes, cups of sugar, and mint leaves to each other over the wall, but they'd never sought out each other's company and Mom always just politely said that *not everybody should be friends with everybody*.

Isla had never taken to Poppy either, and the thought of being near her house filled Isla with a low-key dread.

She didn't stop but drove right on by. After all, it didn't matter what order she worked through her list. She'd come back here after hunting down the mysterious Eli.

· · · · ·•·•· · · ·

Griffin washed his hands, working the soap into every crease between his fingers. He held them under the hot water for longer than he should have, his mind was elsewhere. This sabbatical was coming at just the right time. As much as he'd kicked against the idea, now that he'd handed his patients over to the next doctor on duty, he already felt lighter.

The receptionist lit up when she saw him. "So Doc, you're on your way out of here, at last." Trish was single and felt compelled to remind him of the fact at least twice a month. "Have you got any plans?"

Griffin wouldn't have told her if he did. "A bit of this, a bit of that. Nothing too carefully orchestrated. Have there been any calls? Can I have my phone?"

"Well, don't rush back to work. But in case you feel lonely, let me give you my number." The screen lit up and she entered her number with ticking fingernails before passing him the phone. He needed to put a password on the thing.

He smiled in the most non-committal way that he could, retrieved his bag from his locker, and waved on his way out.

He stopped for a moment, just to breathe the fresh air outside the hospital. Three months. What was the best way to make them count?

"God, you organized this sabbatical. If I know you, you'll have a mission or two lined up for me. All I know is, I'm tired of a life that doesn't set me on fire inside. Whatever it is, bring it on." He glanced around to make sure nobody had overheard him praying out loud, slid into his pick-up truck, and drove off.

· · · · ● · ● · · ·

The annoyingly cheerful GPS lady and her hoity-toity accent informed her that *her destination was on the right.*

Isla pulled up and checked the area. There was no house nearby, nothing but some rundown shops with broken windows and rusted burglar bars.

A beggar huddled next to a collection of garbage cans, hunkered down over his knees. Thick dirt caked both the man's skin and the tattered clothes he wore. She tapped her phone to see if the map application had malfunctioned, or was lagging, but it all seemed in perfect working order.

Maybe this Eli wasn't altogether sane. Or he was a conman down to the bottom of his evil heart. Isla snapped her fingers at her epiphany. That was it. She called up the emergency number for the police and sat with her finger hovering over dial. If something illegal went down, she was ready for it.

She should phone Craig, but she'd chosen not to tell her big brother what she was planning. Her resolve to do this odd road trip was flimsy enough without his common sense getting involved. If he'd said three words to change her mind, she would have been home right now in that awfully big, quiet, house going slowly nuts.

"Eleanor, what on earth did you get yourself into?" She clucked her tongue at her mom's lack of street smarts.

A frizzy-haired woman stuffed into a coral business suit that looked two sizes too small came walking towards the bins where the beggar sat. She was digging through her coral-colored leather bag, muttering under her breath. When she saw the filthy old man, she did a little back step that made her totter in her heels. She sped up, walking a wide arc around him, shooting back little nervous glances.

The beggar lifted his head as she passed and Isla froze. His eyes were bright and focused, they didn't belong to someone so poor and lost.

She sank back into her seat, put her phone down so that she didn't summon up the flying squad by accident, and watched. Time ticked by slowly and an hour later, the man hadn't received a single coin. At best, passers-by ignored him, but some people made their lack of trust painfully obvious. The man looked too old and brittle to move fast enough to keep up with anyone, let alone rob them.

Eli must have sent the wrong digits.

She'd seen enough. It wasn't great to strike out on the first clue of her quest, but a bit of kindness wouldn't hurt. Isla unzipped the cooler bag of snacks she'd bought for the trip and took out an apple, a cheese-and-ham sandwich, and a bottle of water.

She slipped out of the car, hunched down by the man, and cleared her throat to get his attention. He didn't respond and for a moment she panicked that he'd passed on.

"Excuse me, sir." Touching him was not on her list of things to do. His eyes opened a fraction and he stared at her through his crusty lashes. She soldiered on. "Here is some food for you."

His eyes opened fully, crystal blue and clear. He held out his hands and she placed the food into them. Their skin touched briefly and she suppressed a shudder, forcing a smile onto her face instead. The old man said nothing but inclined his head with a gracious nod worthy of a king.

Should she ask him about Eli? It was pointless, but it also wouldn't cost her anything. "I'm looking for Eli Connock. I don't suppose ..." Stupid question. She'd better get back on the road. Her next stop was another two hours drive away. "Never mind."

"Who's asking?"

"I have news for him concerning one of his friends. Do you know Eli?"

"I could take you to him. For a small fee."

There it was. The catch. She should just get on with her trip, the day was ticking past at a speed. *Indulge the man, Isla. Just for a laugh.*

"And what would you charge?"

"Lunch."

He was loopy. Life on the street had messed with his mind. "I just brought you lunch."

The man nodded. "I want you to have lunch with me. Just around the corner."

Every nerve ending vibrated on high alert. This was how people ended up in alleyways with their throats slit. "Just so you know, I have no money. There's nothing valuable on me for you to ste ... er, want."

His eyes narrowed and Isla could have kicked herself for offending the man.

"I'm sorry. I'll come. Let's go. Can we make it quick? I have some traveling to do."

The beggar shoved the food into his coat pocket and unfolded his ancient body with creaks and snaps that made Isla wince. Finally upright, he crooked a finger at her and shuffled along the broken pavement, side-stepping an open manhole.

The overwhelming urge to dart back to her car and run away washed over her, strong enough to steal her breath. A tiny, sneaky, traitorous part of her kicked in and she followed him anyway, all the while composing her final message to Craig just in case this beggar had bad intentions. If this was how she met her end, it would probably be her own fault for naively following a stranger.

Chapter Three

The old man kept up his determined shuffle, grunting now and then with the effort. Isla kept her strides small and slow to keep in step with him.

There was nothing in her that felt right about this, yet she didn't leave. She was officially as loopy as he was.

Walking these streets caused a trickle of panic through her that she fought hard to ignore. Isla usually avoided this part of town. Not out of fear exactly, but more a logical sense of self-preservation.

The man shuffled to a stop and stared up towards the top of the four-story building. It looked like a hollow, abandoned warehouse. Not Isla's first choice of where she'd like to die. Why wasn't she running away?

The air smelled of soup, possibly vegetable soup, wholesome and nutritious, completely at odds with the dirty environment. It was a strange contrast.

"We're here. Come on."

The old man led her through the cavernous mouth of the building as if into the belly of a beast. Isla had no intention of staying outside on the pavement by herself so she hurried in behind him and walked into a different world.

Rows of tables and mismatched chairs sat in neat, orderly rows, bordered by serving tables that ran along two sides of the hall. Most of the chairs were already occupied by folk dressed exactly like Isla's beggar. Enormous pots of soup dotted the serving tables, manned by ladle-wielding volunteers in red shirts with *Welcome to the Souper-duper Soup Kitchen* printed on them in white.

Isla went to tap the beggar on his shoulder, stopped, and coughed instead. "Excuse me? Why are we here? Also, what is your name?"

The beggar grinned without showing his teeth and didn't respond. He lined up at the closest soup station and handed

Isla a bowl. His hands were filthy, dirt caked under his nails, but the bowl was clean, and Isla took it, proud of herself for not flinching.

The volunteer greeted them cheerfully, cheerfully enough to grate Isla's soul. The poor boy had acne all across his forehead and cheeks, even down his neck. He stirred and slopped tomato soup into the beggar's bowl, handed over a slice of buttered bread, and glanced at Isla. If he was surprised to see her, he didn't show it.

"I see you brought a different friend today?"

The beggar thumbed over his shoulder. "Mark, meet Isla-Skye. Isla, meet Mark."

He knew her name. Her mind scrambled back through the few words they'd traded. She didn't remember telling him her name, not even once. She politely accepted her slice of bread from Mark with the shirt that clashed violently with his acne. She flashed a quick smile, just enough not to appear rude.

Her old man shuffled towards the table and sat down at a single open seat, waving her to the other side. There was another seat open much further down, wedged between a silent African man in a weathered, threadbare suit, and a sad, round, woman with frizzy gray hair.

Isla sighed, questioned all her life choices to date, and squeezed in between the suit and the gray-haired lady. The man in the suit tipped his head towards her and the gray-haired lady huddled over her soup as if Isla would steal it.

They ate in silence while Isla's mind ran in circles. The gray-haired lady had all but turned her back on Isla. There'd be no chatting with her. She turned to the African gentleman sitting on her right.

"Hi, my name is Isla." She held out her hand and to her surprise, he shook it.

"Themba." His face was a wrinkled road map of a hard life, but his eyes were kind and his voice gentle. A deep scar ran across his forehead, from hairline to eyebrow.

"Themba, do you know a man named Eli Connock?" It was a long shot but she had to try.

Themba waved his spoon in a wide circle that ended with a stab towards the beggar that had brought Isla here. How was that possible?

"That's Eli? Are you sure?"

The old man paused and squinted. "That's Eli." He went back to his soup, leaving Isla to wonder about the sanity of her mom. It couldn't possibly be the same man. She was wasting her time here. Why would a beggar email her mom? More like, how? Yet this is where the coordinates had led her.

Isla had just decided it was time to move on when not-the-right-Eli finally finished eating. The man had lingered over his bowl of soup and only finished it once the room had emptied and the others had left.

He hobbled over with his left shoe flapping. It was only a matter of time until the shoe sole parted company with the rest of the shoe. So far, she'd tried two names on her list and both had bombed out spectacularly. This trip was not working out the way she'd intended but she was too stubborn to admit defeat.

She'd buy fake-Eli a pair of shoes and then be on her way to number three.

"I'll take you to Eli now. Come."

Sure, and I'll see pink unicorns along the way. "I don't know if that's a good idea. Thank you, but—"

Fake-Eli looked her straight in the eye and there was something deeply compelling about him. He was a large man with many stories written into the tired lines of his face, stories that nobody stopped long enough to listen to. It also seemed deeply rude not to humor him.

"Come, it's not far." His voice was gentle and his eyes twinkled with unexpected life.

Isla took him to her car. They made a quick stop at a street vendor where she guessed his size and bought a pair of trainers to replace his tired shoes. As they climbed in the car, she dumped them unceremoniously on his lap. "These are for you. I hope they keep your feet warm."

He nodded once and hugged the shoes to his chest while he directed her through the cluttered streets.

· · · · ● · ● · ● · ·

The drive home took Griffin past his old high school where guys ran across a field, tossing a rugby ball between them. As he waited for the light to change, a young couple came out of the gate, the body language between them told a story that was as easy to read as the newspaper headline on the streetlight.

The guy was lanky and tall and she was a slight little thing, almost pixie-like. He leaned in close to whisper in her ear and she giggled behind her hand, fiddling with her long hair the way girls sometimes do.

At a glance, it could have been Isla and himself all those years ago.

He waited for the stab in his chest. There it was. The pain was less crippling now, but still there. Probably just because it was all so unresolved. They never got to talk about what had happened. She'd left the school and he never saw her at home anymore. He'd never got the chance to tell her how the whole disaster had changed his life.

Their long years of friendship just sat there in his memories like a brick in a dark passage that he fell over now and then.

Griffin wasn't a romantic and he didn't harbor any pipe dreams that life would reunite them one day. It would be a tall order to trust her after the way she'd dumped him and run away. Yes, he'd loved her, and losing her had devastated him. But over time, he'd managed to pull himself back together again and put her out of his mind.

Until he hit a trigger, like the two lovebirds outside school. Isla-Skye Whittaker. Rolling the name around in his mind gathered tattered fragments of memory from over a decade ago.

Maybe she would forever be the thorn in his flesh. He laughed dryly at his sense of melodrama and pulled off as the light changed to green.

· · · ● · ● · ● · · ·

"This can't be the place. I think you've misunderstood me." Isla's heart sank as she pulled up to a mansion firmly locked away behind tall gates and guarded by security personnel.

Eli said nothing, only grinned at her. The sparkle in his eye was back and Isla's frustration levels climbed through the roof. Indulging this man's fantasies had cost her hours.

A security guard leaned in close and she scrambled for a way to tell her story that wouldn't make her sound like the one of those who spent their lives reading those advice columns her mom had loved so much.

To her surprise, he tipped his hat and waved them through the gates that swung open in a smooth, well-oiled swish.

Made in the USA
Las Vegas, NV
27 December 2023

83565989R00246